FIRST COMES BABY
Janice Kay Johnson

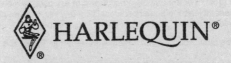

HARLEQUIN®

TORONTO • NEW YORK • LONDON
AMSTERDAM • PARIS • SYDNEY • HAMBURG
STOCKHOLM • ATHENS • TOKYO • MILAN • MADRID
PRAGUE • WARSAW • BUDAPEST • AUCKLAND

ISBN-13: 978-0-373-71405-6
ISBN-10:   0-373-71405-X

FIRST COMES BABY

www.eHarlequin.com

Printed in U.S.A.

ABOUT THE AUTHOR

Janice Kay Johnson is the author of nearly sixty books for adults and children. She has been a finalist for the Romance Writers of America RITA® Award for four of her Harlequin Superromance novels. A former librarian, she lives north of Seattle, Washington, and is an active volunteer at and board member of Purrfect Pals, a no-kill cat shelter. When not fostering kittens or writing, she gardens, quilts, reads and e-mails her two daughters, who are both in Southern California.

Books by Janice Kay Johnson

HARLEQUIN SUPERROMANCE

HARLEQUIN SINGLE TITLE

SIGNATURE SELECT SAGA

†Three Good Cops
††Under One Roof
**Lost…But Not Forgotten

Dedicated with love to Mom,
my best friend and constant support

CHAPTER ONE

LAUREL WOODALL had been sure that asking a man to father her baby—*without* any sexual privileges—had to be the hardest thing she'd ever done.

But no. That conversation paled in comparison to this one.

Asking said man's wife whether it was okay with *her* was definitely worse.

The two sat across their dining room table from Laurel, their chairs placed so close together that their shoulders touched. After dinner, they'd sent the kids to do homework, take baths and get ready for bed. Sheila and Laurel had cleared the dirty dishes and loaded the dishwasher, chatting in the way of two people determined to pretend they didn't feel at all uncomfortable with each other, even though that was a flat-out lie on both their parts. Then they'd poured coffee and returned to the table.

Laurel took a deep breath, clasped her hands in her lap and said, "Well, I assume Matt told you what I wanted to talk about."

Sheila, a freckle-faced redhead, nodded.

"Um…how do you feel about it?"

It. Great word. It could sum up anything from a brightly wrapped package to a great big favor. Like the donation of sperm, the fathering of a baby. But *it,* little tiny word that it was, implied the request was nothing special.

Beside his wife, Matt all but quivered like a tuning fork. He must know what she thought, but not necessarily what she'd say.

"I have a few questions."

"Of course." Laurel smiled as if they were talking about vacation plans, not something so desperately vital to her.

"Would your child know Matt was his father?"

"That would be entirely up to you. I was hoping that he—or she—would." Secretly, she wanted a girl. "That we could be pretty matter-of-fact. I could say, 'I wasn't married and I wanted a child, so I asked one of my best friends if he would be your daddy.' There are plenty of other alternative families around."

"That means our children would have to know, too."

"Yes, I suppose so. But you could explain the circumstances to them the same way."

"Are you expecting Matt to take any real role as father?"

"Again, that would be up to him, and to you, of course. If he was around, a friendly uncle kind of figure, that would be great. Am I expecting him to want joint custody or every other weekend? No."

"Wow." Sheila looked into her coffee cup as if for answers.

Wrong beverage. No tea leaves there.

Laurel leaned forward. "What if I were sitting here tonight telling you I'm pregnant? Wouldn't you gather my baby into your family, the way you always have me? If I were asking you to be godparents…"

"I wouldn't hesitate," Sheila admitted. "But…this is different."

"I asked Matt because I know him. I'm comfortable with him. And…well, honestly, because your kids are so fantastic."

It was the right thing to say. Sheila's face softened.

Matt puffed out his chest. "I'm a proven stud."

His wife elbowed him. "They are fantastic, aren't they? Although I'm inclined to think I'm more responsible than he is."

They grinned at each other, as in love, Laurel suspected, as they'd been on their wedding day. That was another reason she'd asked them. Their marriage was solid, their relationship trusting. Sheila wouldn't wonder even for a second if there was anything funny going on between her husband and Laurel.

She sighed then. "I'm sure most of my hesitation is based on some kind of atavistic response. You know. He's my man, and I don't want to share his genes. But another part of me knows that's silly. He wants to do this for you, and it's not as if I don't love you, too, so… Sure. Okay."

Breath catching, Laurel sat up straighter. "Really? You mean it?"

Sheila smiled. "I said yes, didn't I?"

"Oh, bless you!" Laurel's chair rocked as she jumped to her feet and raced around the table to hug first Sheila, then Matt. "This is so amazing! It's really going to happen. Wow. I'm in shock."

"You're crying," Matt said in alarm.

"What? Oh." She swiped at tears. They didn't matter. Nothing mattered but this. Knowing that soon, she'd be a mother.

Eventually she stopped smiling and wiped away the

tears enough so that she could tell them what she knew about the procedure.

"You could go in with Matt," she said to Sheila. "Help him, um, you know."

"Produce the little guys?" Sheila said just a little sardonically.

The big, brawny, bearded guy blushed, Laurel would have sworn he did.

"Yeah. That." She didn't actually want to think about that part of the "procedure." It was too close to sex, something else she never, ever thought about. Not when she could help it. "If you were there, it would be as if…oh, as if his, uh, contribution came from both of you."

"I don't know. That seems weird. Well, all of it does. But I'll think about it. Okay?"

Laurel nodded.

"Now, how about some dessert? I made a coffee cake today."

Stomach knotted with the aftermath of nerves and maybe a new case of them—she was going to have a baby!—Laurel still smiled and said, "Sounds great."

This had been the hardest part, she reminded herself—and kept reminding herself, even after she'd said goodbye to Sheila and Matt's brood, hugged both of them again and gotten behind the wheel of the car.

She'd had alternatives in mind, but Matt had been first on her list. They'd been friends since she'd taken her first job after the rape in a legal aid office. He was great: smart, good-looking in a teddy-bearish way, gentle, kind and healthy. She knew his parents were still alive and going strong in their seventies—tonight Sheila had mentioned they were on a cruise in the Caribbean—and that his grandmother had lived into her nineties. She knew *him*. The essence of him.

Of course, she'd considered going the sperm bank route. Had even called a couple of places. She'd almost convinced herself that she balked because she could never know how much in each donor's profile was true and how much false. Graduate student in astrophysics. Sure. But maybe he worked at the local Brown Bear car wash. I.Q. of 154. Uh-huh. And how did he measure it? An online pop quiz?

But that wasn't really it. Some of those donors probably were graduate students who needed some bucks to supplement their fellowships. No, what mattered was that they were strangers.

Strange men.

However clinical the *procedure*—there was that word again—she would still be taking a part of him inside her. Her skin crawled at the idea.

But a friend… A friend for whom she had no sexual feelings. That was different. She could hug Matt, and his sperm she could accept.

And he'd said yes. *They'd* said yes. Tears burned behind her eyelids when she let herself into her small house in Lake City.

LAUREL DIDN'T TELL anyone what she planned. Not her father, not her younger sister. Once it was a done deal and she was pregnant would be soon enough. They couldn't try to talk her out of it then.

And they would. Even Matt had, in his gentle way.

He'd cleared his throat apologetically. "I know you don't see a sexual relationship in your near future. But you're still young, Laurel. It's not as if your childbearing years are passing. You've done a lot of healing. You'll do more. Becoming a parent with someone you love…"

She'd shaken her head. "No. It's not going to happen, Matt. And…I need someone to love. Someone I *can* love."

She guessed the certainty in her voice had swayed him. Or the plea, she wasn't sure. All she knew was, she didn't want to argue with anyone else. Explain. Justify.

Nope, she would just announce, "I'm pregnant," and have faith they'd be happy for her.

Caleb was different. She wouldn't tell him when he called or she responded to his e-mails, but in person, it would be hard *not* to. Fortunately, he was out of the country, as he often was, so she hadn't had to make an excuse to avoid seeing him.

She didn't know what he'd say, whether he'd understand or would try to talk her out of a decision she'd already made. He was less predictable than her dad or her sister.

Part of her wanted to tell him. He'd been the most amazing friend she'd ever had, and had been since the second week of their freshman year of college.

Laurel still remembered the first time she'd seen him. Their dorm at Pacific Lutheran University had a rec room in the basement, complete with a Ping-Pong table and a dozen sagging sofas and chairs too grungy even for the local thrift store. She had wandered down, feeling shy but acting on faith that, since nobody here knew her, if she forced herself to *pretend* to be outgoing she might actually be popular. A bunch of kids were draped on the sofas, one reading and nodding in time to music that played through her headphones, some arguing about whether any curriculum should be required—how funny that she remembered that—and two boys played Ping-Pong.

One of those two was in her intro to psych class. They'd sat next to each other and exchanged a few words, so she felt comfortable pausing to watch the game. Until the second boy aced his serve and taunted the guy she knew, then grinned at her. She looked at him, he looked at her and… It wasn't true love at first sight, even though the girlfriends she made in the weeks to come believed through all four years that she had a crush on Caleb Manes. What they'd done was fall into *like*. There was a connection. They were instant friends, this tall, lanky boy with curly dark hair and electric-blue eyes and former high school nerd Laurel Woodall, in those days carrying an extra twenty-five pounds.

She could talk to Caleb; he really listened. And he talked to her, telling her stuff no guy ever had before. They advised each other through girlfriends and boyfriends, first kisses and breakups. He'd slipped a note into her hand when all the seniors in their graduation robes milled like sheep impervious to attempts to herd them into order. She had waved and smiled at her dad, snapping pictures, then peeked at the note.

Friends forever, it said.

She'd felt a tiny glow of warmth and relief at his reassurance that somehow they would stay connected even though they were going in different directions. Caleb had signed up for the Peace Corps and was going to bum around Europe with a buddy until he had to report for training. She had a summer job lined up and was heading to law school at the University of Washington come fall.

But…*friends forever.* Of course they would be.

They almost hadn't been. The irony was, she'd been the one who tried to shut him out, along with all her other friends. But Caleb hadn't let her, a fact that to this day still filled her with misgiving and relief and probably a dozen other emotions mixed into a brew as murky as folk cures for hangovers: weird looking, vile tasting, not so easy on the stomach, but in the end, settling in there.

They'd never been quite as close as when they could drop by each other's dorm rooms and later apartments at PLU. But that would have happened anyway. By the time he came back from Ecuador, she hadn't seen him in two years. They were adults, embarked on careers, or at least— in her case—a job. He'd become engaged once, although the wedding had kept getting postponed and never did happen. Once his import business took off, Caleb had bought a house on Vashon Island, a twenty-minute ferry ride plus a half-hour drive from her north Seattle neighborhood. She saw him maybe once a month. Sometimes less.

They were casual friends, Laurel concluded, refusing to listen to any dissenting voices. She had no obligation to tell him anything.

It had taken her so long to work up the courage to ask Matt to donate sperm, her most fertile time of the month had come and gone. So now she had a month to second-guess herself, suffer daily panic attacks and pray that he and Sheila didn't change their minds. Laurel didn't think they would, but that fear had to be part of those panic attacks that hit her unpredictably.

She'd be sitting on the Metro bus she took every morning to work at the downtown law firm, hip to hip with some old lady gripping her purse and shooting glares at everyone who walked down the aisle, or some guy in cornrows blasting rap from headphones and bobbing in time. She'd be minding her own business, looking out the window and seeing the cross streets pass, wishing she'd had time for a second cup of coffee. She'd vowed to save her money and not stop every day at the Tully's on the corner where she got off, but maybe today…

And it would hit her, a tsunami of doubt and fear, heralded by no warning. The cold constricted her breathing, raised goose bumps that traveled down her arms and then her legs. She would be paralyzed in place, gripped by the shock and the power of the current, aware of light above, but unable to swim to it.

Laurel knew panic, had once recognized the trigger. But she'd gotten better, so much better, until now. This time, she didn't understand.

She *wanted* a baby. She wasn't afraid of having one, of being able to cope as a single mother. She had complete faith she could do it.

Matt and Sheila might back out. But if they did, she still had her list. Or she would pick a donor from one of those trumped-up profiles and buy sperm. There were other ways.

Was Matt the wrong choice? At the question, her anxiety ratcheted up a notch, but she couldn't think why. Like a mantra, she repeated to herself: he's smart, good-looking, nice, healthy. Everything she wanted her child's father to be.

Was she afraid of problems down the line? Her child being hurt because Matt wasn't really interested in being a father? Or worse, Matt deciding to contest Laurel for custody? Claiming her to be unfit?

In her calmer moments, she knew he'd never do anything like that. He was a friend. That's why she'd asked him. Anyway, Sheila wouldn't want to raise his child with another woman as her own. She'd been worried already that Laurel would seek too much involvement from Matt in the baby's life.

Was she scared about the procedure? Laurel did hate annual exams, but she liked the woman doctor she saw at the Women's Health Clinic. She trusted her to be gentle and as unobtrusive as possible. While it was happening, veiled from the doctor by the white sheet, she would close her eyes and think, *A baby. Soon, soon, I'll feel movement inside, and my belly will swell and you'll hear my voice.* She *wasn't* afraid.

But she was, of something. She just didn't know what.

If she stayed very still, the wave would slowly ebb away, leaving her sitting on the bus, her stop still to come, her seatmate unaware of the terror that had swept over her. She would sag the slightest bit in relief, perhaps lean her head against the thick glass of the window, the cool smooth surface more comforting than a hug.

Soon, soon. Then I won't be afraid.

She hated being afraid, feeling vulnerable, and refused to surrender to these panic attacks in any way.

Her period came on time, to the day when she'd expected it. Her last in a year or more, she hoped. She intended to breast-feed, and she knew that often delayed the resumption of menstruation, sometimes for six months or more after delivery.

Of course, she might not get pregnant the first month. There were no guarantees. She wouldn't get discouraged. She could afford the additional procedures.

But she wasn't sure she could bear the panic attacks, day after day, for another month. Or one after that.

They didn't come when she was home alone, thank goodness. She didn't like it when the wind scratched the branches of the maple against her bedroom window at night, or when the house settled and creaked. When she heard a cough outside, late, or the clatter of a garbage can as if someone had brushed it. She was a woman who lived alone in a city that was safer than many, but still a city, so of course she had those anxieties. The important part was, they no longer paralyzed her.

It was the idea of getting pregnant that did. Something about her plan wasn't quite right. Maybe it was only the unconventional way, the impersonality. Not how a young woman dreamed of conceiving her first child.

Once it was done, Laurel was convinced, she'd be okay.

Just today, she'd talked to Matt. She hadn't seen him or Sheila in the two weeks since she'd had dinner at their house and asked them for the ultimate favor. But she called legal aid, where Matt still worked and said, "Just wanted to say hi."

"Hey." He sounded distracted. "Got a doozy today. Landlord from hell. Mildewed, sagging ceiling collapsed and badly hurt a toddler. A few rats fell with the ceiling. Sounds Third World, doesn't it?"

"At the very least. Will the child be okay?"

"Doctor thinks so. But I'm going to nail the landlord's hide to the wall."

"You go get 'em." Laurel felt a momentary pang for the days when she'd imagined that someday she, too, would be a crusading attorney.

"We still on?"

There was something in his voice. Lack of enthusiasm? Hope that they *weren't* still on? Or was her paranoia reading shades of gray into a casual question?

"Yep. Two more weeks."

She heard a muffled voice.

"Listen. Got to go. We'll talk again?"

"Next week," Laurel promised.

Disquiet made her chest feel hollow. Had she ruined a friendship she valued by asking this of Matt? Or would everything be fine, once it was done?

She turned back to her computer and made herself concentrate on the will she was writing. She worked as a paralegal for a firm of attorneys, but most often with Malcolm Hern, whose scrawled notes about the clients' wishes she peered at frequently.

Nonetheless, she was relieved when five o'clock came and she could shut down her computer, don her raincoat, grab her purse and join the other flunkies leaving. This was one of the few times a day she was glad not to have her law degree. If she was working here as an attorney, there'd be no five o'clock departures for her. Nope, she'd be putting in sixty- or seventy-hour workweeks. She *couldn't* be a single parent.

The elevator moved slowly, even after it was full, stopping at nearly every floor between the thirty-fifth, where her firm was located, and the ground floor. She hated being pressed against strangers this way, and always chose a corner if she could get into one. Even so, the man behind her had nearly full-body contact with her and his breath stirred the hair at her nape. Her relief when the light flashed on *L* and the elevator dinged and the doors slid open was profound. Still, she had to wait for others to exit ahead of her, had to suffer more jostling.

Laurel joined the exodus into the marble lobby, heading for the rotating glass doors. She hadn't gone more than a few steps when a man fell into step with her.

"Can I offer the lady a ride home?"

"Caleb!" she exclaimed in delight. "You're back in town."

He wrapped a long arm around her shoulders and gave her a squeeze even as they kept walking. "Yep. Good trip. How are *you?*"

Oh, planning to get myself impregnated two weeks from tomorrow. Having daily panic attacks.

"I'm good. Can I offer you dinner?"

"I was planning to take you out."

"I have beef stroganoff simmering in my Crock-Pot as we speak."

"Deal."

His smile was as amazing as ever although the effect was somewhat different now that he was a man rather than a boy. Most of his travels took him to Central and South America, which meant he was perpetually tanned, paler laugh lines fanning out from his blue, blue eyes. But the dimple still deepened in one cheek whenever he offered his beguiling, lopsided grin.

Caleb wore his hair longer than did most of the attorneys and businessmen in the lobby, not ponytail length, just a little shaggy, the curls making it constantly disheveled. He'd filled out a little in the years since college, but was still lean, and at a couple of inches over six feet he towered over her five foot four or so. Laurel was always aware of women's heads turning when she was with him, not just because he was handsome, although he was. He had that indefinable quality that in an actor or public speaker would be labeled charisma. He exuded some kind of life force, perhaps a belief in himself that drew the stares.

And she was in trouble, she realized suddenly. Was she going to try to get through the evening without telling him what she was up to?

If she kept silent, he'd be hurt later, and for good reason. They'd always told each other everything important.

Everything but what she'd thought and felt when she'd been brutally raped during her first and only year of law school. That single subject was taboo. Only in her rape support group could she talk about that day, because every woman there understood in a way no man ever would.

Okay, this she'd tell him. She didn't like explaining herself, hated the idea of having to tell him to butt out, it was none of his business. But secrecy would bother him more, she knew it would.

Typical Caleb, he'd found a parking spot on the street not half a block from the Drohman Tower where she worked. *Nobody* found street parking at this time of day downtown.

Nobody but Caleb, charmed as always.

"How was your trip?" she asked, once he'd pulled out into traffic.

"Really good. Haiti is always depressing. The poverty." He shook his head. "But I'm excited about the cooperative we've got going there. Not just drum art, although the artisans in the group are making some wall sculptures that are different from the more common ones. But we've added a guy who makes the most extraordinary stone sculptures. Wait'll you see them."

In college, Caleb had been determined to work for a humanitarian organization like Save the Children. But during his time in Ecuador with the Peace Corps, he'd had what he'd described as a revelation. Outside aid wasn't the key, self-sufficiency was. Every country in Latin and South America had unique, beautiful crafts that would bring high prices from Americans if they were made accessible to them. Instead of just buying from artists, he helped organize cooperatives, often village- and even region-wide with profit sharing. Some were comprised only of women, many of whom had lost their husbands to war.

Caleb had started with a tiny store on University Avenue in Seattle, expanding it within a year and adding a second two years later in Portland. Now he had another in upscale Bellevue and a fourth in Tacoma, with a fifth planned for San Francisco. He also put out a catalog and sold through a Web site. He made a good living but passed on profits to the artisans in the cooperatives on a scale that stunned Haitians and Guatemalans who were accustomed to getting pennies for work that sold for a hundred dollars in the United States.

Caleb loved what he did and what he'd accomplished. Every time she saw him, Laurel felt an ache of regret and disappointment in herself. Her dreams had been as vivid as his, and now where was she? Working a nine-to-five job, getting through each day as well as she could.

Choosing to become a mother was the first decision she'd made in a long time that looked ahead, that said, *I have hope.* Maybe, just maybe, Caleb would be glad for her.

Traffic on I-5 was stop-and-go. Laurel could have gotten home nearly as fast on the bus that ambled down Eastlake and through the University District. But she didn't care if the traffic ever opened up. It was wonderful just to be sitting next to Caleb, hearing him talk about the wretchedness he'd seen side by side with the need to create something beautiful. He spoke with admiration of the warmth of community he saw down there and felt Americans had lost, but he also told her about glorious Caribbean beaches littered with bits of Styrofoam and hypodermic needles, about the children and the politics and the disease. He was passionate, angry, awed—and still able to believe he could make a difference.

A few times she'd imagined traveling with him, seeing with her own eyes everything he described. Once he'd tentatively suggested she join him on a trip to Honduras and Guatemala. He'd talked about monkeys leaping through branches above crumbling Mayan ruins, patient women weaving all day long to provide for their families, sunshine and darting fish in coral reefs.

But by then, all Laurel had to buttress herself from the world was her routine. The safety of eating the same cereal every morning, sitting in the same chair at the table, catching the bus at the same time, knowing the faces of the other riders at her stop. She hadn't been able to imagine herself catching a plane, going to a foreign country where she didn't speak the language, taking a boat upriver to places without cars or telephones, to a place where her own life didn't make sense. So she'd made an excuse. He'd looked at her for a grave moment with eyes that saw more than she wanted them to and he hadn't asked again.

Laurel lived in a neighborhood off Lake City Way in north Seattle that had been built in the thirties and forties. The houses were modest but charming, wood-framed, owned mainly by young families. Hers was the anomaly, a homely 1950s addition with a flat roof, a one-car garage made of cinder blocks and a chain-link fence. She'd been lucky to be able to afford it with her father's help. So far, her budget hadn't allowed anything that could be called remodeling, but the chain-link fence was disappearing beneath the honeysuckle and climbing roses and clematis she'd planted along it, and she'd painted the formerly street-sign-yellow garage a more unobtrusive coffee-brown. Trellises and more climbers were masking its ugly facade.

Inside, she'd torn up the shag carpets to expose oak floors that needed refinishing but were still beautiful; however, she was living with 1950s-era plywood and veneer kitchen and bathroom cabinets, aluminum-frame windows that dripped and a shower so tiny and dark it gave her claustrophobia.

Caleb parked on the street and commented on the shoots coming up in her garden.

"I planted a bunch of bulbs last fall. Mostly hyacinths and daffodils."

"Did I tell you that you inspired me?" he said, as she unlocked the door. "I planted a couple hundred tulips in October. With my luck, the moles have eaten them, but I tried."

She laughed, not showing her astonishment at his choice of words. She had inspired *him?*

Comfortable in her house, he found the corkscrew in a drawer and opened a bottle of wine while she changed into jeans, a sweater and slip-on shoes, then put on water to boil for noodles.

"So," Caleb said, "enough about me. Tell me about your life."

He always put it that way, as if she *had* a life.

Today, Laurel thought with a tinge of defiance, she'd prove that she did.

"I've decided to have a baby."

He swore, and she saw that he'd poured wine on the counter. He grabbed the sponge, mopped up, then handed her a glass.

"You didn't just tell me you're pregnant."

"No, I told you I'm going to *get* pregnant."

His eyes narrowed. "Just like that."

"It happens really quickly," she assured him.

"And usually requires a woman *and* a man."

"You know I can't… I don't want…"

What she could have sworn was anger faded from his face. "I know. So you're—what?—planning to find a donor?"

"I already have." She busied herself dumping noodles into the now-boiling water. "You know Matt Baker? My friend from legal aid?"

Caleb's tone was careful, controlled. "Isn't he married?"

"Yes, that's the beauty of it. I already spend a lot of time at their house. They have great kids. I'm Madison's godmother. So it'll give my child a sort of extended family." Beginning to cut up broccoli, she hurried on. "I thought of going the anonymous-donor route, but that made me nervous. It's like, every guy who donates is a future Nobel Prize winner. Brilliant, of course, handsome, athletic, a Ph.D. candidate in something or other. I mean, what are the odds? Some of them have to be ordinary. Or worse than ordinary. Schmucks. I wanted my baby's father to be somebody…" *Somebody, in another life, I might have loved.*

Standing there in the kitchen, the knife poised above a clump of broccoli, she thought, *But Matt isn't.*

Well, she did love him, of course. But not…not that way. He wasn't anybody who ever would have attracted her, not even before. Was *that* the problem?

Caleb muttered a word she couldn't quite catch. "I didn't know you were thinking about anything like this."

"It's been just the past few months."

"Why Matt?"

It was the last thing she'd expected him to ask.

"Well," she faltered, "he's a friend. And smart. He's nice. Healthy. His grandmother lived into her nineties."

"What does Sheila feel about this, Laurel?"

"She agreed…"

"That isn't what I asked."

Her breath caught; she had to face him. His eyes were steady. A couple of creases between his brows had deepened.

"I don't really know," she admitted. "She seemed okay…" She couldn't finish the lie. Sheila had agreed, but she *hadn't* seemed comfortable with the idea. She'd said yes with reluctance, Laurel guessed, perhaps in part out of pity.

Laurel hated knowing that.

Her cheeks heated and she looked away from Caleb, not wanting to see pity in his eyes, too.

There was a long silence. Neither of them moved. The water boiled beside her, and she stood there with the knife in her hand.

"Did you consider asking other friends?" Caleb's voice was deep, quiet.

"I had a list…"

"Was I on it?"

The air had been sucked from the room. She couldn't answer.

"Did you consider asking me, Laurel?" he persisted.

From somewhere, she found the courage to whisper, "What would you have said if I had asked?"

"I would have said yes." He paused. "I'd like to have a baby with you, Laurel."

CHAPTER TWO

"DO YOU MEAN THAT?" Laurel's question came out, a mere thread of sound.

"I mean it." He nodded at the glass. "Have a drink of wine."

She gulped, grateful for the warmth that flowed to her stomach. Her emotions were in such turmoil she had no idea how she felt about his offer.

Caleb wasn't on her list. The only guy she'd put on it who wasn't married was George, who was gay and therefore safe.

Caleb wasn't safe. She knew that much, from the panic and exhilaration and excitement ricocheting through her.

"Hey," he said, voice gentle. "We'd better finish dinner."

"Dinner?" She turned her head and stared blankly at the water boiling over on the stove and sizzling on the burner. "Oh. Yeah." But she didn't move.

"Broccoli," he suggested, and squeezed by her in the narrow galley kitchen to take the lid off the noodles and turn the burner off. "Colander?"

"Um…bottom cupboard." She pointed.

He drained while she hurriedly chopped and put the broccoli on to cook.

Caleb got plates out and said, "We don't have to be

fancy. Let's just dish up here. We can come back for the broccoli."

"Oh. Okay."

She got out silverware while he dished up, and then followed him to the table.

There she studied him as if for the first time, seeing again the changes maturity had brought to his face. He'd become the man he had hoped to be, something not many people could say. His eyes were more serious, sometimes wary; his smiles still lit up a room, but came more rarely. He thought about what he did and said now, and what had once been idealism had now become acknowledgment of the responsibility he had taken on for so many other people. Once, when she'd looked at him like this, Laurel would have been able to read everything he felt on his face. Sometime in the past ten years, he had learned to shield his emotions. She hadn't noticed that until now.

He watched her, his expression merely rueful.

"I wasn't on your list, was I? You wouldn't be so stunned if you'd ever thought about asking me."

She struggled to pull herself together. "I didn't consider asking any single guys. I thought…" Laurel managed a laugh. "Well, that it would send you running in terror."

"I'm not running." *Why not?*

"No. I see."

"But you're not saying what you think."

She let out a shaky breath. "That's because I have no idea what I do think! I figured you'd try to talk me out of the whole idea. I haven't even told Dad or Megan. I was sure they'd both say, 'You're only twenty-eight, Laurel. Give yourself time. You want a family, not the responsibility of raising a child alone.'"

His mouth quirked. "Been airing all the con arguments to yourself, have you?"

"I've been around and around, but I really want to do this." She raised her chin, letting him see that he couldn't sway her.

He shrugged. "This is a normal age to start a family. I've been wondering about myself, too. What's stopping me? Is it the travel? I've been thinking I'd like kids. You're my best friend, Laurel. I can't think of anyone I'd rather have them with."

Them. Not just one. What kind of future was he imagining? With them as a family?

Laurel felt a funny cramp start low in her belly. And even though her emotions were still pinging off each other, she knew: this was right.

A little girl or boy with Caleb's bright blue eyes instead of her hazel ones, his dark curly hair, his height and athleticism instead of her klutziness. A child who would dream, who'd become passionate about something like Egyptian mummies or dinosaurs by the time he or she was four years old, who would dazzle and annoy teachers all at the same time, who would make Laurel laugh.

Until now, she'd wanted a baby, but that baby had been an abstract concept. Suddenly, the child she would carry would be Caleb's. Caleb's and hers.

Goose bumps walked over her skin, and she shivered.

"But…you're bound to get married."

He shrugged. "I don't know. I'm twenty-nine. Hasn't happened yet. The more business expands, the more time I spend on airplanes. Who am I going to marry? A flight attendant? I'm gone too much, Laurel. But I wouldn't mind having a picture of my own kid to carry in my wallet.

Having someone to spend time with when I'm in town."
He frowned. "Or am I making a big assumption here?
Maybe you didn't have any contact with the father in
mind."

"If that's what I wanted, I would have gone with a
sperm bank. I actually was hoping that Matt—that the
father," she corrected herself, "would at least be a friendly
figure in my child's life."

"You know, our food is getting cold."

Trust a man to be thinking about eating. But she shot
to her feet. "The broccoli."

SHE PICKED at her dinner.

In contrast, Caleb ate with a good appetite. "I think they
gave me some peanuts somewhere about lunchtime. Breakfast was…I don't even remember when. A long time ago."

He'd flown from Santo Domingo, Laurel remembered,
via Miami. He probably *was* starving. She decided to for-
give him.

Neither talked much as they ate. She mentioned hearing
that a mutual acquaintance from college had decided to go
back to graduate school. "Oh, and I got an e-mail from
Nadia. I haven't heard from her in ages."

"Your choice, as I recall."

It had been. At first Laurel had turned to her best
friends, but finally one day she'd looked at herself in the
mirror and saw what they did: a woman who bore no resemblance to the Laurel they'd known in college. There
was a Before, and an After, and the After was a painful
contrast. It was easier, somehow, to be with people who
hadn't known the Before version. Who didn't ask difficult
questions, didn't look puzzled at her new timidity, didn't

keep expecting her to become herself again. Old friends had refused to understand that this was who she was now, that the old Laurel had died that night in the parking garage. So she made new friends, like Matt Baker. They knew she had been raped and that she hadn't gone back to law school, but didn't see the painful contrast. She could feel comfortable with them in a way she would never be able to again with people like Nadia and even Caleb.

"It was still nice to hear from her," she said, quietly.

His gaze rested on her face, but she couldn't tell what he was thinking. "What did she have to say?"

"It's funny, but she just got pregnant. She said they weren't planning to start a family yet, but it happened and now they're excited."

"Does she still live on Bainbridge?"

Laurel nodded. "I was thinking of giving her a call."

"You were good friends."

They'd been more than that. Paired by the college as roommates their freshman year, the two, at first sight ill-matched, had continued to room together the entire four years. Nadia's parents were Russian immigrants, and she'd grown up deferring to men in a way that infuriated Laurel, who had been a militant feminist. But they both liked the window open at night, they laughed at the same things and they committed to listening to each other. By graduation, Nadia had been more willing to stand up for herself, and Laurel had begun to see shades of gray instead of stark black and white.

Laurel realized suddenly how much she missed Nadia. Who else could she call and say, *I'm pregnant, and guess who the dad is?*

Caleb pushed his plate away and said, "So."

She gave up moving her food around and set down her fork. "So."

"Have I been persuasive? Or are you going to stick with Matt?"

She shook her head. "No. Unless you want to think about it for a few days?"

"No thinking." He held out his hand, laying it on the table, palm up. "I'm ready when you're ready."

Her chest felt as if it might have a helium balloon in it. She reached out her left hand and laid it on his, then almost jumped at how sensitive she was to such simple, everyday contact. The pads of his fingers tickled her skin, and when he wrapped his hand around her much smaller one, the scrape of his calluses might as well have been fingernails slowly, sensuously, drawn down her spine.

Something flared in his eyes, too, perhaps only awareness of how startled she was. But his voice, if anything, was pitched to soothe her.

"We've been good friends for a long time, Laurel. We'll make this work."

She gave a jerky nod. "I think we can."

"So when? How?"

The procedure sounded even more appallingly clinical, even degrading, when she described it to Caleb.

"Does your insurance cover this? Or will it cost you?" he asked.

"It costs, but it's not that much." She hoped he wasn't planning to offer money.

"Because I'm thinking, why can't we do it ourselves?"

Her chair lurched as she jerked back, pulling her hand free. That quickly, her breath came fast, shuddery, and she stared at him in shock.

"Laurel." He started to stand, but when she shrank further into herself he stopped, then sat again. "I didn't mean that way. God! Do you really think I'm that big a jackass?"

"No! Of course not!"

"Then why are you cringing?"

"You know I can't…"

A muscle spasmed in his cheek, and he closed his eyes for a moment. "I know. I do know. That's not what I was suggesting. Only that we go the do-it-yourself route. Save bucks. I give you the sperm, you, uh, use a—I don't know what—a turkey baster or something and squirt it in." He winced at the imagery. "I'm just saying, it can't be that hard to do."

As rattled as she'd been a second ago, Laurel started to think. He was right; it couldn't be hard. Women got pregnant even when their boyfriends had used condoms. It might be…nicer, yes, nicer to get pregnant at home. They could laugh at the awkwardness and their own embarrassment, instead of him having to get aroused in some examining room at the clinic, and her having to lie on her back with her feet in the stirrups with the doctor and nurses snapping on latex gloves and speculating about why she'd chosen this route to motherhood.

It wasn't as if she was afraid of sperm. Only of men's bodies, of being overpowered, of…

No. Don't think about it. Don't remember. Not now.

"Crap," he said, shaking his head. "I'm being insensitive, aren't I? The last thing you want is me handing you…I don't know what. A baggie of… Jeez. Forget I suggested it."

"No, I kind of like the idea. If you won't be embarrassed. We could try, and then if I don't get pregnant we could go to the clinic the next month."

"You're sure? Wow." A grin broke out. "Hey! We're going to be a mom and dad."

"Together, to see our kid graduate from high school and college."

They were smiling at each other, foolishly.

"An adventure," Caleb said.

Finally, one she could take with him.

"An adventure," Laurel agreed.

THAT EVENING, AFTER HE LEFT, she called Matt.

"Hey," she said. "Listen, I hope this won't break your heart, but Caleb and I talked, and… Well, he volunteered to father my baby."

Long silence. Waiting in apprehension, she feared she was hurting his feelings. She'd asked, he'd accepted and now she was saying, *By the way, I don't need you after all.*

"Got to tell you, that's a little bit of a relief. Sheila wouldn't have withdrawn her blessing, but she keeps suggesting other ideas for you. I don't think she was happy."

"No, I got that impression. Tell her… Well, I'll tell her myself. The fact that both of you agreed was incredibly generous. You're good friends."

"But you found a better stud, huh?" He was grinning, she could tell.

"A single one. Probably better all around."

"But you're still going ahead with this?"

Her fingers tightened on the phone. "It wasn't a whim, you know."

He fumbled through an apology. She assured him she hadn't taken offense. How could she? He *was* a good friend.

But…he wasn't the right man to be the father of her baby.

NOT AT ALL TO CALEB'S SURPRISE, Laurel insisted on a parenting plan, with rights and responsibilities down on paper, signed and even witnessed by a next-door neighbor. The one part included at his insistence was the child support he intended to pay, although they finally compromised on an amount less than he liked. The plan was Laurel through and through. She liked everything hashed out thoroughly, no detail misplaced, everyone crystal clear on where they stood.

Caleb had known within the first week of meeting her that she would end up a lawyer.

It broke his heart that she hadn't.

No, what really broke his heart was *why* she hadn't.

A 4.0 student at PLU, she'd scored high on the LSATs and been promptly accepted at the University of Washington Law School, one of the top handful in the nation. She'd e-mailed him often that first semester and into the second one, excited and energized, thriving in the competitive, challenging environment.

Traveling weekly to Quito to check e-mail and respond to friends, he'd been first puzzled and then alarmed by her silence, which started in early April. *Tough exams coming up?* he'd e-mailed. No answer. Three weeks later, he'd heard from Nadia. Laurel had been attacked in the parking garage on the UW campus late at night, after she'd stayed studying at the law library. Brutally raped and beaten, she was left for dead. Not until morning had someone seen her feet sticking out from behind her car and called 9-1-1. She hadn't come out of the coma for a week. Her face was damaged—cheekbone shattered, eyes swollen shut, three ribs broken, one penetrating a lung. She was expected to recover, Nadia had written, but…

Caleb had almost flown home. But when he'd called,

her dad had said she didn't want to see anybody. She was confused, struggling to remember what had happened. A few days later, in a second phone call, he'd told Caleb she didn't want him to come.

"She's proud of what you're doing there," he'd said. "She says she's okay. She has Meggie and me, of course." Laurel's mom had died of cancer when Laurel was a girl. "Nadia has been at the hospital almost daily. There's nothing you can do, Caleb. Not right now. She'll need all her friends later."

When she'd finally e-mailed, near the end of May, she'd told him that the police hadn't arrested anybody, and she'd missed too many classes to go back to school. Maybe in the fall. Her message had concluded, *Thanks for the flowers and your good wishes, Caleb. But...can we not talk about what happened?*

Their e-mail conversations over the next year had been surreal. She wanted to hear every detail about his village, from the goat that chased toddlers and finally ended up in the dinner pot to his work organizing schools. She was evasive about her own life except for the most superficial details. He knew she'd given up her apartment and was living with her father in Shoreline, just north of Seattle. She had decided not to go back to school that fall.

I'm still feeling some physical effects, she'd written, in what he guessed was a masterly understatement. *The dean says whenever I'm ready. Next fall looks better.*

She talked about autumn leaves and lilacs coming into bloom, about windstorms and politics, but not herself. Mention of mutual friends became rare. In fact, he began to suspect she wasn't seeing anyone but her father and sister.

She always responded to his e-mails, but started to take

a couple of weeks to do so. When the time for his return to the States neared, she wrote, *So, are you coming back to the Seattle area? If so, we'll have to get together some time.*

Some time? They were best friends. What did she mean, *some time?*

A couple of his buddies were at the airport along with his parents to greet him when he landed at Sea-Tac. Not Laurel. When he called and tried to set up a dinner, lunch or anything else, she had excuses. Caleb called Nadia and found out that she hadn't seen Laurel in six months. She'd given up. Finally, he just went by her dad's house.

Laurel was shocked to find him on her doorstep, but not as much as he was by the sight of her. It wasn't so much the injuries—he'd expected those. A scar ran from the crest of her cheekbone into her hairline. Her face wasn't as perfectly sculpted as it had been. But that didn't matter.

What got him was the weight she'd lost, the paleness of her face, the dullness in her eyes. She was thin, washed out. Her arms were wrapped around her waist instead of outstretched to draw him into a big hug. Her smile didn't reach her eyes.

He couldn't say, *What in hell happened to you?* He already knew. He just hadn't known how far the effects went beyond the physical.

He hugged her, pretending he didn't notice the way she shrank away. He talked about his flight, about his culture shock, persuaded her to take a walk to a small park he'd noticed driving there.

The next time he called, she made excuses again. He dropped by again. And again.

She quit even talking about going back to law school,

but she did heal to the point where she got a job at a downtown law firm and with her dad's help bought the house and moved out on her own once again. By that time, few of her old friends came around anymore. Even Nadia, now married and working full-time as a marketing executive, had given up. Only Caleb stuck it out. Sometimes he wondered why he persisted. But…she was Laurel. He'd known from the first time he saw her that she was special. He'd said friends forever, and meant it.

He used to think they might get together sometime. As in, sleep together, or maybe even fall in love and go off into the sunset. At first it didn't happen because their timing wasn't right. He had a high school girlfriend when they first met; by the time he and Danica called it quits at October break, Laurel was dating some guy. It worked that way until their senior year, when they were both briefly single. He thought about making a move on her. He *wanted* to make a move on her. Damn, he'd wanted to. But then he looked at her and thought, *Yeah, but she's my best friend. It can't work out long term. I'm leaving for two years. What if screwing her now ruins what we have?*

In the end, it hadn't seemed worth it. But he'd left for a summer in Europe believing that someday Laurel would be the girl for him. If he had a choice between time spent with Laurel and anyone else, Laurel always won. Once he got back, he thought, then he'd get bold.

That wasn't how it happened, of course, or how it ever would happen. They'd stayed friends, since he wouldn't let her quit on them. But romance was not a possibility anymore. She wouldn't let it be.

Nonetheless, he'd been royally pissed when she told him she had chosen Matt Baker to father her baby. She'd decided to pick a friend, and she hadn't picked *him?* He hadn't even made her goddamn list? For a minute, he'd seen red. Or maybe green, because he was jealous as hell. If any man's sperm was swimming inside Laurel Woodall, it was going to be his.

It would, that is, if he could get it up and manage to jack off in her bathroom, knowing she was sitting out in the living room pretending to watch TV. Him, he'd never felt less aroused in his life.

And this was the big day, outlined in red on his calendar. The day of the month she deemed her most fertile. Something he had never expected to know about her.

Of course, instead of being the big day, it was going to be a humiliating one for him if he couldn't perform.

To start with, her bathroom wasn't conducive to erotic activities, even self-managed ones. The damn room was tiny—as in, you could wash your hands while you were still sitting on the toilet. For that matter, you could stick your head in the shower and wash your hair without leaving the toilet, either. Good thing if he ever had to take a shower here, because his entire body sure wouldn't fit in that stall.

His real problem, though, was that the bathroom felt virginal. White-painted cabinets, wallpaper—although there wasn't much wall—that was also white strewn with violets. He used to think it was funny that tough, argumentative, take-no-prisoners Laurel had a secret girlie side. Right now, gaze on the tiny, green-glass bottle with tiny white bell-shaped flowers in it that sat next to the sink, Caleb wasn't so amused. Trying to get worked up, he felt as if he was raping her in a figurative if not literal sense.

She wants your damn sperm.

No, she didn't. She wanted an immaculate conception. But she couldn't have one, so she was hoping for the next best thing. A tube of some unacknowledged substance that she could use like a douche. She didn't want *him,* she wanted a baby.

Well, if that was all she'd take from him, that's what he'd give her, Caleb thought grimly, and unzipped his jeans.

Think about that beauty who flirted with you in Santo Domingo.

The idea of sitting here in this girlie bathroom, Laurel a room away, getting aroused by imagining the exotic, coffee-skinned beauty who had tried to lure him into her rooms on a back street in the colonial Dominican Republic city struck him as dirty.

It had to be Laurel, Caleb realized, desperate. How could he give her a baby if it wasn't even her he was thinking about? Whether she would like it or not, he was going to close his eyes and imagine making love with her. Maybe this wasn't the normal way for a man and woman to conceive a child, but he figured it wasn't as much the physical act as the emotions that were important. By God, he was going to *feel* as close to what he should be as he could manage.

But it was the old Laurel he pictured, the one who laughed at him and challenged him and, yes, flirted with him. He fantasized about the young woman he remembered from brief glimpses, in tiny panties and bra. By her senior year, her body was slim and pale but for nicely rounded hips she grumbled about, but looked more than fine to him, and generous breasts she tried to minimize with baggy shirts. It was the sexy Laurel he saw when he closed his eyes, not the traumatized one who shrank from all contact.

Thinking about her that way…well, it wasn't as much of a reach as he'd thought it would be. And it worked.

No problem.

COULD HER CHEEKS get any hotter without sizzling like meat on a grill? Laurel didn't want to know.

She accepted the big plastic syringe Caleb had gotten from a veterinarian friend, tried not to look at the milky liquid inside and said, all bright and chirpy, "Oh, good. I hope it wasn't too…well, hard."

Humiliation swept over her. *Bad pun.* Really, really bad.

Yes, her cheeks *could* get hotter. And did.

"Your turn." Darned if his cheeks weren't stained dark red, too. So, okay, this wasn't an everyday happening for him, either. "You want me to stay?"

And hold her hand?

She shook her head quick. "No, I'll be fine."

Caleb was already backing up. "Then, uh, I'll give you a call."

"Okay. Sure."

He had the front door open. "I'll lock."

"Good."

But she was talking to herself. He was gone, duty performed. So much for them laughing together at the awkwardness.

She stared down at the object in her hand before remembering exactly what it was and averting her gaze.

Laurel lay on her bed to insert the syringe, then remembered that standing on your head was supposed to help speed the sperm on their way. She'd been able to stand on her head when she was a kid, but hadn't in years. Could she still?

She finally slithered off the bed, using it to brace herself, and managed to keep her feet in the air for several minutes. That *had* to be long enough. Then she read in bed for a while, knowing full well that she wouldn't remember a word later, and finally dozed off even though it was still early evening.

She woke up later, blinking fuzzily and trying to remember why she was in bed and whether the 8:13 on the clock was morning or evening.

Evening. Oh, God. She was pregnant. Maybe. She hoped. Or at least, in the process of *getting* pregnant.

She splayed her hands over her belly, a smile curving her mouth as she imagined life inside her, however tiny.

"Are you in there?" she whispered, as if the cells that held the possibility of life could hear. "If you are, welcome. I really want you. And…I think your daddy does, too."

She had that helium-balloon sensation again, chest swelling with an emotion that felt perilously like happiness. When was the last time she'd been happy? Really, truly, happy? The After Laurel didn't know. A long, long time. Realizing that she was happy actually scared her a little. Being careful, guarded, made her feel safe. Happiness made you careless.

But she had to open herself to it, if she was to be a mother. She could never let her child realize how vulnerable she felt. Knowing your mom was scared of the world was no way to grow up.

And maybe she could rediscover not just herself, but

how it felt to let even something small, like watching a butterfly, make you happy. A child could do that for you, open your eyes to sensations and wonders you'd come to take for granted.

And she, who took so little for granted anymore, was more than ready to rediscover the wonders and not just the dangers of the world around her.

CHAPTER THREE

LAUREL KNEW SHE WAS pregnant within two weeks. She couldn't verify it, and she didn't call Caleb with the big news. Not when she'd have to say, *It's actually too early for a pregnancy test. I just have a feeling...*

But her period came as reliably as Monday mornings. On Wednesday, when it should have started with a flood, it didn't. Not Thursday, either, or Friday, Saturday or Sunday.

The following Wednesday, she was so queasy she couldn't eat her morning oatmeal. A banana was the best she could do.

Caleb had had to fly to South America unexpectedly, promising he wouldn't be gone for more than a couple of weeks, so telling him she thought she was pregnant wasn't an option anyway. Not if she didn't want to make the announcement via e-mail.

She hadn't actually seen him since the evening he'd disappeared into her bathroom and emerged a half hour later, red-faced, with the syringe he all but flung at her before he fled. Or maybe, left quickly out of consideration for her feelings. Laurel wasn't sure.

He'd called a couple of times, and they'd had stilted conversations. It was almost as bad as when he'd first come back from his stint in the Peace Corps and been so familiar she felt even more like a stranger to herself.

After a week of nausea, she did tell her rape support group that she thought she was pregnant. The group of nine other women gazed at her in surprise and speculation, waiting for the details.

She'd intended to keep it brief—*I want to start a family, I had sperm donated*—but once she'd started, Laurel had found herself spilling everything. Her choice of one friend to be donor, and then her decision to change to her oldest, dearest friend, despite the fact that he was single. The only thing she didn't say was that there'd once been sexual chemistry between them. Because that didn't matter anymore, did it?

They congratulated her, but they also asked questions, and some surprised her.

Marie, one of the women who was most reticent about the details of her own rape, asked, "Why didn't you tell us sooner?"

"You mean, before I got pregnant?"

There were nods all around.

"Because..." She didn't know why.

"You thought we'd try to talk you out of it," Marie said.

"That's why I didn't tell my dad, but..." She looked around the circle. "*Would* you have tried?"

At least half the women nodded.

"But...why?" she asked.

Again, it was Marie who spoke. "You're the only one of us who hasn't had a relationship since her rape." They'd been meeting for a long time now, with Cherie the most recent addition two and a half years ago.

"A lot of you are married," Laurel argued. "That's different."

"I'm not married," Jennifer said. She was a quiet blonde about Laurel's age.

Three others reminded her they weren't married, either.

"And I *wasn't* married when I got raped," Cherie said. "I met Greg later."

Laurel lifted her chin. "What's your point?"

Marie spoke for all of them. "That sex and relationships with men are harder for us than they used to be, but not impossible. Having a kid is great. Just….don't give up on men until you've given 'em a fair try. Okay?"

How was it that she hadn't realized she was the only one in the group who had resolved to stay celibate?

She nodded, although she hadn't changed her mind.

"When are you due?" someone asked then.

In chatter about bottle-feeding versus breast, offers of hand-me-down clothes, even a stroller and tales about their own children, Laurel almost forgot their reservations.

Almost.

DESPITE HER CERTAINTY, she was so nervous when she went into her doctor's office to take the pregnancy test, she couldn't just sit and wait for the results, pretending she cared what *Good Housekeeping* said about organizing closets. She went for a walk, just a couple of blocks, but it was easier to reason with herself when she was moving than sitting still in a waiting room full of other people.

You think *you're pregnant,* her doubting inner self said, *but so did Bloody Mary. Haven't you ever heard of hysterical pregnancy?*

She had, and she might be a good candidate, as desperate as she was to be pregnant.

"I'll bet Queen Mary didn't have morning sickness," she argued with herself.

A couple of passing teenage boys in gigantic pants and black bandannas gave her a "yo, you're crazy, lady" look.

Maybe she was. Her breath came short. Thank God she hadn't told Caleb.

There was one way to settle this.

Laurel turned resolutely and went back to the clinic.

The receptionist didn't even let her sit down. "Dr. Schapiro will see you now."

She escorted Laurel to an office rather than an examining room.

The doctor was perhaps fifty, with a dark bob of hair, crinkles beside her eyes and a warmth that seemed genuine. She stood and shook hands with Laurel across the desk.

"I know this is good news for you. You're pregnant."

Laurel closed her eyes momentarily against a wave of joy and relief.

"It is good news?"

"Yes, I…yes."

Her gaze was curious, but she didn't ask why Laurel hadn't been back to have the sperm implanted here. "We'll get you scheduled for your first prenatal exam, and I've already written you a prescription for vitamins. How are you feeling?"

"Nauseated." Laurel made a face. "Pretty much constantly. Or maybe I should say, unpredictably. I thought it was called morning sickness. Shouldn't I feel great in the afternoon?"

Dr. Schapiro laughed. "Unfortunately, it's called that only because nausea on first rising is common. There are women who tell me they feel dandy in the morning and then can't eat dinner, and others who suffer from a certain level of nausea pretty much all day. I take it you're one of those?"

Laurel nodded. "I'm trying to keep eating. I know it's important. But it's hard. Every so often I'm suddenly starved, but if I eat very much I throw it up an hour later."

"The good news is, morning sickness usually only lasts through the first trimester. But it's really important that you're able to keep food down." She talked for a few minutes about eating small amounts, what foods were least likely to cause nausea and which were most important for the fetus's development.

Armed with a pile of handouts and an appointment a month later, Laurel walked out of the clinic in a daze. She was pregnant. First try. She'd *known* she was pregnant. So why the sense of unreality now?

Because she hadn't gotten pregnant the usual way? Well, yeah. The big event had borne more resemblance to treating herself for a yeast infection. Except for the standing-on-her-head part.

A chilly trickle down her spine made her wonder whether she was really feeling fear. She'd taken a huge step, and now had to live with the consequences. *And* she had to tell everybody, starting with her dad and sister. She'd have to suffer the questions and curiosity of everybody at work. She wasn't even sure how the women in her support group truly felt about her decision.

But it's my decision, she reminded herself. Nobody but hers. Which, when she got right down to it, was what made it so scary.

Managing financially was a worry, of course. She made a decent living at Vallone, Penn and Cooper, the law firm, but she'd need to take maternity leave, and then find reliable day care. Caleb had insisted on paying child support at a very minimum. She knew he'd give her more if she'd take it, but the reality was, Caleb had fathered her baby out of kindness, no matter what he'd said to the contrary. What happened once he got married and had other children? What if his wife resented the existence of this child that wasn't even the vestige of a former relationship? Laurel had to be self-supporting. She wanted to be able to put away a good deal of the money from Caleb in a college fund.

When she got home, Laurel called first her father and then her sister and invited them to dinner Saturday night.

"I have news," she admitted to Megan. "No, not a word until Saturday."

"You're going back to law school!" her sister crowed.

The pain took her by surprise. She should have realized that's what Meg would assume. Why did it hurt so much? Because her own sister didn't know her well enough to understand why she couldn't go back? Because a part of her hadn't quite let go of the dream?

She managed to say, "No. It's not that. Sorry."

"Oh. Well," Meg rallied, "don't be sorry. I can't wait to hear what the news is. Dad's coming, you said?"

Friday afternoon, as she left work, Caleb fell in step with her in the lobby. "You going to let a guy take you out to dinner?"

Startled, she spun so quickly her ankle turned and she would have gone down but for his quick grip on her arm. "You always manage to sneak up on me!"

"What better place to lie in wait for you?"

"Did you just get in?"

"12:16 p.m. I went home, took a shower, changed clothes, then headed here."

They emerged onto Fourth Street, where traffic was bumper to bumper and the sidewalks jammed. Caleb laid a hand on her back to steer her. "I'm a block down."

"Of course you are."

His grin flashed. As long as she'd known him, everyone had teased him about his luck.

In the crowd, talking wasn't practical. Horns sounded, bus brakes squealed and the sound of a deep bass pounded from a car that was stuck in traffic. Neither Caleb nor Laurel said a word until Caleb unlocked his Prius and they both got in and the racket of the outside world was buffered. He put the key in the ignition, but didn't turn it. Instead, he looked at her. "So?"

She knew what he was asking. "I'm pregnant."

His smile was a glorious burst of delight. "Really? Now?"

"No, tomorrow." She poked him. "Of course, now."

"You've had a pregnancy test?"

"Yes, and I'm spending half my time hugging toilets."

"Morning sickness?"

Laurel sighed. "In lieu of rejecting the fetus, my body is rejecting everything else I put in it."

"My mom swears morning sickness is why she never had another kid. She actually ended up in the hospital when she got dehydrated."

Great. She'd needed to hear this.

"Most women go through it and come out just fine on the other side." She was counting on it. "Which is usually after three months."

"And right now, you're—" he frowned, calculating "—five weeks?"

"Six."

"Have you told anyone?"

She took a deep breath. "Tomorrow is the big day. I'm having my dad and Meg over to dinner. I admitted to Meg that I had a big announcement."

He must have heard something in her tone. "Did she guess?"

"She assumed I was going back to law school."

"Ah." Caleb studied her, but said nothing.

"What?"

His eyebrows rose. "I didn't say anything."

"But you were thinking it." Laurel knew she sounded bellicose.

"I was thinking, My God, we're having a baby."

Tears abruptly filled her eyes, and she bit her lip. "We are, aren't we?"

He reached out and took her hand. "Did you ever think, back in college, that we'd come to this?"

"Not that you'd donate sperm." She had sometimes dreamed that one day they would look at each other and realize that the *like* they'd fallen into had become *love*. Maybe it had, on her side. Or at least, she'd become aware of the possibility. But that she'd cold-bloodedly choose him to father her baby because he was handsome, smart and healthy… No, never that.

"Yeah, that one would have taken me by surprise, too." Still smiling, he started the engine. "Do you want me to be there tomorrow night?"

She turned her whole upper body. "Would you?" Hope trembled in her voice.

"I'd like to be." He looked over his shoulder to merge into traffic. "I was afraid…"

"What?"

His shoulders moved, a small jerk. "That you wouldn't want to be open about me being the father."

Nonplussed, she realized she had never really thought it through. If Matt had fathered her baby, she'd intended to keep the knowledge among a chosen few. Probably her dad and sister. They'd met Matt a few times and knew he and Laurel were friends. But a more public announcement would have been awkward all around. Either she explained to everyone that it was just sperm, or people would think he and she had had a fling, which wasn't kind to Sheila.

But with Caleb… It wouldn't matter if most people assumed they'd had a brief relationship. At least, it wouldn't to her.

She sneaked a glance at his profile.

He turned his head, his blue eyes meeting hers. "This taking deep thought?"

"No, I was just realizing that it didn't. Unless you'd rather I kept it to myself, I don't mind if everyone knows you're the father."

"Like I told you, I want to *be* a father. In every sense of the word."

If he hadn't signed a contract and parenting plan—well, okay, if he wasn't Caleb—that might have scared her. If Matt had started talking like that, she would have freaked. She'd wanted the baby to be *hers*. Hers alone.

How funny that now she was okay with this baby being *theirs*.

Unaware of her reverie, Caleb muttered a profanity as a hulking SUV cut him off on the freeway.

"Have you told *your* parents?" she asked.

He shook his head. "I figured I'd wait until it happened."

She couldn't blame him, since she'd done the same. Almost at random, Laurel said, "I'm planning dinner for six tomorrow."

"Cooking doesn't nauseate you?"

"Yeah, but I'll survive."

"Why don't I cook? You have to admit, my sweet-and-sour pork is to die for."

"Why *aren't* you married?"

"Huh?"

"Do you know how many women would kill for a man who'd make that kind of offer?"

This grin was faintly wicked. "Yeah, I'm one of a kind. Women do propose all the time. But I'm saving myself for…" He broke off.

"For?"

"God knows. An octogenarian wedding?"

"You and a little white-haired lady in a nursing home?"

"Maybe." He growled something under his breath. "Does traffic get worse every day, or is it my imagination?"

Contemplating the giant parking lot I-5 had become, Laurel said, "It gets worse, I think. That's why I ride the bus."

His face settled into a frown. "I don't like the idea of you having to take buses when you're really pregnant."

"As opposed to only a tiny bit pregnant?"

He ignored her flippancy. "What if you have a long wait? And the Metro buses have lousy shock absorbers." He wasn't done. "What if you have to stand? And you know how you get jostled getting on and off."

She did know, and wasn't looking forward to it. But the idea of squeezing herself behind the wheel of a car, only to inch along the freeway, was even less appealing.

"The bus is actually pretty relaxing. And people are nice. Somebody would give up their seat for me."

"Hell, let's get off here." He took the Forty-fifth Street exit and got in the left lane to head west, toward the Sound. "What do you feel like eating?"

Her stomach quivered. "A piece of dry toast?"

"In other words, don't bother taking you to Le Gourmand?"

She groped through her purse for the soda crackers she'd taken to carrying. "Really, really no."

"Ah, well, let me get some takeout and we'll go to your place."

Even the smell of his Korean takeout upset her stomach. She had to crack her window, which would have helped more if the air outside hadn't been diesel-laden. But she made it home and curled up on her couch a safe distance from Caleb while he ate. Her stomach had settled enough to accept a piece of toast, which he made for her, and some strawberries.

He didn't stay long, promising to be back by four tomorrow with the groceries he needed to make dinner. "You don't have to do a thing" were his last words.

The next afternoon, Caleb returned so vibrantly full of life and energy Laurel felt washed out in comparison. She'd been so tired all day that she'd already taken a nap. She only hoped today was an anomaly. How would she get through a day at work if all she wanted to do was crawl under her desk and snooze?

She left him to cook while she showered and then fortified herself with a couple of crackers. She wouldn't even *have* to make an announcement if she had to dash off and puke the minute Dad and Meg walked through the door.

They arrived separately. Megan, four years younger than Laurel, was a hotshot software designer for a small firm that existed in Microsoft's shadow in Redmond, just across Lake Washington from Seattle. She was currently working on a team designing some kind of management software that she claimed would be a big seller thanks to flexibility from a rules-based interface.

Whatever that was. Laurel was embarrassed to have so little grasp of what her sister actually did.

Both sisters had had dishwater-blond hair when they were toddlers—the kind that the sun bleached to silver-blond every summer. Laurel's had stayed somewhere between blond and light brown, while Megan's had darkened to a rich shade of mahogany. Megan was, in Laurel's admittedly biased opinion, a beauty. She had inherited their mother's slim build instead of Grandma Woodall's buxom one, which Laurel considered something of a curse.

In low-cut jeans, heels, a cropped lime-green blazer and big gold-hoop earrings, Megan strolled in, dropped a huge purse and hugged first Caleb and then Laurel.

"You didn't say Caleb would be here."

"He invited himself yesterday. And then offered to cook."

"What a man," her sister said admiringly.

Laurel laughed. "That's what I told him."

"You know, if you don't want him…" Megan gave him a saucy look.

He grinned at her. "One Woodall sister is enough for me, thanks."

Laurel suspected that he saw Megan as a little sister, and for all her teasing, Meg had never given the slightest sign of a crush on Caleb. She was currently dating another computer geek, a guy who would have been handsome if he'd ever comb his hair or thought about what he was putting on in the morning. Apparently his virtuosity in HTML and a dozen other computer languages offset his stylistic lack for a girl who'd cared deeply what she put on in the morning from about her second birthday on.

Dad arrived grumbling about traffic. "I had to go in to work today. Somebody screwed up."

He was an engineer at Boeing, working on a new fuel-efficient plane that was to be built in Everett. In his mid-fifties, he had to be the catch of the Boeing plant, single, nice looking if not exactly handsome and still possessing all his hair. It was the color of Megan's, and turning silver dramatically at the temples. As far as Laurel could tell, he had never considered remarrying. She knew he dated, but not once since her mom had died when she was eleven had he introduced a woman to his daughters.

"Smells good," he said, shaking Caleb's hand. "Thank God you took over the kitchen."

Laurel threw a magazine at him. He laughed when it fell short.

"So what's the news?" he asked. "Meggie told me last night that you have an announcement."

Caleb clanged a pan lid. "Why don't we wait until we sit down?"

"So you can listen? Or has she already told you?" Megan asked.

He smiled at her. "Not saying."

"Pooh."

"Anybody want some wine?" Laurel stood. "Caleb, how far away from sitting down are we?"

"Five minutes. In fact, you can take the salad to the table."

Laurel's father opened the wine and poured, and a few minutes later they were seated. The food did smell good. So good, she was having one of her brief and usually foolish moments of genuine hunger.

Meg leveled a look at her. "Out with it. We're ready to toast. Assuming it's good news?"

"It's good news." Laurel met Caleb's gaze and drew strength from the encouragement she saw in his eyes. Then she bit her lip, looked at her dad and said, "I'm pregnant."

There was an awful moment of silence. He stared at her, as if uncomprehending. "Pregnant?"

"I should have told you I was going to try. But I was afraid you'd want to talk me out of it."

"I didn't know you were even dating…" His dazed stare swung to the fourth person at the table. "Caleb?"

Laurel decided to be blunt. "No, we aren't sleeping together. Yes, Caleb's the father. I asked him to donate sperm."

"You mean?" Megan looked stunned.

"Yes. I chose to be a single mother. Instead of going to a donor bank, I decided to ask a friend. Caleb wants to be involved in my baby's life."

He spoke up then. "As I told Laurel, there's no one I'd rather have a child with."

Her father half rose. "You got my daughter pregnant?"

"Daddy!" She grabbed his arm. "He didn't 'get' me pregnant. Not the way you mean. At my request, he donated sperm."

Her father sagged back into his seat. "Good God, Laurel! You're twenty-eight. Have you given up on life?"

That hurt. It would have hurt worse if Caleb hadn't said quietly, "Seems to me she's embracing it."

"But you're writing off any possibility of falling in love and getting married."

She wanted to say no, but that would be a lie.

"You didn't believe me when I told you before. I just…I can't imagine it, Dad." Her voice was small, shaky. She might have fallen apart if Caleb hadn't been there offering steady support by his mere presence. "But I want children. I want a family. And I can have that without getting married. Is that so awful?"

He scrubbed a hand over his face. "No. No, of course not. You'll be a hell of a mother, Laurel."

Tears in her eyes, Megan stood and hugged Laurel. "I should have said this first. Congratulations."

"Thank you," she whispered.

Her father lifted his wineglass. "To my first grandchild."

They all drank, Laurel taking the tiniest of sips before setting her glass down again.

Caleb handed Megan the bowl of rice to begin dishing up, then the salad to George Woodall.

He took it, but seemed unaware it was in his hand. "I don't like the idea of you managing on your own, Laurel. Being a parent…it's hard work."

"You managed on your own, after Mommy died."

"You girls were eleven and seven. And don't you remember how tough that first year was? Meggie had to drop out of soccer. I just couldn't get her to practices. You two went off to school every day in mismatched outfits, your hair barely brushed."

"But in the end, you were a great parent."

"You weren't babies. Laurel, no matter how beat you

are, there'll be no one besides you to get up in the middle of the night, no one to give a bottle, get to day care when you're held up…" He shook his head. "You know I'll do what I can, but I'm a long way from retirement age. And Meggie seems to work twelve-hour days."

"It's not that bad," Laurel's sister said. "Although… Honestly, I'm not sure I've ever actually held a baby. You know I never babysat."

Megan hadn't liked little kids. By the time she was ten or twelve, she'd curl her lip and say, "Ew, kids." Laurel wasn't expecting a whole lot in the babysitting department from her sister, at least until her child was of an age to start learning to navigate the Internet.

"I don't expect a lot of help." Laurel accepted the rice from her sister. "Daddy, dish up."

He looked down uncomprehendingly at the bowl still in his hand, then transferred some salad to his plate and handed it to Caleb. Poor Caleb, who had slaved in the kitchen and was probably starving. He always was.

To reassure her father, Laurel talked about some of the research she'd done on maternity leave, neighborhood day-care centers and mothers' groups.

"I do plan to be here," Caleb interrupted, when she was waxing eloquent about her ability to handle her job and a baby with one hand tied behind her back.

His scowl was for her. He wasn't jumping in to make her dad feel better, he was irked at her for leaving him out of her calculations.

As if the two of them were alone at the table, she said, "You travel so much."

"I can curtail it when you need me. I have people working for me who'll be glad to take over."

"But…I didn't ask you to change your life."

His face darkened. "I thought I made it clear that I wasn't going to be just a biological father. That if I signed on, it was going to be the real deal."

"I didn't expect you to change diapers, either."

"Why not? Don't fathers do that?" He shot a glance at George.

"I did," her dad agreed.

"I'll be here, Laurel," Caleb repeated.

Absurdly, her eyes were filling with tears. Pressing her lips together, she nodded, then dabbed at her eyes with her napkin.

As touched as she was, Laurel was a bit annoyed when her father seemed to relax after this exchange, apparently reassured that Caleb intended to do his manly duty. Hadn't he raised her and Megan to be strong, independent women who could cope with whatever life threw at them? Apparently, single parenting wasn't one of those things.

She tried to excuse him. He was from another generation that still had faith in traditional two-parent homes. But the world had changed. Look how many gay and lesbian couples had children, how well open adoption was working, how single mothers banded together to share their loads.

But Laurel couldn't shake the feeling that if Meg had made the same announcement, he wouldn't have been so alarmed. Her father doubted *her* ability to handle the stress of single parenthood, not the ability of women in general or even of his daughters in particular. Despite his support, in the end he was just like everyone else. He didn't understand why she couldn't go back to being herself, the Laurel who hadn't been taught how powerless she really was, who hadn't faced death, who hadn't spent weeks in the hospital recovering from broken bones and swelling that compressed her brain. And because she couldn't, he assumed she was weak, that she would falter as a mom.

Knowing he thought like that stung.

But her father being her father, he disarmed her hurt and resentment before dinner was over. He set down his fork, looked at her and said, "Laurel, I want you to know that I didn't mean to imply you can't do this on your own." His smile held regret and remembered grief. "I just wish you didn't have to."

"Oh, Daddy!" Blinking back more tears—damn, she wished she didn't cry so easily these days—Laurel stood and hugged him. With her eyes closed, the familiar scent of him in her nostrils, and his strong arms closed around her, she felt so safe.

Straightening away from him was a wrench, just as moving out of his house the second time had been. She couldn't be Daddy's little girl forever, and she would forever know she wasn't really safe.

"Thank you," she whispered, and went back to her place at the table.

When he and Megan left an hour later, Caleb was at her side to wave goodbye.

"I really appreciate you coming," she told him, assuming he was leaving, too.

"Hmm? Oh, no problem."

"Are you taking off, too?"

"I thought I'd hang around for a while."

"Okay," she said, although he hadn't asked for permission.

Inside, he asked, "How's the stomach?"

She'd remembered what the doctor said and barely nibbled. "Actually, I feel fine," she said with surprise.

"Good. Why don't you sit down and I'll get you some herbal tea?"

That sounded nice. Grateful everyone had helped clean up, Laurel headed toward the couch, ready to relax.

That is, until behind her Caleb continued, his tone flat. Maybe even hard. "And then, you and I need to have a talk."

CHAPTER FOUR

LAUREL'S VOICE ROSE. "What do you mean, I'm trying to shut you out?"

"That seems clear enough to me." Caleb paced her miniature living room, three steps one way, three the other. He considered himself an easygoing guy, but tonight she'd enraged him almost as much as she had when she asked another man to father her baby. "Didn't you just spend the last two hours trying to convince your dad how competent you are to single-handedly raise our child?"

"I was trying to make him understand my decision!" She sat on the couch, glaring up at him, her head turning as he passed in front of her.

"I thought it had become *our* decision."

"I made the decision to have a baby long before…"

"I butted into it?" he interrupted.

"I didn't say that!"

"But you meant it!"

Her lower lip stuck out in a way that was familiar to him from the thousand maddening arguments during their PLU years. "Maybe I did."

Ready to yank on his hair in frustration, Caleb was struck by a sudden thought: he hadn't seen Laurel look so stubborn, even combative, so *alive*, since they'd hugged goodbye at Sea-Tac Airport the summer she saw him off to Ecuador.

His Laurel, who had felt powerless since even the choice of life and death had been taken out of her hands in that parking garage, was grabbing for control, because something mattered a whole hell of a lot to her.

Next to that, his hurt feelings didn't count.

He stopped midroom and shook his head. "Listen to us. We haven't squabbled like this in years."

She sniffed. "We never *squabbled*. We debated. And I usually won."

"Yet another subject open to argument."

She bit her lip to hide her smile. Seeing it, he couldn't help laughing.

"Okay, okay. This one you can win. I understand why you felt you had to convince your dad that you're superhuman."

She gave a queenly inclination of her head. "Thank you."

Anger gone, Caleb dropped into her single easy chair and slid low, spine curved. "Just...don't forget I'm here, Laurel. For you, any time. You know I mean that."

Abruptly, tears sparkled in her eyes. She swiped at them impatiently. "Darn it, Caleb! I'm trying to be mad at you!"

"Yeah? You can quit any time."

"I don't want to quit! I *am* competent to raise this baby alone. I swear my father relaxed the minute you stepped in." She lowered her voice to a gruff note that failed to echo her dad's. "'Ah, she has a man after all. I don't need to worry.'"

She looked cute trying to scowl at him, her lashes still damp, her hair sagging sideways from the elegant topknot she'd earlier achieved.

Caleb found himself smiling. "You do have a man. You don't have to worry."

"Aargh!" Laurel jumped to her feet.

"Now, now," he soothed. "Don't upset the baby."

She picked up a pile of magazines from the coffee table and flung them at him.

Caleb laughed as they rained down on him, slithering to the floor and to each side of him in the chair. "Temper, temper."

She stamped her foot. "Nobody could ever make me as mad as you do!"

"Isn't that what best friends are for?"

"No! They're supposed to support each other!"

His amusement vanished, and he was dead serious when he said, "That's what I'm trying to do. But I can't support you if you won't lean, just a bit."

Her expression changed, and they stared at each other for a wondering moment. She moaned. "I knew I shouldn't eat dinner," she said, then dashed to the bathroom.

By the time Caleb got to his feet, she'd dropped to her knees in front of the toilet and was heaving up what she'd just eaten. Even as she puked, she was poking behind her with one foot trying to shut the bathroom door.

He didn't let her. Because he couldn't get into the bathroom, Caleb sank to his haunches behind her and laid a gentle hand on her back. He waited until she was done and her body sagged, then rubbed.

She groped with one hand until she found the lever and flushed the toilet. "I'm disgusting!"

"It's not the first time I've seen you puke," he reminded her.

Laurel never had handled booze well. They hadn't been

friends a month when she'd drunk too much beer at a kegger and hadn't made it back to the dorm before she'd had to vomit. Caleb remembered the night, the day's heat lingering, lights in dorm buildings around them, Laurel's soft whimper as she sank to her knees beside a towering rhododendron. Him leading her home, taking her to the bathroom and helping her rinse her mouth before he tucked her into her bed and left her already falling asleep.

"Don't remind me," she mumbled now.

"Yeah, but just think." He kneaded her shoulders as she slumped against the toilet. "That time you were sick because you'd done something stupid. This time, it's because you did something smart."

"You think?" she whispered.

"I think."

After a moment, she said, "I liked what you said to Dad. About how I'm embracing life."

"Isn't that what you're doing?"

Again, she was silent for a moment. "I don't know," she said at last. "I hope so." Her shoulders rose and fell in a deep sigh. "Thanks, Caleb." She began to struggle to her feet. "I'll feel better once I've brushed my teeth."

He hated taking his hands from her, but rose, too, and let her shut the bathroom door this time.

Outside, in the tiny nook that passed for a hall in her house, Caleb realized he was going to be shut out often. He *had* to let her shut those doors, real and metaphorical, or she might believe that he didn't have faith in her ability to cope.

On the other hand, he wasn't going to be waiting for her to invite him in, either. Or she'd be raising his kid alone, and he'd be wondering how it happened. Because if there was one thing Laurel had become good at, it was shutting other people out.

Through the door, he asked, "You ever call Nadia?"

Silence. Water ran, then was turned off. Laurel finally came out of the bathroom. "No, but I will," she said, gaze sliding from his. "Do you want another cup of coffee?"

"Doesn't the smell make you sick?"

"No, now that my stomach is empty, I'm starved again. Coffee would smell good."

He patted her on the back. "Six, seven more weeks. You'll make it."

On her way to the kitchen, Laurel cast him a look that verged on dislike. "Easy for you to say. You'll be out of the country for most of it."

"I don't have to be," he repeated. "I can delegate."

Still prickly, she said, "I'm not very good company these days. You might as well travel now. If you plan to be around more after the baby is first born."

If he planned to be around. Caleb counted silently to ten.

"I plan to be around. But I think I'll skip the coffee tonight, head on home."

"Oh?" She didn't sound as if she cared. "I'll walk you out."

"No." Once upon a time, he might have wrapped her in a hug or kissed her cheek. Now he only nodded toward the refrigerator. "Get yourself something to eat. But call me if you want me, Laurel. I mean it."

Her voice softened, or at least he imagined it did. "I know you do, Caleb. Thank you for coming tonight."

"Any time," he told her, and let himself out.

Time to tell his own parents.

HIS FATHER SET DOWN his drink so hard, liquid splashed onto the table. "Are you crazy?"

Caleb had braced himself for their questions and concern, but he hadn't anticipated the genuine shock on their faces when he told them right before dinner at their house.

"You know how long Laurel and I have been friends."

"Friends don't impregnate friends."

"Clay." His wife shook her head in warning.

"What?" he asked her. "I'm supposed to smile and say, Isn't that nice? Do *you* think it's nice that some woman who isn't married to our son is going to be raising our grandchild?"

"Some woman?" Caleb's temper sparked. "Laurel's a hell of a lot more than that! You claimed to like her!"

"We do like her…" his mother began, but was interrupted by her husband.

"What does liking her have to do with anything? She's not our daughter-in-law. Hell, she could decide we shouldn't see the baby if she feels like it."

"We have a parenting plan…"

"Were you smart enough to lock in some legal rights?" He saw the answer on Caleb's face. "No, she was hurt five years ago, and you still feel so bad you gave her everything she wanted. A baby and a check every month."

Caleb stood. "She didn't want the check. I had to insist."

"Ever occur to you that you were reeled in like a big, flopping rainbow trout?"

They shouted then, father and son, until Caleb's mother stood, too.

"Both of you, sit down!"

They were surprised enough to comply.

"Do *I* have permission to speak?"

Two nods.

"Caleb, what your father is saying very poorly—" she narrowed her gaze at him "—is that we worry about you getting hurt. It's not that we don't like Laurel. You know we always have. And we feel sorry for her. But once you hold your baby, you won't want to let go. You don't understand yet what you've given away."

He started to speak and she shook her head.

"What if she marries someone else? If she no longer wants you to spend significant time with your child? Will you take her to court? Will you walk away?"

"It won't come to that…"

"How do you know?"

How did he know? Laurel had tried to sever their friendship once, so he knew she was capable of it. Had he been a fool, giving a gift this huge?

No. He shook his head, refusing to believe it. They were best friends. The other time, she'd tried to shut him out because she hurt, not as a cold-blooded choice. They were having a baby *together*.

Caleb stood again. "I hoped you'd be happy. But I can't make you accept your grandchild. I guess you'll have a choice to make."

He walked out, snagging his coat from the tree in the front hall and quietly shut the front door behind him.

BIG SURPRISE, CALEB LEFT her a phone message only three days later to tell her he had to go to Costa Rica. "It'll be a short trip," he promised. "I'll check e-mail a couple of times a day."

In a way, she wasn't surprised that he was fleeing the country. He'd told her tersely a few days before that his parents weren't happy he'd donated sperm. She could tell they'd had a hurtful scene, one for which she was to blame. Caleb probably welcomed a distraction.

The "short trip" lasted a week. He was home ten days, then gone to Paraguay and Uruguay for two weeks.

Not that she had the energy for him anyway. Laurel was exhausted. She nibbled a cracker before stumbling out of bed in the morning. Somehow she put herself together enough to make it to work, laid her head on her desk and napped during her lunch break and robotlike caught the bus for the long ride home. She might or might not get something to eat, then fell into bed until her alarm shrilled at her to wake up the next morning. She was alternately starved, queasy and so nauseated she had to vomit. Eating became a grim matter of choosing foods her stomach would tolerate that also provided adequate nutrition for the fetus.

She tried not to look at herself in the mirror, because all she saw was a pale, exhausted shadow of herself, a wraith. When she saw the doctor again she'd lost weight, not gained.

Dr. Schapiro was satisfied with the diet she described, and decided to hold off on antinausea medication for another month. "But if you've lost weight again…"

Laurel talked to Caleb several times during the ten days he was back from his travels and he came over on Saturday and ended up helping her with yard work.

Which was nice of him, but she would have appreciated him keeping his opinion of how she looked to himself.

Comparing her to survivors of malaria was unkind.

Weren't pregnant women supposed to *bloom?* Why wasn't she blooming? Why was her body screaming, "Intruder alert! Intruder alert! Eject! Eject!"

The next time Caleb appeared, it was in the lobby again as she was leaving work.

Laurel didn't even have the energy to be startled.

"Caleb."

Although he'd already fallen into step with her, he stopped abruptly and swung her to face him. "Good God. You look like you'd topple over if the breeze picks up."

"I'm tired."

"You know what? I can tell." His mouth a tight line, his brows pulled together in a frown, he steered her toward the revolving doors and then down the street a block and a half to his parked car. When he unlocked the door, she sank into the passenger seat gratefully.

He started the car. "It's Friday. You're taking next week off."

"No, I'm not."

Taking his gaze from the rearview mirror, he surveyed her with disconcerting thoroughness. "You don't look tired. You look like hell. If you won't take care of yourself, I'm going to make you."

The angry, stern man beside her bore no resemblance to the laid-back Caleb she knew. Through her fog of exhaustion, Laurel once again was forced to realize that he was now a man, and one she didn't know as well as she had that happy-go-lucky, idealistic boy.

"I just need to catch up on sleep this weekend."

"Are you still sick to your stomach?"

The organ in question lurched, and she clapped a hand to her mouth.

Swearing, he braked with the car halfway into traffic and grabbed for a bag in the backseat. He dumped something out—she heard objects fall—then thrust it at her.

Horns sounded.

"Shove it up your…" Caleb muttered, then pulled out even as she hunched over the bag.

Somehow she kept from vomiting, perhaps because she'd barely nibbled at lunch.

"What does the doctor say?" Caleb asked, that same hard edge to his voice.

Swallowing to quell the nausea, Laurel said, "She thought it sounded as if I'm eating enough. She'd rather I was gaining weight."

He shook his head. "She can't do anything about the nausea?"

"There's medication, but I hate to take anything I can avoid."

Frowning, he said nothing for several blocks.

"When do you see her again?"

"Um…" Laurel pictured the calendar by her phone at home. "Almost three more weeks."

She received an incredulous stare.

"Did you admit to her how crappy you feel?"

"Uh…"

"Didn't think so." Caleb brooded until he reached the entrance to the freeway express lanes and was able to accelerate.

"Take some vacation days. Come and stay at my place next week."

Looking down into the plastic bag, a wave of longing struck Laurel. To have nine whole days with no alarm going off, to be able to sleep all she wanted, to have Caleb pampering her…

Fighting the weakness, she shook her head. "I'm going to need all my vacation time when I have the baby."

"Then you'll take some leave without pay after the baby is born. Laurel, you know I want to help with more than that damn child support you so reluctantly agreed to take. I have plenty. Believe me, you can afford to take a few months off. You need the break *now*."

She ought to be offended by his attempt to play the autocrat, but honestly…she was relieved. The first trimester was almost over. In another week, the nausea and exhaustion might pass.

"My garden…"

"Will survive without you. If you're bored, you can pull weeds in my flower beds."

"Do you *have* flower beds?"

"Remember the tulip bulbs I planted?"

"Oh, right."

"They're about to bloom, and I've got over fifty rhododendrons now. My yard is going to be spectacular."

She hadn't seen his house in ages. She remembered a glorious view across the Sound toward Bremerton and Port Orchard. Built of wood and glass, his home had seemed like a natural outgrowth among the Douglas firs and cedars on the acreage he owned on Vashon Island. When she was last there, half the rooms were still unfurnished, and she was sure there hadn't been more than a few scraggly shrubs that he'd inherited when he bought the place.

"I haven't been there in…" Laurel paused, trying to remember.

"Years? I know. You never seem interested."

"I'm just…set in my ways."

"I know," he said again. "It's okay. I haven't minded coming to see you instead of the other way around. I know Vashon is a trek."

It really wasn't. The ferry ride from Fauntleroy in west Seattle was only about twenty minutes. She couldn't use that as an excuse.

The truth was, he'd made all the effort to maintain their friendship. She was glad to see him when he appeared, but had never roused herself to do more than e-mail when she hadn't heard from him in a while.

Laurel was ashamed to see how much he'd given, and how much she'd taken. And now he was trying to do more for her.

Not just for her, she reminded herself. For the baby, too. For *his* baby. She didn't have to feel entirely selfish if she let him help.

She was aware of a wash of anxiety at the idea of going away—even if "away" was only a twenty-minute ferry ride from Seattle. She hadn't spent the night anywhere but her father's house and then hers since she'd been released from the hospital. In fact, it had been five years, Laurel realized in astonishment. And it wasn't even that she was afraid to spend the night elsewhere, that was the odd thing. She hadn't really turned down invitations, except Caleb's to join him on a trip to Central America. Rather, she just hadn't *considered* going anywhere. She liked her routine.

Although truth be known, she was getting awfully tired of that routine.

She didn't really want to spend the rest of her life tied to her homely flat-roofed house, did she?

Without giving herself time for second thought, she said, "Okay. I'd really like to stay with you. This has been a pretty rotten few weeks. I'll e-mail as soon as I get home to let my boss know I'm taking next week off. Honestly, I doubt anyone will mind. I haven't told them I'm pregnant yet, so they think I'm fighting some horrible flu. Nobody wants to come near me. I can clear the lunchroom just by walking in."

"And the restroom by tearing in and lunging for the toilet."

She gave a tiny giggle. "Well…yeah. A few days ago a couple of attorneys were putting on makeup and gossiping, and boy did they exit fast when they heard me start to puke."

"You *will* start feeling better?"

"So all the books say." Laurel sighed. "But most women don't seem to feel this lousy the first trimester, either, so who knows?"

"Maybe my sperm is toxic."

She rolled her head to give him the evil eye. "Oh, that's a comforting thought. I suppose there is awful pollution in some of the places you visit."

"It's especially nice when the planes dump chemicals on the marijuana fields. And on anyone and anything that happens to be nearby."

"You've seen it?"

"Can't miss it. Lethal crop-dusting."

"Maybe your DNA *has* mutated."

He flashed her a cross-eyed look with his tongue dangling out of his mouth. "Maybe he'll look like me."

She was startled into a laugh. "No, *she'll* probably inherit my limp, dishwater hair and eyes of such an indeterminate color the people at the DMV argue over what to put down."

His hand closed over hers. "*She* will be beautiful, just like her mommy. With hair the color of honey and eyes that change color depending on her mood."

Tears filled her eyes. "That's the nicest thing anyone has said to me, ever."

Caleb laughed, a deep, merry sound. "Remind me not to compliment you again."

Embarrassed, she wiped her eyes and sniffed. "I'm sorry. Everything makes me cry lately."

"That's traditional, I hear."

Now that she thought of it, the books said that, too, but she'd just assumed she was depressed. "How do you know?"

"You've met Stewart, right?"

She nodded. Stewart Deaver was a friend of Caleb's from… Laurel couldn't remember. The Peace Corps? She knew he had helped Caleb set up his Web site.

"His wife just had their second kid. He claims to be scared of her when she's pregnant. If she isn't crying, she's mad. Sara has always said she wants to have three kids. Stewart says no way."

It would take courage to get pregnant a second time, Laurel already knew. Three times? Her stomach wobbled. *Nope.* But maybe she'd change her mind after the baby was born.

Voice soft, Caleb asked, "Do you know how often you touch your stomach?"

Surprised, she looked down to see that, indeed, her hand was splayed over her abdomen. Her fingers curled, and she lifted her hand.

"Oh, dear. Maybe people at work have guessed."

"Is it a secret?"

"No-o…" She pursed her lips. "But I should officially give warning before everyone starts gossiping."

"And what are the odds you'll manage that?"

Remembering the two attorneys in the restroom, Laurel conceded, "Slim to none. Unless I make a preemptive strike."

"Do it as soon as you get back. You'll start showing pretty soon anyway."

She would. It wasn't lost on her that the waistbands of her pants and skirts hadn't gotten loose as weight fell off her. If she ever started really eating again, she was going to get well-rounded fast.

"We're here," Caleb said, pulling her from her reverie. "How quick can you pack?"

"It won't take long," she promised. "Why don't you find yourself something to eat while I throw stuff in a suitcase? I'll grab a box from the garage, too. We might as well bring all the perishable food."

He grinned at her over the roof of the car after they got out. "If I don't eat it first."

She packed in about ten minutes, taking only jeans, T-shirts and a couple of sweaters, sloppy canvas tennis shoes and sandals. Nine whole days without her having to squeeze into panty hose! No heels, no suits, maybe not even any makeup.

She added toiletries and half a dozen books to keep her happy while Caleb was working, then pulled her suitcase out to the living room to find that he had the box of food set on the table.

He loaded everything in the trunk while she e-mailed her boss and shut down her computer. Then she locked her front door and left a note at her closest neighbor's to say she'd be away for a week, and they drove away with her refusing to turn her head to look back even though anxiety had once again balled in her chest.

I can lounge around and be taken care of, she reminded herself. *Sleep in. Take walks. Laugh with Caleb.*

Gradually, she relaxed, until she found herself childishly excited about riding on the ferry.

Her enthusiasm suffered a jolt when they drove onto the dock and she saw how choppy the Sound was. Already queasy, she was bound to get seasick.

"It's such a short ride, I don't usually go up, but sure," Caleb said, when she asked if they could go up to the passenger deck.

Looking amused, he went outside with her, where they leaned against the railing and looked ahead as the ferry horn sounded and water churned. Seagulls swooped around them, and the dark creosoted pilings fell behind.

The cold, salty wind whipped Laurel's hair and seemed to cleanse her lungs. Instead of the motion increasing her nausea, it seemed to be settling her stomach. Clutching the railing, she drew in great breaths of air and laughed.

Beside her, Caleb turned his head and smiled. With the wind in his hair and the sun on his face, he looked more at home here than he did in the lobby of her office building.

"How long since you've been on a ferry?"

"Forever," she admitted, looking ahead toward the green hump that was Vashon. She'd closed herself in, she realized. She lived in a city surrounded by water and mountains, and she couldn't remember the last time she'd gone for a hike, or accepted an invitation to sail or even walked on the beach. This summer, she would do more, she vowed. Instead of catching the bus home, she'd go down to the waterfront and take the ferry to Bainbridge and back, just for fun. Maybe she'd drive up to Paradise on the flank of Mount Rainier and hike when the avalanche lilies were in bloom as much as a pregnant woman could.

The memory of the last time she'd been up to Rainier floated into her mind. She'd been with Caleb, of course. They'd just finished their sophomore or junior year in college.

How much of what she'd done or thought or felt seemed to be related to Caleb.

As if it were a natural corollary, she asked, "Have you talked to your parents since you got back?" She hated knowing that she'd damaged his relationship with them. One more thing she hadn't thought of when she'd asked first Matt and then Caleb to father her child.

He shrugged, not looking at her. "My mother."

Laurel's heart sank. "I take it they're not any happier about this?" She indicated her belly.

"They don't get how close we are." He paused. "Mom did ask about you. She'll come around."

Laurel nodded, not trusting her voice. Knowing how much his parents loved Caleb, she supposed they would. But they would always regret that this grandchild hadn't been born under more normal circumstances, that he or she wouldn't grow up under Caleb's roof. Thinking about them gave her a twist of guilt.

When the ferry landing and the tiny town grew near, Laurel let Caleb urge her down to the car. They drove off the ferry, in line with other islanders on their way home.

Vashon was beautiful, wooded from end to end with occasional pastures, businesses clustered in a couple of tiny communities, most of the homes on acreage like Caleb's. His was down a long gravel drive that felt as if it was plunging into a tunnel through a stand of mature Douglas firs and cedars, the understory thick and green, made up of ferns and salal and huckleberries.

When the car emerged from the trees and she saw the house ahead amid curved beds filled with naturalistic groupings of rhododendrons underplanted with tulips, lawn winding between the mulched beds, Laurel gasped.

"It's spectacular! Caleb! You let me brag about my teeny garden, and yours looks like…like…" Words failed her. "The Arboretum, or Olmstead Gardens or…"

"You notice everything I planted is easy care." Caleb shrugged, but his voice held a note that told her he was pleased by her awe.

"I've never seen so many varieties of rhody." When he stopped the car by the front porch, she got out.

When this property was logged, it had been done skillfully, leaving clusters of four and five firs or cedars here and there rather than stripping the land bare. Rough grass had once grown between, but now Caleb had dug out the shrubbery borders in long, graceful curves. Leggier rhododendrons grew in the shade close to the trees, thicker bushes in sunnier spots. She saw an amazing diversity of foliage, and huge clusters of blooms in pale pink, buttery yellow, lavender and fuchsia. Other shrubs and small trees were interplanted, she saw, with Japanese maples having deep red leaves and flowering cherries or plums that had likely already bloomed. At the lowest level, he'd added the salal and ferns native to the Northwest forest, as well as the tulips. From the size of the rhododendrons, she realized Caleb had to have been planting them ever since he'd bought the house.

A glorious fragrance wafted to her, and she identified the humming she'd been vaguely aware of as bees buzzing in the blooms.

Aware that Caleb had come around the car to stand beside her, Laurel turned to him. "You never said."

"Yeah, I did."

"You talked about digging and planting, but I thought just a bed or two. I had no idea you'd been so ambitious."

His shoulders moved, as if he was embarrassed. "I wasn't ambitious. I started because, jeez, I was a home owner and home owners should landscape. Right? But then I found out it's good therapy."

She nodded. Therapy was exactly what gardening had become to her, as well. Using her muscles, sweating, being outside in the sun or mist, creating earth richer than she'd started with, watching leaves unfurl, vines clamber, flowers open—all had given her a sense of purpose and of rightness she never felt when concrete was underfoot.

"So I finished the first bed," he gestured at one close to the house, "and decided it looked weird all by itself. I bought a book about rhododendrons, started making a game of finding new varieties. Somehow—" he rotated as if surprised himself to see the extent of his labors "—I just kept going."

"I keep realizing," Laurel heard herself say softly, "how much I don't know about you."

"You know me better than anyone else."

She shook her head. "I did, maybe, when you were twenty-two. But not anymore."

His expression when his eyes met hers was inscrutable. "I've always been here, Laurel."

She nodded, unable to say anything. Or, perhaps, unwilling to say, *I guess that means I was so self-absorbed I didn't bother seeing how you'd changed.*

"You're not the same person you were, either." His gaze was steady, his eyes so blue.

"No." They both heard her sadness. "I'm not."

"It doesn't matter, though." His hand caught hers. "What was it I said?"

She tried to smile, but felt her lips quiver. "'Friends forever.'"

"That hasn't changed."

"Thanks to you." Grief welled in her at the thought of how much she had lost, and how close she'd come to Caleb, too, being no more than a memory of a fun college friendship. And it would have been her fault.

"Now we're tied together once and for all." His gaze lowered deliberately to her stomach, then back to her face. "Our very genes have mingled."

Laurel felt that squeeze again in her belly she knew was sexual. She ignored it. Her body didn't understand that this baby was being born out of friendship, not lust.

"That's a funny thought, isn't it?" Laurel said.

"Not funny. Nice."

This smile came more easily. "It is nice."

His gaze moved over her face with an intensity that caused another odd cramp low down.

"You have color in your cheeks."

She reached up to find them warm. "I feel good. Hey! Really good," she said in surprise.

Caleb grinned, that dimple deepening, for a moment the boy a part of her wanted him to be forever. *"Mi casa es su casa."*

"Gracias" was the limit of her Spanish.

"Let's get your stuff inside," he said practically, and she followed him to the trunk of the car.

CHAPTER FIVE

ON THE SECOND FLOOR, Caleb stood at the window of his office and watched Laurel out in the yard. Every morning, sometime after breakfast, she'd taken to putting on gloves and going out with a knee pad and an old bucket to hand-pick weeds from shrub borders.

He'd argued the first morning or two, telling her she didn't need to feel as if she had to work for her keep, that she could just lie around, et cetera et cetera. He had finally figured out that she was *happy* puttering outside, that she was no fonder of lounging now than she had been when he first knew her.

Kneeling in a sunny spot between two drifts of tulips, she tossed some weeds—probably dandelions, his bane—in the bucket, then paused, her face tilted up and her eyes closed. Enjoying the sun on her face, she had an expression of quiet pleasure.

He hated like hell that he had to take her home tomorrow, that the day after she'd be back at work, with a forty-five-minute bus ride each way. She looked a hundred times better than she had a week ago. He wanted her to quit the damn job and stay.

Caleb also had the sense not to tell her that. For half a dozen good reasons, with three predominating.

For one, she had fought hard to maintain her independence and dignity, and he respected her for that.

Two, Laurel would resent being told what was best for her, and he would once again be invited to butt out.

And finally, the very suggestion that she stay—how long?—held implications he wasn't yet comfortable with, or willing to put into words. Even touching on the idea in his thoughts made him shy away. Wanting Laurel to stay for good... They were friends, no more, and likely never *would* be more.

He'd always felt protective of her. Since finding out his bright, confident Laurel had been left for dead, Caleb had worried about her. He was finding now that he hated thinking about her and his kid living an hour away, pretty much on their own. She wasn't willing to take enough money from him to allow her to quit her job. Which meant six weeks or so after giving birth, she'd be putting the baby in day care for ten- or eleven-hour days, then coming home to be a great mom as long as she could stay awake. Day after exhausting day.

No, the life he imagined her and the baby living didn't sit well with him, but he didn't know what he could do about it. He'd offered sperm and some involvement in their child's life, and that's what Laurel had accepted. That's all she'd wanted from *any* man, and he'd jumped in without taking the time to think through how left out he was going to feel.

His father's words drifted through his mind. *Ever occur to you that you were reeled in like a big, flopping rainbow trout?*

And his mother's. *You don't understand yet what you've given away.*

Frowning, he watched as Laurel bent her head and began plucking weeds again. Caleb didn't even have to ask himself whether he'd have kept his mouth shut even if he *had* talked to his parents in advance and thought all this through. Of course he wouldn't have. Picturing her pregnant with Matt Baker's baby was still enough to raise his hackles.

No, what really ticked him off was knowing she'd planned to get pregnant with another guy's baby, that if he hadn't happened to drop by, she would have done it.

If the first he'd heard about it was a joyous "I'm pregnant," the news would have damn near killed him.

Which circled back to the huge problem of why he was the only man who could father Laurel's babies, and why he'd face a lifetime of misery if he said the words aloud even to himself.

He swore softly and made himself turn away from the window. He had plenty of work to do. Sitting down at his desk, he tried to concentrate.

Sales weren't what he'd hoped for in the Tacoma store, and he was analyzing the problem. Wrong location? Inadequate advertisement? The store had a different layout than the others he owned. Unappealing for some reason? Was it the manager? Staff?

The San Francisco store was less than a month away from a grand opening, and he probably should have flown down there this month. He'd been more hands-on with his other stores in their early months. This one was by way of an experiment. He couldn't keep expanding if he had to micromanage every step. There was only so far he could stretch himself. The question had become, what did he give up? Choosing merchandise, nurturing the co-ops, meeting with the artists? Not a chance. Yet every new store meant more sales, more opportunities he could offer to the artists, more villages he could work with.

All this going on with Laurel had brought to a boil his time-management issues. He'd promised to be here for her when she needed him. He was going to want to be here even more when the baby was born.

The only answer was to hire good people, provide support but oversee from a distance, and let them do the job. Caleb was finding that to be harder than it might sound. He was *used* to doing everything.

On the other hand… He was glad not to have to be in San Francisco this week. His hands-off policy with it gave him time to concentrate on the disappointing sales at the Tacoma store, and most of all, to be here with Laurel.

She had entertained herself happily. He'd gone one day to Tacoma, one to Bellevue. Otherwise, he'd spent a few hours of every day shut in his office studying figures, making phone calls, taking faxes. Then he and she had gone for walks, taken a picnic to the beach, browsed antique stores here on the island, cooked together and gone out for a couple of lunches.

He'd noticed that her nausea had diminished from the minute she set foot on the island. She was still tired; she'd taken to napping for at least an hour, sometimes longer, every afternoon, but she looked rested when she got up. More than rested—satisfied. She would wander into his office and yawn and stretch luxuriantly, sometimes lifting her T-shirt to bare a strip of pale stomach.

He would look at it and feel a jolt. *My baby is inside her.* Caleb was still stunned by how powerful that knowledge was, how primitive his response to it.

My baby. My woman.

Sorry, buddy, he reminded himself. No such luck.

She'd smile at him lazily and just a little secretively, as if she had kept a private tryst. But then she would say with open delight, "That was a lovely nap," and bend over so that her hair flowed toward the floor and she could grab it and bundle it into a scrunchie. "What's for dinner?" were always the next words out of her mouth.

He wondered if she had realized how much hungrier she'd gotten. He would swear her face had filled out in just the one week. Her color was certainly healthier. A couple of times, he'd thought of suggesting she use suntan lotion, considering how much time she was spending outside, but she looked better with her cheeks rosy and the beginnings of a tan on her arms and legs.

It was almost lunchtime now. He hit Send on an e-mail he'd wasted a half hour composing—or, more accurately, *not* composing, because his thoughts had been on Laurel instead. Then he went downstairs just as she came in the back door.

"Caleb." Her face lit at the sight of him. "Want to go out for lunch? I have a craving for another of those veggie melt sandwiches."

"Why not?" he said lazily, glad she couldn't see the way his heart bumped because she smiled that way, just for him.

"Give me a minute to clean up." As usual, she slipped past him without actually touching him. She didn't like touching, he'd noticed, if she could avoid it.

"Take your time."

He stayed where he was as she climbed the stairs. *Damn,* Caleb thought in faint shock, *I'm in deep.*

ONLY A FEW DAYS AFTER he'd taken her home, Caleb flew out to San Francisco with the intention of continuing on from there to El Salvador, a country where he had just established a fledgling co-op.

With her nausea having vanished virtually overnight, Laurel recovered her excitement. *I'm pregnant!* she found herself thinking with delight again. Six more months, five, four.

On a Saturday morning in July, she awakened with a sense of anticipation. Not about the weather: forecasters were promising near ninety-degree temperatures by noon. But earlier in the week, Meg and Laurel had talked on the phone about doing something undefined. Maybe Summerfest, the art fair in Kirkland this weekend; maybe the aquarium, something Laurel hadn't done in years, and lunch at Ivar's. Megan arrived in her usual breezy fashion, to find her sister still in her shorty pajamas and robe.

"You're pregnant," she declared, giving Laurel the once-over.

"You think?"

Her grin flashed. "Get dressed. Quit lazing around. Time's a-wasting."

"Yeah, yeah." Pretending to grumble, Laurel went to the bedroom and grabbed jeans from a drawer. Her loosest jeans—she'd already given up on several pairs that had been favorites. She managed to get them up, started to zip them, then stared down in shock at the gap where the zipper clearly wasn't going to close. How could they have gotten too small in a *week?*

She moaned. Okay, she'd been leaving buttons unfastened for several weeks on slacks and skirts for work, but this was ridiculous!

"Are you all right?" Meg stood in the doorway to the bedroom. Her gaze went straight to the gap. "You look like…well, not a house, not yet, maybe just a cottage, but you're five months along, and you're still trying to get into your old jeans? Jeez, Laurel. Don't you have some with that ugly stretch panel? Or do you plan to go à la Kate Hudson and bare the belly?"

Laurel rolled her eyes. "Gee, you make both alternatives sound fun. Do I look like Kate Hudson?"

Megan turned to her dresser. "Well, then, where's the maternity clothes?"

"Um…I haven't bought any?"

Her sister looked genuinely stunned. "Because you thought you were going to have an exceptionally tiny baby and never get big?"

"You know I don't like to shop. Besides," she grumbled, "I'm always tired." How could she leave the house with no clothes?

"Guess what we're going to do today, like it or not?" Meg went to the closet and rifled through the shirts on hangers, finally selecting a peasant-style tunic in a not-quite-sheer cotton that was embroidered around the hem and neck. She tossed it to Laurel. "Wear this. It'll hide the waistband."

Laurel tried to balk. "What about Summerfest?"

Her little sister made a rude sound. "Like either of us needs another pretty something to put on a shelf. Whereas you, sweetie, do need clothes. And my advice about what to buy, of course."

Laurel meekly followed orders. While she finished getting dressed, Meg checked the Yellow Pages.

They started at a shop in University Village that also sold baby clothes and toys. Laurel fingered rattles and tiny socks until her sister dragged her to the racks of clothes. Meg made her model everything that wasn't first rejected for being too cutesy.

"You will not," she ordered, "wear a T-shirt that says Baby On Board."

"Now I *have* to buy one."

She spent an outrageous amount of money, loaded her purchases in the trunk of Meg's sports car, then suggested the aquarium.

Meg hardly glanced at her. "Don't be silly. We've barely begun."

Next on the list, apparently, was a shop on Pine called A Pea in the Pod.

"Isn't that cutesy?" Laurel asked hopefully.

"No, it's just cute," she was told.

Another small fortune later, she was outfitted. If she did laundry regularly.

"You can pick up some practical stuff at Macy's," Meg said as they got back in the car. "More jeans, bras, whatever."

"Really? I'm allowed?"

"Come on. Admit it. If I'd left you to your own devices, you would have gone to the department store and bought the absolute minimum, and everything would have been drab. Why not be stylish?"

"Because I never am?"

Meg patted her. "You would be if you listened to me more often."

"Can we have lunch now?"

They continued down Pine and parked under the viaduct, decided they weren't in the mood for the aquarium anymore, but did go to Ivar's for chowder, clams and chips.

They took carryout down to the harbor steps, where a

breeze off the Sound made the temperature bearable, and sat there to watch boat traffic.

They ate in contented silence, entertained by the array of humanity that wandered—or skated—by, as well as the marine traffic.

After downing a French fry, Meg asked, "So where's Caleb?"

"Um." Laurel had to think. "Ecuador. No, maybe Bolivia by now." And she didn't like to admit how much she missed him.

"Why isn't he hanging around holding your hand?"

"You think because he donated sperm he should be constantly at my side?"

"He's a little more than a sperm donor."

Laurel didn't argue. Caleb was…Caleb. Her best friend. Now the father of her unborn child.

"Traveling is what he does," she said simply. "It's why he agreed to be the father. He isn't sure he sees himself getting married or having kids otherwise."

Her sister gave her an incredulous look. "Men who travel for business get married."

"Successfully?"

Her sister mulled that over. "Maybe it's tougher."

"He doesn't see it right now. That's all I know."

"Hmm."

Laurel narrowed her eyes. "What's that mean?"

"Nothing." Meg widened her eyes in a way that told Laurel she was lying and it had meant something for sure. "Back to Caleb. He's just planning to stop by once in a while?"

"He's planning to be here when I need him. I don't right now."

They'd talked about it a couple of times. He'd been reluctant to make this trip, but she felt good right now. Sometimes she still napped at her desk, but mostly she was fine. "When I get mountainous," she'd told him, "you can grocery shop for me. And I know you want to be here for the birth."

She had mixed feelings about that, torn between wanting him holding her hand and not liking the idea of him seeing her so vulnerable. But she was learning that the adult Caleb was stubborn. He intended to be there, and that was that.

Plus…she thought she wanted him there more than she *didn't* want him.

About her last remark, Meg conceded, "I suppose it makes sense for him to get his trips out of the way during the easiest part of your pregnancy. I was starting to develop a grudge."

"Don't. He saved my life when he made me take that week off."

She hadn't been so happy in a long time as she'd been during that week. Maybe not since she'd graduated from PLU and hugged all her friends goodbye.

"You never do anything fun," Meg said.

"I'm trying to do better." And she was. Last weekend she'd gone on a west Seattle garden tour, getting the chance to see glorious, small gardens that had given her a million ideas. Two weeks before that, she'd spent a few hours wandering the Pike Place Market. Another day, she'd ridden the ferry to Bremerton and back, as she'd promised herself. She'd loved the sunshine and salt air, but missed having Caleb beside her.

"Do you ever hear from your college roommate?" Meg

asked, as if she sensed how close Laurel's thoughts had edged to her loneliness. To the fact that she'd done all those things by herself.

"Oh, I got an e-mail a while back," she said vaguely.

Five months back, to be precise. And she'd meant to call or e-mail in response, to say, *Guess what! I'm pregnant, too.* But she hadn't, because…oh, she hardly knew why. Because she didn't want to talk about why she *hadn't* responded to Nadia's overtures in the previous years?

Probably, Laurel admitted to herself. She already knew she had created a whole life around her cowardice. The counselor she'd seen for several years had supported her venturing back into life one toe at a time rather than diving in. Laurel wasn't sure she'd meant the kind of caution that shut out old friends, though, and she'd sometimes used the word *temporary.* As if she assumed Laurel would someday take up her life where she'd left off, if wiser and sadder.

That evening, after Meg had gone home, Laurel made herself a salad for dinner and thought more about Nadia. That day when she'd taken the ferry just for fun, she could have gotten on the one going to Bainbridge Island. She'd chosen the Bremerton ferry instead because the ride was longer, she'd told herself, but now she thought it was also another form of mental avoidance. Nadia lived on Bainbridge. Laurel would have *had* to think about her if she'd seen the island rearing up. It would have been so easy to call and say, *I thought I'd hop on a ferry. Want to have lunch?*

What would Nadia have said? Had she given up on Laurel, after yet another friendly approach was rebuffed?

What would she say if Laurel called now? As in, this evening now? As soon as she finished eating now?

Familiar anxiety climbed into Laurel's throat. Of course, she could e-mail instead. It was so much easier to explain herself when she could reread and edit than when words just came out and couldn't be taken back. That made sense, she thought, relieved. Maybe later tonight she'd see if there was an e-mail from Caleb and then she could compose one to Nadia. Or tomorrow.

Her tension eased.

Soon, anyway.

Relaxed again, she had stood to take her dishes to the sink when she heard again the tendrils of her self-dialogue as if an echo had returned to her. Laurel stopped halfway into the kitchen. How many times had she soothed herself that way? Her favorite words were *soon, someday* and *maybe next year.*

Cowardly words. The kind she would have despised when she was twenty-two and ready to take on the world.

They were the kind of words that let her off the hook. *Next year* could be renewed every year. *Soon* was ill-defined enough that it might never come and that was okay.

What was she afraid of? That Nadia would be angry? That she would have plainly lost interest in their friend-ship?

Or that she'd want to renew it?

Laurel honestly didn't know. But she felt something she hardly recognized: a stiffening of her backbone, maybe. A determination to *ignore* this anxiety instead of deferring to it.

It would be nice to talk to Nadia. All the time she'd been spending with Caleb had reminded her of the fun they'd had, of the hours out on the lawn or slouched on dorm beds when they'd debated and dreamed and schemed. Not just Laurel and Caleb, but also Laurel and Nadia. They'd become like sisters.

Nadia, she vaguely remembered, had barely left her side at the hospital. Laurel was the one to let it be known that she needed some space, that old friends made her uncomfortable.

As compared to new friends?

She wouldn't know. Matt was the only real friend Laurel had made since she was released from the hospital. She'd had high school friends, college friends and legal aid friends. Except for him, the last new ones she'd made had been other first-year law students. They'd rallied, too, but drifted away when she didn't return phone calls and their lives moved on while hers didn't.

Only family had stuck. Family, and Caleb. But she'd never felt really easy even with Caleb until these last months, when she'd spent so much time with him. *He* didn't seem disappointed in her. Maybe Nadia wouldn't be, either.

Would she love Nadia any less if she'd gotten a waitress job out of school instead of acting on her dreams?

Of course not. That's not what friendship was about.

No, she reminded herself, but friends couldn't help but be mirrors she would see herself in.

And that, in a nutshell, was what created the anxiety. *She* didn't want to compare herself to who she'd once been, and who she might have been.

Well, duh. She'd known that, in a way. But maybe she was ready to start peering at herself in those mirrors, if obliquely. Remembering, she'd discovered with Caleb, wasn't all bad.

Heart pounding, she found herself picking up the phone with no memory of having set down her dishes. She had never once called Nadia at the Bainbridge home she shared with her husband and had to look up the phone number.

She dialed and listened as the phone rang once, twice, three times. Then it was picked up and a man said, "Hello?"

Taken aback, forgetting there *was* a husband, Laurel fumbled, "Um, may I speak to Nadia?"

"Let me check and see if she's lying down. May I ask who's calling?"

On a flare of alarm, Laurel thought, *Lying down?* Then, *Wait. She told me she was pregnant five months ago. That must mean she's at least eight months along.*

"Laurel," she said. "Laurel Woodall."

"Really." There was a significant pause. "Hello, Laurel Woodall. You, she'll get up for."

So Nadia had talked about her. Was that good, or bad? She waited, rigid, fingers tight on the phone.

After at least a minute, Nadia came on the line. Her voice was cautious, but also thick, as if she was on the verge of tears. "Laurel? Is it really you?"

"It's me." What else could she—should she—say? "I'm sorry."

"Sorry? For what?"

"That I haven't called in years."

"But you're calling now." Definitely teary.

Shying from the emotion, Laurel said, "And you, you're pregnant."

"Due in less than two weeks. Can you believe it? You wouldn't recognize me! I'm a hippo. I keep expecting the doctor to tell me he's hearing two heartbeats, but no. Apparently I'm just bearing a baby who'll be featured on a tabloid cover. 'Newborn ready for preschool,' obstetrician says."

Laurel laughed, wondering how she could have forgotten how funny Nadia was.

"Do you know if it's a girl or boy?"

"Nope. Mystery kid." Nadia told her she'd be coming over to Seattle to have her baby at Swedish, contractions and ferry schedules permitting.

"I'll come and see you. *And* your baby."

"You could come sooner than that. I'm dying of boredom. I'm a mere ferry ride away."

Rather than answering directly, Laurel blurted, "I'm pregnant, too."

"Really?" Nadia said in amazement. "Oh, Lord. I didn't mean that the way it sounded! Just that you swore you'd never…"

"It's okay," Laurel assured her. "Actually…I haven't. I did it the high-tech way. Well, really not that high tech, because I…" She didn't have to explain that she'd inseminated herself, for goodness' sake! "Caleb donated sperm."

This final, bald statement brought silence. Finally, *"Caleb?"*

"We've stayed friends." She knew she sounded defensive.

"With Caleb." It wasn't a question. Instead, Nadia was making a small, sad statement. *With him, but not with me.*

"He wouldn't go away."

"You mean, he didn't give up like I did?"

This was harder to explain than she'd expected. "He just kept showing up no matter how rude I was to him."

Another moment of silence. "I'm sorry I did give up, Laurel. We were better friends than that."

"He was always stubborn."

"You love Caleb."

Willfully, Laurel misunderstood. "I love you, too."

"No, I mean…" Nadia stopped. "You're having Caleb's baby. Damn. I wish we'd set up a pool. I'd be raking in dough."

"You thought I'd have Caleb's baby?"

"I thought you'd end up with him. Having his baby being the *finale*."

"But I'm not with him. We're still just friends."

"Same result, though."

Laurel looked down at her swelling stomach. "Well… yeah."

"How far along are you?"

They spent a happy ten minutes comparing symptoms and complaining about the myriad miseries they'd encountered since conceiving.

"You *lost* weight?" Nadia said incredulously. "God. All I've done is gain! My doctor has been nagging me since month three. I don't *want* to count calories. I just want to eat."

"Now that I've gotten over puking, me, too. I'm making up for lost time."

"Just think. We're pregnant at the same time."

It was true. Maybe their lives hadn't diverged so very far.

"Can you make it over here?"

"You're not working?"

"Through my seventh month. Then I took a leave of absence. Honestly, I may not go back for a year or more. What about you?"

"I can't afford not to go back."

"Isn't Caleb doing really well? I keep reading about his stores expanding."

To yet another person, Laurel had to explain that she couldn't let a man who wasn't her husband or even lover support her just because she'd asked him to donate sperm.

"Is that how he feels about it?"

"It's how I feel."

"You always had trouble taking favors. Even compliments. So I guess money isn't any surprise."

Favors? So she liked to make her own way. That was a failing? And the compliments she'd had trouble taking were the ones on her appearance. She knew she wasn't anything special to look at, and didn't appreciate insincerity. So what?

"I'd really like to see you," Nadia continued.

"I'd like to see you, too."

"It needs to be soon. I've been getting twinges."

Sunday was her day for grocery shopping, but she could put it off. "Tomorrow?"

"Really?" Nadia sounded weepy again. "I've been wanting to talk to you so much!"

They discussed the ferry schedule, and Nadia called to her husband who agreed to meet Laurel at the dock.

Dazed, Laurel hung up. She sagged into a chair and searched for the familiar anxiety only to find it missing. She'd called Nadia. She was fine. Better than fine. She was excited.

She had to tell Caleb.

Only minutes later, she was online.

I called Nadia, she typed. And guess what? I'm going to take the ferry to Bainbridge tomorrow to see her.

CHAPTER SIX

UNNOTICED, LAUREL STOOD in the door to the hospital room and stared in amazement at Nadia nursing her newborn child. For a moment, she forgot that Caleb waited down the hall.

Just last Sunday, she'd taken the ferry to Bainbridge Island, met Nadia's husband, Darren, an orthopedic surgeon, and had a tearful reunion with her best friend in the world, next to Caleb.

Pregnancy had given them an instant bond that erased the lost years. In no time, they'd been laughing and talking as if there'd been no interruption in their friendship.

Now here it was, only Thursday, and Laurel had gotten a call on her cell phone from Darren.

"She went into labor yesterday, and she just had a nine-pound, five-ounce boy." He had sounded both exhausted and exhilarated, the words coming fast. "Nadia asked me to call you. She said to tell you it was worth every minute."

"Nine pounds, five ounces? She wasn't kidding about having a huge baby."

"The doctor's thinking we miscalculated on when he was conceived. But I was a big baby, too."

He was also a big man, easily six foot three or four, dwarfing his petite wife. Laurel had liked him.

"Is she staying at the hospital?"

"Probably just overnight. Alex is a little jaundiced and they want to keep an eye on him."

"Would she like a visitor?"

"She'd love one."

So she'd come after work, and now stood gazing at her dark-haired friend, whose head was bent as she looked down at the swaddled infant seemingly latched on to her nipple. The expression on her face was so tender, Laurel felt tears prick in her eyes.

"Hi," she said softly.

Nadia's head came up and she gave a glowing smile. "You're here! Come and sit down. Isn't he the most beautiful baby you've ever seen?"

She couldn't see him all that well, but…no, he wasn't. Laurel hadn't actually set eyes on that many newborns before. She assumed she'd be prejudiced when her baby was born, too. Actually, little Alex's head was somewhat misshapen, his dark hair patchy and his skin blotchy. And he looked so tiny!

"He's a *big* baby?" she said, looking down at the tiny hand that had crept from beneath the receiving blanket to flex like a kitten's paw when it nursed.

"Really, really big." Nadia laughed up at her. "Isn't it amazing? He'll be walking before I know it."

"And wanting his driver's license."

"Even if you understand intellectually…"

"Emotionally it doesn't seem possible," Laurel agreed. "Wow." Her legs felt weak, and she sank down in a chair beside the bed. "Suddenly it's become real."

"I'm not sure I believed it, either." Nadia's dark hair was sweaty and disheveled, she wore no makeup, according to her husband she'd been in labor for twenty-six hours, and yet she was radiant, her brown eyes glowing, her smile soft. "But, Laurel, now I do. And the way I feel about him…" Her gaze caressed her infant son. "No matter what you read about it, you're not prepared."

"Is Darren jealous?" Laurel asked, only half kidding.

"He's too in love." Nadia laughed gently. "He keeps wanting to unwrap him so he can see him better. I accused him of wanting to count toes."

"He does have the regulation ten?"

"Mmm." She eased her son from her breast. "He's asleep."

His tiny face was screwed up as if he had a thousand worries, but then he'd had a tough day so far, too. What must babies think, thrust into light and noise and the chill of air outside their mother's bodies.

"Caleb came with me. He's down the hall," Laurel said.

"Really?" Nadia looked up. "Well, for heaven's sake, go get him."

"Are you sure? He thought you might not want too many visitors."

"Are you kidding? I'd love to see him!"

When Laurel came back down the hall, Caleb rose from the hard plastic chair. "That was a short visit."

"She's not going to let you get away without admiring her baby."

He laughed and followed her, a big, vibrant man who strode the hospital's corridors with the confidence of a doctor. In Nadia's room, he went right to the bed and bent to kiss her cheek. Then he straightened and studied the crumpled face of her newborn son.

"He looks like you." Pause. "At the end of finals week."

She punched him and he dodged, laughing.

"Seriously. He does look like you. Shape of his eyebrows, nose, even his mouth."

Laurel looked more closely and saw that he was right. "Except for his chin. Does he have a cleft like his daddy?"

"I think so." Nadia gazed bemusedly at her sleeping son's face. "I hope he's tall like his dad, too."

"That'll mean having your kid looking down at you by the time he's eleven or twelve."

"Did that bother your mom?" Nadia asked.

"Nah. She knew who had the real power."

He pulled up a second chair and they chatted for a few minutes. Then Laurel noticed the smudges of tiredness under Nadia's eyes and the way she began to pause before she answered a question, as if her brain felt filled with sludge.

A nurse came in and took Alex away, and even without her significant glance, Laurel had begun to rise. "You need a nap, sweetie."

"You don't have to go…"

"Yes, we do. What better chance will you have to rest up for the long nights ahead?"

The two women hugged goodbye, Caleb kissed her cheek again and then he and Laurel left the room. They paused at the window to the nursery to look at the half dozen swaddled babies sleeping, knit caps on their small heads, identical expressions of fierce concentration on their faces.

"Just think," Caleb murmured.

She was thinking, had been thinking for five months, and increasingly so recently. At first she'd been so miserable, focusing on the baby had been impossible. But now, since she'd begun to feel the flutter of movement inside her, she found herself daydreaming constantly.

Was her child a girl or boy? She kept imagining a girl, for no logical reason. Laurel wondered what she'd be like. Would she have her daddy's idealism? Mom's insistence on nailing down the details? Would she be creative, silly, earnest? A social butterfly or an introvert? Would she be cautious with money, or a spendthrift?

What would she become? Would she find something in life she wanted passionately to do? Would she get married, have children, be fulfilled?

Laurel felt herself poised on the brink of wondrous discoveries. Right now, she was almost jealous of Nadia, who had begun making them.

"Let's get a bite to eat and go to a movie," Caleb said suddenly.

"I have work tomorrow…"

His eyes were so blue and beguiling. "We won't be out that late."

"What do you want to see?"

He laughed and gave her a quick hug, releasing her before she could feel the first flicker of alarm. "That's my Laurel. Ever suspicious."

How often had he said that to her? And how often had she argued the same way?

"I'm not suspicious. I just like to know what I'm getting into."

The moment she said that, she had an insight.

Oh. So that's *why I lost my ability to be even the tiniest bit reckless. Because it never came naturally to me in the first place.*

Not profound, but something that hadn't occurred to her

before. She had been the cautious toddler, the reserved child, liking all her *t*'s crossed and her *i*'s dotted, as her father had put it. She had eventually persuaded herself that she could take chances. Then, in one horrifying hour, she had learned that even studying late, even walking out to her car alone, had been too great a chance.

So now, she didn't take even minute chances. She didn't try new grocery stores, didn't risk missing the same bus she took every day, had a routine for locking up at night and one for getting dressed in the morning.

Whereas someone less cautious in the first place might have rebounded more readily.

"What are you thinking?" Caleb asked.

"That I'd forgotten I was always chicken."

"You weren't chicken. You just didn't like surprises."

"But surprises can be good."

His forehead creased a little as he studied her. "Yeah, they can."

"Surprise me," she said impulsively. "Whatever movie you want to see."

His grin warmed her heart. "Thatta girl."

He grabbed a newspaper on the way out of the hospital. In the car, he opened it to the movie section, pages rustling, and studied it for a minute before saying, "How does Serafina sound?"

"*Melanzane alla Serafina?* It *always* sounds good."

Caleb made a rude noise and folded the paper. "By any name, still eggplant."

"So sue me. I like eggplant." Laurel buckled her seat belt. "I haven't been to a movie in ages."

"I haven't, either."

Caleb found parking on a steep hill not a block from

the Tuscan-style restaurant on Eastlake that was a favorite of theirs. Dinner was as good as she'd anticipated, conversation better with Caleb telling her about his latest trip, and her telling him about how it had felt to see Nadia again after nearly five years. At the end they shared some divine cream puffs filled with caramel ice cream and topped with bittersweet chocolate sauce.

"Yum," she murmured, licking her lips. "I've never been a huge chocolate fan, but lately I crave it."

It seemed to her Caleb's eyes had darkened, and for a moment his gaze lingered on her mouth. His voice was huskier than usual, too. "I can tell."

Laurel felt a tiny thrill, as if...oh, she held some power she hadn't known she possessed.

But the moment passed, he smiled and thanked the waiter who brought their tab, and she decided she'd imagined any charge in the air between them.

She braced herself for some peculiar independent film. Caleb claimed to like his movies challenging. Instead, he took her to the Metro to see a film from Denmark she remembered reading about. "Sweet" the reviewer had called it.

Settled in their theater seats, Caleb laid his hand, palm up, on the armrest between them. "You remember our 'dates'?"

A funny bubble of happiness made her want to hiccup. They'd done that, even when one or the other of them was going with someone else. He'd stop by her room, or she'd stop by his, and they'd say, "Date night!"

In their poverty-stricken college days, that had meant pizza or a burger, maybe, instead of dining hall food, and then a movie at the local multiplex. They would always hold hands during the movie. "Because it's a date," Caleb would explain.

She supposed whichever one felt insecure about their relationship had demanded the date night. It had been a way of reclaiming *them,* Caleb and Laurel, even when they'd both known that the current boyfriend or girlfriend would resent their bond.

Laughing, now she held out her hand in turn and felt his engulf it. She hadn't held hands with anyone in…oh, forever. Probably not since the last movie she and Caleb had seen the spring of their senior year. After that, he was gone, and although she'd dated during her first year of law school, that had mostly meant intense conversations over cappuccinos.

The theater darkened, previews played and then the movie unfolded. Caleb never let her hand go, holding it on her thigh. His shoulder and upper arm brushed hers. But she didn't feel trapped. Instead, the contact was reassuring, a recovery of good times past, a way to enhance the closeness they had begun again to share.

The movie was delightful and as sweet as the reviewer promised. The thing Laurel liked about many foreign films was that they weren't about gorgeous movie stars. The people seemed ordinary, sometimes homely, their problems modest but real. This couple found each other even though they didn't speak the same language. The obstacles to their happiness were sometimes absurd, yet also believable. Laurel was smiling when the credits rolled and the lights came up.

She turned to Caleb. "You chose that movie for me."

"Yeah, I did. I figured your first surprise in a long time should be a good one."

"Was it too corny for you?"

"Actually, I liked it." He gave her hand a squeeze, then released it, reaching toward the ceiling for a stretch. "Time to get you home."

He walked her to her door, as if the date was just that. Laurel was glad. She didn't like coming home at night alone. Once she'd unlocked and turned on lights, he smiled, said, "That was fun," and kissed her cheek, just as he had Nadia's earlier.

She jumped, startled by having his face come toward hers, by the warmth of his breath on her cheek, the brush of his mouth, the faintest scrape of whiskers as he drew away.

As if he hadn't noticed, Caleb said, "'Night," and left.

Laurel locked up, then went straight to the bathroom to brush her teeth and get ready for bed.

Why had he done that? she wondered. Had he thought she might be hurt if he seemed more affectionate toward Nadia than he was toward her? It had seemed perfectly natural when he greeted Nadia that way, so she didn't know why she was making a big deal out of this.

Yes, she did. It was because they'd never kissed before, even on date nights. There'd been a few times she had ached for him to bend his head, for his mouth to cover hers. And she'd seen in his eyes that he'd wanted that, too. But they had both known that it couldn't be just fun, that they didn't dare go beyond a certain point with their flirting. To stay friends, they couldn't cross that line.

But tonight, he had. It hadn't been a romantic kiss. Maybe she was making too much of it. Maybe it was a Latin American thing, as casual as a handshake to him now.

But if so, you'd think he'd have kissed her cheek without thinking sometime in the past five years. So why now?

Because it was a date night? Because they were now adults? Because she'd been comfortable with holding hands, so he thought it wouldn't scare her?

Laurel set her alarm and turned out her bedside lamp. In the dark, she admitted to herself that she'd liked having him kiss her. She'd missed physical intimacies even as she shied from them.

Her dad was a wonderful man, but he wasn't physically demonstrative. It wasn't until college that she'd learned that other people, even just friends, hugged easily, snuggled when they watched movies even if they weren't boyfriend/girlfriend, put on each other's suntan lotion, gave neck and shoulder massages, walked with their arms wrapped around each other's waists.

Maybe, she thought, maybe she could learn to enjoy that kind of intimacy again. Maybe that was all Caleb was trying to show her.

But a picture of him at dinner flashed into her mind. His eyes darkening, his sudden stillness creating tension, making her see anew that he was a man now. One who on a certain level was…a threat.

Staring at the ceiling, she worried: What if all the time he was spending with her *wasn't* just about friendship, or even about the baby? How would she feel if the next time, he really kissed her?

CALEB DIDN'T WANT to leave town right now, when Laurel was coming to trust him, but if he was going to squeeze all this year's travels into a compressed few months, he had to go.

"You're okay without me?" he asked her on the phone when he called to tell her about his projected trip.

"Of course I'm okay!"

"Geez, leave me my illusions. I thought I was essential to your very existence." Light tone, but he winced anyway. *Shouldn't have said that.* Too close to wish fulfillment.

But her voice softened. "Being friends doesn't mean you have to check in three times a week. An import business means traveling."

Yeah, and he wouldn't want to give it all up, but his attitude toward these trips was changing. He hadn't noticed, until Laurel asked him to become a daddy, but Caleb realized now that his enthusiasm had been waning already. The excitement and passion of the first couple years had mellowed into satisfaction somewhere along the line. Lately, even that wasn't driving him as effectively. He had to brace himself to head for the airport again.

He had become less patient with the squabbles among his co-ops, too, with missed deliveries, with the mindless interference of bureaucrats.

A week later, wasting a day negotiating with a local functionary in Ecuador who wanted to be bribed so that he wouldn't insist on meticulously searching shipments for drugs—and breaking half the ceramic items—Caleb was well aware of how different he would have felt once upon a time. Fuming behind his smiles and handshakes, he thought, *Does this goddamn idiot* want *the villagers in his district to die because they can't afford TB medicine or to own a couple of alpacas to shear?*

The goddamn idiot probably didn't. He was just too consumed with solidifying the tiny amount of power that separated him from the impoverished to see the greater good.

Not that many years ago, Caleb had believed he could convert bureaucrats like this jackass and infect them with his belief in how the world could be changed. Today, having succumbed and "thanked" his nemesis with a wad of bills, he shook hands, exchanged grandiloquent promises of eternal friendship and left the government offices. His Ecuadorian driver was waiting for him. Quito was still a mix of modern and ancient, and not many miles out of the city they were on a dirt track. Dust bloomed behind them, and the Jeep swayed through ruts and jolted over rocks and potholes in the dirt track that would become a sea of mud the next time it rained.

Feet braced on the rusting floorboard, Caleb seethed with frustration to the point where he wasn't aware when they slowed to go through a village of the colorfully garbed women walking to the well with pots on their heads, naked children laughing and darting out of the way. He was oblivious to the sight of the terraced fields rising toward the Andes.

That night, sleeping on a mat on the floor, he thought, *Maybe I've expanded too much.* The joy of the early days was gone. Challenges didn't get his juices flowing anymore; they were irritating obstacles. He no longer flew down here to spend three relaxed weeks in Ecuador. No, instead he had a planned itinerary of four countries in that same period of time, and a wasted day like this screwed up his whole schedule.

Once, he would have talked about how he felt with his father, also a businessman. Even if—when—his parents came around, he was going to have a hard time forgiving their reaction to the news that Laurel was pregnant. With his anger running so deep, he and his father weren't doing much talking at all. This was something he had to work out on his own.

His next stop was Cuzco, the ancient city in Peru he'd grown to love. In part thanks to tourism, it had held on to its charm.

Again, he faced delays and frustration. He had no time for strolls through the narrow, cobblestoned streets, or for browsing open-air markets in search of new craftspeople. Nope, he dealt with business, and four days later had to leave.

He loved this city, but flying in and out of here was something else again. Buying a ticket on any of the small South American airlines was like bargaining with God.

Today he took his seat, then watched with incredulity as the flight attendant used a bungee cord to secure the door. He actually unbuckled his seatbelt and started to stand, then thought, *Crap, who knows when I can catch another flight?* They'd probably been securing the damn door this way for months. What were the odds the cabin would lose pressure this time?

Those odds were higher than he liked, Caleb admitted to himself as he sat back down, buckled up tightly, gritted his teeth and closed his eyes in anticipation of takeoff. The airport here was notorious, because planes had to climb so steeply to make it over the ridges surrounding the city. Flying in felt like a plunge into hell. The plane went so low over ridges you could study the leaves on the trees. No matter how many times you did it, you knew the next time there was no way in God's green earth the pilot was going to be able to abort the descent, lift the nose and land.

Caleb wasn't a praying man, except at times like this. More bargains: *I'll be good if you'll let me survive* this *flight*.

This was another way in which he'd changed: he worried about dying now.

He couldn't be as philosophical about the risk of one of these duct-taped-together airplanes falling from the sky, or the fact that he knew his dead body might be found someday in a Jeep beside the road in one of the many countries where government forces and rebel guerrillas waged constant war.

Peasants who were economically well off were unlikely to support antigovernment forces, which made him unpopular with them. Brutal bands of the *Senderistas* in Peru, better known as Shining Path, the National Liberation Army in Colombia and their counterparts in half a dozen other Central and South American nations roamed at will, terrorizing villagers and conducting bloody skirmishes against Army units. In countries like Haiti, it was the government forces Caleb had to worry about, as brutally as they worked to suppress the peasants whose lot in life he aimed to improve.

Over the years, Caleb had had several near misses. In Guatemala he'd managed to convince a small band holding guns on him that he, too, thought the government needed overthrowing, that he was here because he sought to undermine it. He'd had death threats, and had slipped into the jungle a couple of times just ahead of guerrillas.

When he was young and foolish, he'd been exhilarated every time he emerged from danger unscathed. But now he was going to be a father. He wanted to be around not just to see his baby born and to support Laurel as much as she'd allow, but to be there when his kid grew up. He was thinking about soccer games and school conferences and high school graduation.

And Laurel. Always Laurel.

She might not think she needed him, but she did.

He had rewritten his will just before he left for this trip, leaving everything he owned to her. He doubted she'd approve if he had asked her, but tough—if this damn plane went down in a fiery ball, at least he'd know she was financially set.

But damned if he was willing to die. She was bound to want a second child, and he'd have to rise from the grave when she asked Matt Baker for sperm again.

The plane felt as if it were climbing straight up, the body shaking and rattling. Even businessmen who flew often sat silent, grips tight on the armrests. When the plane cleared the mountainous rim of the bowl that held Cuzco, the sighs of released breath were audible the length of the plane.

Caleb kept an eye on the door secured by the bungee cord, but it held until the plane landed in Bogotá, Colombia. A week here, then on to Honduras, then home.

He strolled down the street from his hotel that evening, enjoying the pleasant temperature that was nearly year-around in Bogotá, and found a small café where he ate *ajiaco,* a traditional chicken-and-potato soup with capers and avocado on the side. Walking back, night air cool on his skin, he thought ruefully about the next day, when he would head for the lower-lying coastal area notorious for sultry heat and 100-plus inches of annual rainfall.

A number of time zones ahead of Seattle, Caleb had to struggle to stay up late enough to call Laurel after she'd be home from work. At last he deemed it worth taking a chance and dialed from his hotel room, waiting through interminable bursts of static and clicks until her phone rang and she picked up.

"Hey," he said.

"Caleb! You sound far away."

"I *am* far away. Bogotá."

"Checking up on me?"

Was he? Maybe. He wasn't sure he'd ever have faith she was safe again. And if he felt that way, it was no wonder *she* fought a myriad of fears.

"I miss you," he said. "The nomadic life is losing its glamour."

"Thinking about your own bed?"

No, yours.

Lucky those words hadn't slipped out.

"I was thinking about our week together. Watching you pull weeds. Going out to lunch together every day. Cooking. Reading. Playing Scrabble."

"It was a lovely week."

Stretched on a lumpy bed in the small hotel off the tourist route that he frequented whenever he was in Bogotá, Caleb listened to the wistful tone of her voice.

"How are you?"

"Good," she said. "Really good. I saw the doctor Tuesday. The baby is getting so active, she wakes me up at night sometimes."

"She? Did you have an ultrasound?"

Laurel laughed. "No, it just gets awkward saying 'he or she' all the time. Besides..."

"You think it's a girl."

"The flutters feel like a girl."

"And aren't you going to feel silly when he turns out to be a big, strapping fellow."

His gaze followed a cockroach that walked into the bedroom from the bathroom, bold as you please. Ah, well. They were a fact of life down here.

"I'll never tell him I thought he was a she. And you can't, either. Cross your heart."

"Consider it done." He wasn't about to say, *Hope to die,* not after his day's ruminations on that very subject.

They talked for a few more minutes. She'd had dinner the night before with Matt and Sheila Baker. Seattle was having a heat wave, which made sleeping hard for an almost-six-months-pregnant woman. When he mentioned the temperature here in Bogotá, she moaned.

Oh, and her sister had broken up with her style-challenged boyfriend and was dating a journalist for the *Seattle P.I.*

"Although the relationship may be short-lived, because the other day he accused her of having her head in the sand because she doesn't share his minute-by-minute fascination with breaking news and was unaware of some subtlety of Capitol Hill wrangling."

"Tact's apparently not his strong suit, either."

Her laugh rippled. "Yeah, but let's face it. It's not Meg's, either. She says what she thinks."

"The first time I met her, she said, 'Wow, you're sure skinny.'"

Another gurgle. "I'd forgotten that. I always suspected her cool up-and-down appraisal had something to do with your decision to prove how rough and tough you were by playing rugby."

He was still too embarrassed to admit she was right.

"What was she? Fifteen?" he complained in remembered indignation. "College guys were supposed to look good to her."

Caleb had lost sight of the cockroach. He wasn't worried. He'd sleep well under mosquito netting that kept out larger insects, too. He carried his own netting, malaria and dengue fever lacking appeal. The Radisson Royal Bogotá Hotel might keep their mosquito nets in good repair, but they tended to be full of holes in places like this.

He said good-night with regret, went to the bathroom one more time, watching where he stepped, then wrapped himself in treated mosquito netting.

Funny, he thought on the edge of sleep, that he never used to feel lonely, either.

CHAPTER SEVEN

PREDICTABLY, CALEB'S MOTHER kept trying to smooth over the rift with him. She started every phone conversation with "How's Laurel?"

Today was the usual after he picked up and she said hello. "How's Laurel? With the weather so hot, I keep thinking about her."

"She's fine," he said shortly, as he continued scanning a spreadsheet open on his computer. Oh, hell, *pretending* to scan.

In the silence, he could feel her hurt feelings.

"Mom…"

"Am I not supposed to mention her name?" she said, with quiet dignity.

Oh, crap. He didn't want to do this. But he also didn't like skating around the subject the way they'd been doing lately.

So he came out and said, "I keep wondering why you are."

"She's carrying our grandchild."

"It's news to me that you and Dad are planning to acknowledge that you have a grandchild." Unfair, he knew, but damn it, he was still mad.

"Caleb, we never said that. You've magnified what we *did* say."

"Have I? It seems to me it came down to you being shocked and disappointed that I'd let that floozy 'reel' me in."

"Your father was tactless."

"Dad tends to say what he means."

"You're sulking. If you'd quit, you might be willing to see that we had reason to be shocked. Were we supposed to be thrilled that our first grandchild is being born because our son donated sperm?"

"It's Laurel."

"Yes," she said. "But we didn't realize what she meant to you. You're not always forthcoming, you know. All we knew is that you still get together sometimes. Do you realize how many years it's been since we saw her?"

The spreadsheet forgotten, he frowned. Was it true that his parents had no idea how much Laurel meant to him? Had they really believed that she was no more than a casual friend?

Maybe. He hadn't been all that sure in his own mind what she *did* mean to him. Not since he was a teenager had he talked much to them about any woman he was seeing.

"No," he admitted.

"Graduation day. When we all went out to dinner together."

Laurel, her dad and sister had joined Caleb, his parents and his grandmother for dinner that night.

"Six years ago?"

"Six years. Your father wasn't suggesting she was a floozy. What he was telling you is that she's a stranger. Think about it, Caleb."

He heard in the quality of the silence that she'd hung up, and did the same himself.

So now it was his fault that his parents had been appalled to hear Laurel was bearing his child?

Caleb ran a hand over his unshaven chin.

Maybe. Partly. But *only* partly. Because while he hadn't said, *I always thought Laurel would end up being your daughter-in-law,* he also knew he'd never given them any reason to think she was the kind of woman who'd use him and then discard him. Or that he himself was capable of judgment so poor.

His father in particular hadn't just been stunned. He'd been angry. And while Caleb's mother had continued to call regularly as if nothing was wrong, his father hadn't gone out of the way to apologize.

His father, apparently, didn't think he had anything to apologize *for.*

Until he did, Caleb wasn't letting go of his anger.

IN PROFILE, LAUREL AT six months pregnant was the graceful personification of pregnancy. She didn't yet lumber or have trouble levering herself from chairs or into cars, but was blatantly *expecting.*

Caleb hadn't expected to find the sight of her carrying his baby so sexy.

Back from the latest trip, already planning the next without even a drop of enthusiasm, he was trying to focus on enjoying the time he had with her. He sure as hell didn't want Laurel to know he sometimes got aroused just watching her stroll to the kitchen.

The pregnancy was amazing enough, the change in only a few weeks dramatic.

They had planned to do something this Saturday. He'd

dropped by late morning, catching her showered but still reading the newspaper.

"Do you still *fit* in that shower?" he asked.

Setting aside the sports section unread, she laughed. "Yes. It's not that much smaller than normal. Not all of us have a shower that's a whole room."

His bathroom was a major indulgence. The windows surrounding the Jacuzzi tub made him feel as if he was in a treetop. The tub was separate from a huge shower tiled in forest green. The vanity was higher than usual so he didn't have to stoop. The towels were huge, thick and luxurious. Laurel had teased him about the bathroom when she stayed with him.

Caleb poured himself a cup of coffee, thinking about the day. "How about the UW bookstore? I've been wanting to go for a while. There must be someplace we can grab a bite to eat on the Ave. Maybe wander a bit."

If he hadn't happened to glance her way when he mentioned the UW bookstore, he wouldn't have seen her flinch. The reaction was so fleeting, the next minute he wondered if he'd imagined it. Because if he hadn't, she'd managed between one blink and the next to relax completely, deliberately.

Maybe she'd just felt a twinge. Didn't women's uterine muscles have warm-outs for the big event?

"I don't know," she said. "I was thinking it might be fun to go see Nadia and the baby. We could stop for lunch somewhere on Bainbridge, say hi and coo to Alex, then do whatever."

That sounded good, too, but something compelled him to push, find out if he *had* imagined her momentary tension.

"Didn't you go over last weekend? I feel lazy. And I'm out of reading material."

She sipped her herbal tea. "How about Elliott Bay instead, then? We know there are good restaurants in Pioneer Square. Trattoria Mitchelli…"

Dangling another longtime favorite of his in front of him was a cheap trick. Caleb carried his coffee over and sat across the table from her.

"I like the University Book Store better," he said perversely.

A flicker of distress marred her serenity. He watched carefully, without appearing to, as she struggled to hide it.

"Stubborn," she murmured.

Caleb reached across the table for the weekly events section that ran in the Thursday *Times*. Laurel had apparently set it aside in case they wanted to consult it about weekend happenings. He found what he wanted quickly.

"Did you notice the Korean dance troupe that's performing next weekend at Meany Hall?" The University of Washington sponsored a world-class lineup of international performers at the theater. "Do you ever go? I haven't been in years."

"Me, either." She was definitely tense now, but trying hard not to show it. "But I'm not sure this one appeals to me."

Cutting to the chase, Caleb set down his coffee cup. "Do you ever go near the campus?"

She sat quiet for a minute, probably tempted to feign ignorance of where he was going. But she had the courage to instead lift her chin and look him in the eye. "No."

"Never?"

"No."

"Not once since…"

"No."

The hard, defiant quality of her single-word answers took him aback.

"Is that healthy? What's your counselor say?"

"I don't see a counselor anymore." Not that it's any of your business, her tone implied. "I haven't in years. I go to a group at a rape center. The subject hasn't come up."

"Are you afraid to go anywhere near the campus?"

Caleb wasn't sure what compelled him to prod for answers, but he felt as if they were important.

Her hands out of sight on her lap, she sat as stiff as a witness on the stand. "No. Just…uncomfortable." Her eyes were dark with hostility. "Is that a crime?"

"What was done to you was the crime."

"It's the criminals that are reputed to go back to the scene. Not the victims."

Should he back off? Was he risking her trust by pushing too hard?

"I wasn't suggesting we go near the garage…"

"How did you know…?" Laurel bit off her question. "I suppose someone told you."

"It sure wasn't you." Buried frustration surfaced. "Do you know, you've never talked about the attack to me? Not once?"

Her shoulders hunched. "I don't like to talk about it."

"We're best friends, Laurel." Caleb pitched his voice low and gentle. "I've always been here for you to talk to."

"I have my group."

"Of other rape survivors."

"Yes."

"And you don't talk to anyone else about it."

"No."

"Why?" he asked, equally blunt.

"Because no one else understands."

"How can we understand if you won't talk to us?"

She shook her head in quick denial. "You're a man."

He thought of the years of restraint it had required to sustain any kind of relationship with her at all and began to feel pissed. "And that equates me with rapists?"

She had to hear the edge in his voice. Her gaze flashed to his. "I didn't mean that."

"What did you mean?"

"You have no idea how it feels to be a victim. You've always been tall, strong, confident."

"My Jeep was pulled over in Peru by Shining Path guerrillas." Actually, he didn't know that the nasty bunch who threatened him were really *Senderistas,* but he wasn't going to tell her that. "Ever hear of them?"

Her hazel eyes widened. "You never told me."

"I didn't want to upset you."

In a near whisper, she asked, "What happened?"

"They shouted about American imperialists. The mood was ugly." His bowels tightened at the memory of feeling the barrel of a submachine gun pressed against his head, while his driver fell to his knees and pleaded for his life. *They're going to kill us both,* he'd thought with youthful incredulity. *This isn't supposed to happen. Don't they know I'm trying to help?*

Looking as shocked as if it had just happened, Laurel said, "But they let you go."

"I managed to persuade them that I was a renegade American. Antigovernment, a man of the people like they were. My outrage at the conditions in the village I'd just departed helped. They seemed to be having a leadership dispute, and someone won. They finally let us go."

He didn't tell her they'd suggested he stay away. He had always figured the odds of running into the same, ragtag group weren't high.

Suddenly, because of Laurel and the baby she carried, none of his odds looked so good anymore.

"Point is," he said, "I know what it feels like to have the crap scared out of me. Damn near literally."

He'd stunk afterward, as if his body had secreted terror in the form of sweat. That night, he'd stood in a tepid shower and scrubbed until his skin was on fire.

Laurel shook her head. She'd heard his claim and was denying it. "But not to be helpless. You've always had the ability to get yourself out of trouble and you did."

What was she saying? That she hadn't had a chance? Or that she hadn't taken the one she had?

"Did you fight?" he asked quietly.

"I said I don't want to talk about it." Her eyes were wide and spooked.

He felt sick, and was almost sorry he'd raised the subject. "Why haven't the police ever been able to find that piece of shit? They must have DNA."

She'd shrunk, as if the very memory of the attack had made her want to become invisible. "No. He wore a condom, they think. And gloves. So no fingerprints, either."

"Are you afraid he'll come after you?" some instinct made him ask.

Laurel was quiet for a minute. "For a long time, I was. But…I doubt he knows who I am. He didn't steal my bag. It got wedged under the car. And…it wasn't even my car.

The papers never printed my name. So I don't see how he'd know."

She was trying to convince herself. Maybe she mostly did believe that. But the victim inside her didn't. Not entirely.

"It's been five years."

Laurel nodded.

"Do the police stay in touch?"

"I hear from that detective every once in a while. The same guy has raped a couple of other women they know of. Maybe more. If they weren't hurt quite as bad, they might not have called the police."

"Or if they were too scared of him to call."

She nodded again, as if that were a given.

"But the cops still don't have any fingerprints."

Laurel shook her head. "They do have DNA from another rape they think he committed, but apparently he's never been arrested. They didn't come up with a match."

Caleb didn't ask if any of the women were able to identify the man. If she would recognize his face. She didn't want to remember. He'd asked enough for one day.

After taking a swallow of now-cooling coffee, he said, "I wasn't thinking. We can do whatever you want today. Visiting Nadia is fine."

Head bent, Laurel had been gently rubbing her belly. She looked up, face pale but determined. "No. You're right. It's silly not to go anywhere near…" She couldn't say 'the garage.' "It's like I've drawn some kind of artificial line. This block is okay. That one not. Let's go to the bookstore. And maybe…" she stumbled but caught herself, "maybe even for a walk on the campus. For *her* sake—" she touched her rounded stomach again "—I've got to quit being afraid."

"Are you sure?"

"I'm sure."

Caleb smiled at her. "You're a gutsy broad, Woodall."

She summoned a weak smile from somewhere. "I know, Manes."

THIS WAS WHAT SHE GOT for agreeing so impulsively. Esophagus burning, she sat beside Caleb as he turned west on Forty-fifth and began the climb from University Village to the campus. Her body ached because she was holding herself together so tightly. The baby, echoing her distress, fluttered nonstop.

When she was driving, she never came this way, though she had with Caleb on occasion. She'd never wanted to give herself away by protesting, even though Forty-fifth went right by the main entrance to the University of Washington and crossed University Avenue—or, in local parlance, the Ave.

"I wonder if we can get street parking," she said, in a voice that hit a shrill, panicked note.

Caleb gave her a sideways glance, but didn't comment. He obviously knew that she'd been attacked in the parking garage on Fifteenth, the street right before University—and the street where the lot for the bookstore was. From that parking lot, she'd be able to see the entrance to the garage. And—oh, God—she didn't think she was ready for that.

He passed Fifteenth and turned left instead on University, joining the slow traffic that had to stop frequently to let people cross. In one way, the Ave hadn't changed at all—panhandlers plied street corners and on rainy days huddled under covered storefronts and the pedestrians were a mix of students, professors and shoppers. What *had* changed were the stores. Hole-in-the-wall places that sold cheap imports from India were now cheek by jowl with upscale boutiques.

"Nicer stores," she said in surprise.

"Yup. I led the way," Caleb said modestly.

Lord. In her turmoil, she hadn't even remembered his flagship store was here on the Ave.

"Wait." She narrowed her eyes at him. "You must be down here all the time! How come you didn't go to the UW bookstore then?"

"That's work. Today's play."

Uh-huh.

"I do, however, have my very own, guaranteed parking spot behind the store."

Buen Viaje—literally, good journey—was on the west side of the street, not, thank goodness, backing on Fifteenth. He circled into the alley behind the store and parked in one of three slots there. Entering through the heavy metal door on the back of the building, they cut through the store so he could say hi. But when Caleb started for the front door Laurel stopped him.

"It's amazing in here!"

"You've been…" he shook himself, "no, of course you haven't."

"I did go see your Bellevue store. But it's different."

Caleb shrugged. "Bellevue itself is different."

The Eastside was money. Microsoft, Bellevue Square, Lake Washington waterfront. Laurel had been surprised at how ritzy his store there had looked, with high-priced sculptures spotlighted, exquisite tapestries artfully arranged, the store feeling more like an art gallery than the slice of Latin American culture she'd expected.

This one was a complete contrast. It was like stepping into a bazaar in Santo Domingo or La Paz or any of the other cities Caleb had described so lovingly over the years. The haunting notes of a flute came from unseen speakers. The clerk had the dark, broad face of a Mayan. Shelves were crammed, cases spilled with a wonderful mishmash of everything from Honduran pottery to whistles in the shapes of birds and animals, from gaudy tin ornaments to racks of colorful embroidered purses and tote bags.

Dazed, she turned to take it all in. Walls were hung with weavings and masks, while one step up from the main room a nook held racks of clothing. Carvings of jaguars, Haitian metal hammered art, a glorious profusion of pottery, extraordinary wood carvings, jewelry…

"You chose all of this."

"Pretty much. Some of it is typical import stuff, some one of a kind. The back room," he nodded, "has the high-end stuff."

They spent a half hour in the store, with Caleb picking items up and telling her stories about the old woman who wove in a dark hut with only two small windows, the young Haitian man with a resistant strain of TB who made striking sculptures at a feverish pace, determined to have something to leave to support his wife and children if he died, about the cooperative in Momostenango, Guatemala, known for their distinctive wool products.

He didn't tell her how the profits had changed the lives of the artisans, but she could imagine wells dug, flocks of goats or chickens, school for the children, medicine when a family member needed it.

"I'm ashamed that I've never come to see your store. I hoped you wouldn't ask what I thought."

"You were sick when I had the grand opening…" He stopped. "Of course you weren't."

"It was silly."

"Not silly. You were attacked a few blocks from here. It's natural that you didn't want to come." He nodded toward the door. "Ready?"

Laurel took a deep breath and nodded.

The minute they stepped out into the sunshine, a grizzled, graying man eased toward them. "Got a buck for a Vietnam vet?"

Caleb dug in his pocket and handed over a five. Leaving him saying "Thanks, man," they turned north toward the bookstore, making their way along the crowded sidewalk.

Laurel's senses felt heightened. Smells played like musical notes: the sour, unwashed odor of the homeless man, the spicy fragrance from a Mongolian restaurant, baking bread from a deli, automobile exhaust from the street.

Voices, snippets of conversation.

A blonde in a halter top and ragged, low-slung camouflage pants to a coterie of friends: "Oh, my God, and then *he* said…"

Impatient: "Mom, I told you!"

A cluster of young men, arguing as they waited in line at Starbucks: "I tell you, partitioning Iraq…"

The brush of arms against hers as people hurried past, smiles when people saw her belly, the fire on the faces of a group picketing a store, all sensations and sounds and sights swelled into a symphony in her head.

There was Bulldog News, where she'd often browsed

the magazines and bought coffee, a favorite pizza joint. Businesses she'd heedlessly passed, ones she'd frequented. She hadn't gone to school at the UW for quite a year, but this was all so familiar.

She was the one who was different. She didn't feel anything like the young woman who had joined in passionate debate with other law students while they grabbed Thai takeout or bought espresso or chai tea to get them through study sessions. Now she felt like one of the middle-aged shoppers, a visitor to a strange land, and she didn't like the sense of not belonging.

Caleb took her hand when they crossed the street to go into the bookstore, a vast mecca for student and reader that occupied three floors.

They started together in the middle, where tables held sale books in front and then carefully arranged displays of new titles. Able to lose herself in the books, Laurel hardly noticed when they separated; she knew Caleb's tastes and where to find him and he knew hers.

She chose a couple of fantasy novels, then browsed aisles on politics and law and sociology, becoming engrossed in a book that explored the biological roots of moral behavior. She had a bigger stack than she should by the time he reappeared with his arms full.

"I haven't even made it upstairs," she protested.

"I'm hungry."

"You're *always* hungry."

"I feel like dolmades."

"Costa's has great salads."

"And souvlaki."

"Oh, fine," she pretended to grumble before admitting, "This is probably all I can afford anyway."

Caleb took their bags to his car while she window-shopped for a block, and then they strolled to Costa's just north of Forty-fifth.

As they were going in, a mixed group was leaving. Laurel had barely registered that one of the faces was familiar when the dark-haired woman turned.

"Laurel? Is that you?" She laughed in delight. "My God! It is! And look at you!"

Sela Sweeney had been Laurel's study partner and best friend at the law school. She was also one of the people Laurel had cut off the quickest, when she'd known she couldn't go back.

"Sela!"

The two women hugged and then stepped back to study each other, the others having continued down the street after a few backward glances.

Skinny in their grad school days, with a mass of unruly dark hair, Sela had become merely slim and chic, with her hair short and stylishly tousled.

But her wide smile and deep-set, intelligent brown eyes were the same.

"How *are* you?" she asked.

"Really good," Laurel said, and was surprised to realize she was telling the truth. "What about you? Where are you practicing?"

"I'm a D.A. And damned good." She indicated Laurel's stomach. "When are you due?"

"November. Oh, this is Caleb Manes. Caleb, Sela Sweeney."

"I remember Laurel talking about you. Don't you own Buen Viaje?"

They talked animatedly for a couple of minutes. After

having to step aside so another group could enter the restaurant, Sela pressed her card on Laurel and said, "Call me. Please. We can have lunch and catch up."

Caleb waited until they'd been seated inside before he asked, "Will you call her?"

She nodded slowly. "It was really nice to see her. It was funny, because I haven't thought about her in years. Not since the *Times* quoted her about the Wattenberg case. Remember that?"

"She was on that legal team?"

"Uh-huh." Laurel skimmed the menu without really seeing it. "What were the chances of running into her today? Although I almost walked right past her, because somehow I still thought of her as the same."

"A perpetual student."

"When you leave people behind, aren't they supposed to stay frozen in time?"

He nodded. "Yeah, it's always a shock to see that they live outside our reality."

"Exactly." From the corner of her eye, she saw the waiter approaching and hastily focused on the menu so she could give her order a minute later.

She talked about some of her other friends from law school days as they ate. Relaxed, she wasn't expecting an ambush.

"Is this why you didn't go back to law school?" Caleb nodded his head toward the entrance, but by the gesture indicating the campus, the Ave, this whole world she had rejected. "Because you were afraid to park here and walk to class?"

She stiffened. "No. I could have transferred to UPS or gone to Willamette."

"Then why?"

"What is it with the twenty questions today?" She sounded hostile and didn't care.

"I know you and yet I don't." His forehead creased, and for a moment his face looked like a stranger's. "I'm just realizing how much is on the 'don't' side of the ledger."

"I changed. I told you that."

"No, actually you didn't. You tried to pretend you hadn't changed at all, that everything was fine. I let you."

The baby swooped in her belly. Or perhaps it was her heart contracting in fear. "And you're suddenly not willing to do that?"

"Oh, I'm not going away." Suddenly he was her Caleb again, smiling at her. "But I won't promise not to keep bugging you for answers, either."

Relief made her dizzy, her voice high. "Oh, good. Something to look forward to."

Their food came, and concentrating on it made a natural break in the conversation. When Caleb talked again, it was to ask questions about the high-profile case that had gotten Sela Sweeney quoted in the *Times*.

Laurel remembered more than she should. She knew she'd read the accounts at the time with fascination, envy, frustration and a jumble of other emotions that had ultimately pushed her outside to dig out a new flower bed.

I could have been in that courtroom. Shovel full of soil tossed aside. *I* should *have been in that courtroom.*

The conversation moved on to politics and then books, but Laurel kept picturing Sela, crackling with energy and intelligence that was harnessed now, mature.

And me, she thought sadly, *I'm a glorified secretary.* By choice.

Why?

Wasn't that the same question Caleb had just asked, but phrased differently?

All she knew was, one of the components of a top-notch lawyer was confidence, even brazenness. She was no longer the woman who had been Sela's match. She was no longer sure of herself, in so many ways.

"Do you still want to walk on the campus?" Caleb asked, after they left the restaurant.

She'd intended to, she really had, but Laurel realized suddenly how tired she was.

"Can we do it another time?" she asked. "I think I've walked about as far as I can today."

Caleb was immediately concerned and offered to go get the car, but she insisted she could certainly waddle four or five blocks.

They argued, she won, with a tart "Caleb, I'm pregnant, not sick."

Some of the spark had gone out of the afternoon for her, though. She'd anticipated feeling triumph, because she'd made herself overcome one layer of her fears, however thin. Instead, as they walked she seemed to see her old self in vivid color and felt like a pale shadow beside her, the real Laurel Woodall.

Caleb had lied when he called her gutsy, she realized, conscious of his hand on her back and his anxious glances. Gutsy? It was laughable. Maybe she had been, but no more.

She shouldn't have come. In these, her old stomping grounds, the wall between Then and Now had become translucent. Blame it on seeing Sela, Laurel thought, depressed.

Was Caleb, too, seeing the old Laurel in Technicolor? Movement stirred inside her, as if in reminder.

She looked down to see her belly lurch, and despite her mood, she smiled. *No, baby, you're not one of my regrets.*

With his big hand on the small of her back, Caleb steered her out of the way of a couple of skateboarders, his body angled to protect her from getting jostled.

Laurel had a melting sensation that made her want to turn and lean against him, burrow her head beneath his chin. Feel his arms around her, strong and encompassing.

They'd made this baby together. That gave them a bond even more lasting than friendship, didn't it? He wouldn't give up on her now.

Even if he was as disappointed in her as she was in herself.

CHAPTER EIGHT

LAUREL'S DAD INSISTED on taking her grocery shopping regularly. He wanted to help her financially and, once she'd started working, she had refused his support. But if they shopped together, she couldn't very well make a scene at the checkout stand when he said, "Let me get it today." Which is what he always said, right after she finished unloading the cart and reached for her wallet.

Pride was all very well, she figured, but he was happier if she'd accept at least this much help.

Today, as she pushed her cart down the cereal aisle, she told him about going to the UW bookstore and having lunch at Costa's a couple of weeks ago.

His eyebrows rose. "Did you." It was commentary; not question.

"Ran into a friend of mine from law school. Sela Sweeney. Remember my mentioning her?"

"I met her at your place a couple of times. It's too bad you lost touch."

He was such a tactful man, his bluntness when she announced her pregnancy atypical. *Lost touch* implied one of those regrettable facts of modern life, an unintended drifting apart, rather than the deliberate act of slicing someone out of your life.

"We may have lunch one of these days. Catch up."

"Nadia and now Sela. I'm glad, Laurel."

His face was so kindly, her eyes prickled with tears. "Aren't you ever tempted to criticize?"

They'd never been a touchy-feely family, but he laid a hand on her shoulder. "You're a lovely young woman, Laurel. I thank God every day that I still have you."

She briefly pressed her cheek to his hand, her eyes misty. "I love you, Daddy."

"And I love you. Now," he said, "get more than one box of cereal. You'll be out in less than a week."

Dutifully Laurel added a second box to her cart.

"The trip to the U District your idea?" he asked casually.

"No, Caleb's," she admitted. "He has a tendency to push."

"Pushing usually makes you dig in your heels."

In the produce department now, she chose a head of lettuce. "It's funny, because he never has before. Maybe it's just because we're spending more time together these days."

Her father put a basket of raspberries in her cart. "More time? Whenever I talk to you, he's in Bolivia and God knows where else."

"I've told you he needs to travel now if he's going to stick around after the baby is born."

"He *is* going to stick around and help?"

She kissed his cheek. "Yes, Daddy, he is. You know Caleb better than that."

If there was one thing Caleb was good at, it was stick-to-itiveness. She hadn't been able to shake him, no matter how hard she tried.

He'd actually backed off since the day they went to the University District. Laurel had expected Caleb to figure he'd scored a triumph. So why shouldn't she drop by the law school for a visit next, or drive through the parking garage just so she could see that it was nothing but concrete and painted lines?

But he hadn't. In fact, he had seemed a little…remote. She frowned, thinking about it. He called every couple of days and had gone with her to her doctor appointment Wednesday. Plus, they'd done stuff. Saturday had become "their" day. Last week he'd helped her divide spring blooming perennials, and then after she took a nap they went out to dinner and a movie. This coming Saturday, they were planning to go see Nadia and her baby.

But they hadn't talked much, or not as easily.

Of course, it probably went both ways. She'd felt… constrained. Wondering whether he thought she was a coward, or whether he was plotting some way to get her over all her fears, make her like her old self. The Laurel he'd obviously liked better than he did the new version.

But she also knew she had let him see an angry side of her she had succeeded in hiding until now. Maybe she'd even sounded irrational. She didn't care. If she didn't want to talk about what happened, she didn't have to. He didn't know, couldn't know, what it was like to be degraded and hurt like that. To be battered into submission, to be raped to your own whispered pleas. "Don't hurt me, don't hurt me, don't hurt me." To have the breath choked out of you until your vision turned red and then darkened, to be dropped like garbage, your head bouncing off the pavement… No. She had no obligation to spill her guts.

That evening, after her dad had gone home and she

was getting ready for bed, Laurel thought more about the flash of anger she'd seen on Caleb's face when she refused to tell him what he wanted to hear.

She had told everything she remembered to the police officers, because she still thought she might die and she wanted them to catch *him*. But then they didn't, even though every word had been agony with her face grotesquely swollen, and every sound she formed with her lips painful to make. Even though the police artist had drawn a picture from her description that looked terrifyingly like him. Afterward…afterward, she never wanted to tell anyone ever again.

Not even the other women in her group. A few of them talked about the rape, over and over. Laurel couldn't imagine why. It seemed compulsive. Any excuse, and the raw story spilled out again. No one ever interrupted. They all nodded, murmured sympathetically, hugged the storyteller when she was done, her eyes stricken and her face wet.

Others, like Laurel, had never told more than the bare bones of their story.

"I was attacked in a parking garage and left for dead."

Nods all around, a respectful acceptance for her reserve.

On most of them, the trauma was invisible. Outside the women's center, they would be like other women, shopping, picking up kids after school, going to work. Only a few of them, like Laurel, bore scars and had aches that would never go away.

What she'd come to realize is that the women like her who'd been badly injured weren't necessarily any more screwed up than the women who described their rapists as apologetic, almost gentle, or the ones raped by a man they knew. If anything, they struggled more with a sense of complicity.

How many times had she heard "I guess I flirted with him." Or "I should have fought." Or screamed. Or been smarter about leaving a porch light on, about leaving a window open on a hot summer night. They all, in greater or lesser degrees, searched for ways they could have prevented what happened. The funny thing was Laurel didn't know why. None of them could go back, or change the ending. So what was the point?

But they all did it.

She picked up her toothbrush, but didn't immediately turn on the water. Instead, Laurel studied her face in the mirror, turning her head and lifting her hair with one hand so that she could see the thin, pale line that ran from what had been her shattered cheekbone up into her hairline above her temple.

The plastic surgeon had done an extraordinary job. She didn't quite look like her old self, but close. Closer than she…no, not deserved. Had *expected*. Still, the reconstruction made her face asymmetrical and the scar tugged at the left corner of her mouth. Sometimes she was almost glad. Her outer self matched her inner self. Scarred.

Maybe *that* was why some of the women felt compelled to retell their stories so often, she thought in surprise. Because their suffering wasn't written on their faces. It must be odd, for them, to look into the mirror expecting to see a face that reflected who they now were, only to see someone who no longer existed.

It would make it easier for other people to forget, too. We humans, she thought, judge so much on appearances. If all looks well, it must be, right?

Perhaps, in this way, she was lucky, she tried to tell herself with dispassion.

Laurel stared at herself even as some emotion swelled in her chest, puffing up larger and larger until it filled her and she recognized rage and hurt.

The toothbrush clattered into the sink and she wrapped her arms around herself. In the mirror she saw her mouth open in a soundless cry.

Lucky?

Tears wet her cheeks, and she gagged, bending over as if with labor pains.

Don't think about it. Think about the baby. Think about Caleb, and the salty smell of the Sound and the sight of hundreds of rhododendrons in bloom in his yard. You don't have *to remember.*

Not lucky, she thought drearily, after she'd run out of tears and had scrubbed them away with a cold, wet washcloth. *Because I can never look in a mirror without remembering.*

CALEB LOVED GOING to her doctor appointments with Laurel. He was sorry every time he had to miss one. It was the only time he got to see her bare belly, for one thing, with mysterious movement beneath the surface, and occasionally a knob would poke up. Once, her entire belly had had this rhythmic jerk, and the doctor had laughed.

"Hiccups."

The doctor, a woman, always let him listen to the heartbeat. She'd move the stethoscope over the swell of Laurel's stomach, her expression inward, and then she'd stop, murmuring, "Ah. There he is."

Then she'd pull the earpieces from her own ears and Caleb would don them.

Thump. Thump. Thump.

"Damn," he'd whispered in wonder the first time.

The wonder hadn't diminished an iota. There was a *baby* in there.

Her baby. His baby.

Maybe some of his surprise was rooted in the unusual way they'd conceived this child, but he suspected most fathers-to-be felt the same awe and even disbelief. Women seemed to take more in stride the whole idea of a real, live kid in there, under their ribs.

Just this past Wednesday when he went with her, he'd looked up with the stethoscope in his ears and met Laurel's eyes. They'd just gazed at each other for a moment, emotions naked, and he had felt a profound relief. Lately, he'd begun to feel some real doubt about how this was going to turn out for him. Maybe his parents had been right. Maybe he *was* just a sperm donor.

Oh, Laurel saw him as a friend, too, but a hell of a lot more casual one than he'd realized. It was his own fault for not seeing sooner how superficial their relationship was. He hadn't let her cut him out of her life when she tried, but she had cut him off from her inner life. He was still stunned by her ferocity when she'd told him he wouldn't understand because he was a man.

In a flash he'd realized she saw him as a threat. That, deny it how she would, Laurel did hold him responsible on some level for the rape. If he had a penis, he must have brutal impulses.

He knew he shouldn't be angry, but he was. Hiding it took some effort. She was his best friend, and here he was waking up and realizing that in the past five years she hadn't told him *anything* meaningful about what she thought and felt. Mr. Sensitive Guy, he'd gently suggested he was available if she ever wanted to tell him about the rape, but had let it be okay that she didn't.

What he hadn't let himself see was that she didn't talk to him about anything else really important, either.

Today, for example.

He picked her up at ten and they drove onto the ferry for Bainbridge. They went up to the observation deck, Caleb buying a cup of coffee. Then they went outside and leaned against the railing.

Even at this hour, the day promised to be hot. The water was unusually still and shiny, the surface almost oily looking, the sky a washed-out blue. Laurel gripped the railing with both hands, tilted her head back as if to receive the sunlight and gazed dreamily ahead, toward the distant bulk of Bainbridge Island.

She wore a thin tank top and a loose jumper over it, flip-flops on her feet. Caleb was ticked to find himself stirred by her body, even as alienated from her as he felt. Her hair, a shining mix of honey and pale brown, was gathered into a ponytail that bared the long, slim line of her neck. Her shoulders and collarbone were as slender as ever. But her breasts, always full and now voluptuous, pressed against the fabric of the jumper. And he kept seeing her belly as she lay on the examining table at the doctor's office, swollen with the life inside.

He faced the railing himself, hoping like hell she didn't glance down and notice his erection. Wouldn't that be wonderful. She'd recoil from the evidence that he was the brute she had feared he was.

"You're quiet," Laurel said at last.

"Nothing to say."

He felt as much as saw the look she flicked at him

before she turned her head again to stare out at the water. Tension gripped his neck and shoulders, braced for…what? Some kind of confrontation?

He should have known better. A confrontation would have required some honest emotion from her. Nope, she just let it drop, let the silence build. By the time the ferry landing neared and they joined the line of people heading down the steep stairs to the car deck, that silence was as thick as a wall stuffed with insulation.

As he drove, she commented brightly on houses and gardens they passed, on peekaboo views, on anything and everything to avoid acknowledging the new tension between them. But he knew she wasn't impervious.

Nadia and her husband owned a beauty of a house on grassy acreage, sharing a pond with one other home. They'd had it built five years before, she had told them the first time Caleb came with Laurel. Shingled, half craftsman, half chalet, it had lots of windows, flowers in window boxes, a wraparound porch and gleaming wood floors. A surgeon and a marketing executive, they must make a damn good living.

When Caleb's car pulled into the circular driveway, Darren waved from his ride-on mower. Much of the grass was left to grow long and go to seed, but perhaps an acre around the house Darren kept as lawn. Caleb parked right in front and they got out to the sound of the mower, seemingly echoed from afar. Sunny Saturday morning, the neighbors were all out mowing, too. With daylight extending well into the evening, Caleb had taken care of his lawn last night.

Darren headed toward them, and Nadia came out the front door holding the baby. She wore a sacky T-shirt and shorts and was barefoot, her short dark hair tousled. She was patting the baby's back, and he let out an inelegant burp just as his dad switched off the John Deere.

"There," Nadia cooed, "you'll feel better now. You know you will. Little pig," she told Laurel and Caleb, "all he wants to do is nurse."

Darren and Caleb shook hands.

"Don't feel you have to stop mowing because of us," Caleb said. "You want to finish before it gets too hot."

"Getting there already," Nadia's husband said. "Won't take me a half hour. If you're sure you don't mind?"

"I'm the only one who'll even notice." Caleb nodded at the women, both cooing at the baby now.

Darren laughed. "Gotta tell you, I never thought I'd descend to baby talk, but you should hear me when I change his diaper. You'll do it, too."

"Goochy goochy goo?"

"Something as bad. I kid you not."

Darren got back on the mower. Caleb followed the two women into the house.

Nadia said, "Lemonade? Iced tea?"

"Iced tea would be great," Caleb said. Laurel asked for lemonade and offered to go pour the drinks.

"No, you can play with Alex, since he's actually awake. Here," she said, holding him out not to Laurel but to Caleb. "Do you want to hold him?"

"Sure." Dealing with as many women's cooperatives as he did in Latin America, he'd become used to toddlers running underfoot, usually wearing T-shirts but no diapers or pants, and the women often carrying babies slung on their backs. He'd held his share. Caleb accepted the slight weight, automatically placing a hand to support Alex's head.

Big dark eyes gazed suspiciously at him, as if unsure whether this face was familiar or not.

"Hey, little guy," Caleb said. "So you're a big baby, huh?"

Laurel had come to stand so close to him, he caught the scent of her shampoo, something flowery. Staring in fascination at Alex, she said, "He's still awfully tiny, isn't he?"

"They all come that way."

"I hadn't actually seen that many newborns before."

In this country, women didn't tend to take their babies out much until they were older. Or they were swaddled so you couldn't glimpse much but a scrunched, sleeping face.

Over his diaper, Alex wore only a thin blue cotton garment with short sleeves and no legs. His bare thighs were chubby, his knees drawn up against Caleb's chest.

A month from now, he'd be holding his own baby.

"Here," he said, transferring Alex to Laurel.

She accepted him with a competence born of her previous visits, and laid her cheek against the baby's downy head. As if instinctively, she rocked slightly on the balls of her feet and murmured silly things in a singsong voice unfamiliar to Caleb.

She already knew on the deepest level, it seemed, how to be a mother, how to connect to her child when the time came. Why was it so easy for mother and child and so difficult for man and woman?

Nadia came back with drinks and they all talked until her husband came in, showered, and said he had the coals hot in his barbecue for hamburgers.

Alex napping in a bassinet, they sat outside in the shade on the porch and ate potato salad, corn on the cob and hamburgers on ciabatta bread instead of regular buns. The hamburgers were unusually good, chopped up onions in them and maybe some spices.

"I love staying home," Nadia was saying. "Big career woman, and I have absolutely no desire to go back right now. I used to talk about waiting until I was in my thirties to start a family. And I was thinking *if* then."

"What changed your mind?" Laurel asked.

Her husband laughed. "She got pregnant."

"It was an accident?"

"Yup. We got careless…" His wife swatted him and he ducked away, laughing. "Next thing we knew, she was pregnant. But, you know, I'm thirty, she's twenty-eight. So we hadn't intended to have a kid for a couple more years. We adjusted our thinking."

"I thought I might at least have a few twinges of regret," Nadia admitted. "But I can't say I feel a one."

Laurel stared at her. "So you're not planning to go back to work?"

"When I first got pregnant, I only intended to stay home until Alex was three months old." She gave her sleeping son a melting look. "Then when he was first born, I thought maybe I could take a year off. Now, I just can't imagine leaving him. Darren and I talked about it last night and we decided I'm going to be a stay-at-home mom for a few years."

Laurel was quiet now.

Caleb opened his big mouth and said, "I'd like Laurel to do the same."

Startled, she looked only at him. "You know I can't."

Forgetting the others were even there, he asked, "Why not?"

"I can't afford…"

"I can."

Her eyes flashed. "We'll talk about it later."

Frustration choked him, but he nodded.

After a moment, Darren made some comment about the Seahawks game on Sunday, Caleb replied, and the awkwardness receded.

Awkwardness for which *he* was responsible. *Stupid, stupid.* She wouldn't appreciate being put on the spot in front of other people, and he couldn't blame her.

On the surface, conversation was easy, and if Caleb and Laurel didn't say much directly to each other, he hoped it wasn't obvious. Eventually, Alex woke up cranky, and Laurel and Caleb said their goodbyes.

The same thick silence descended the minute they got in the car again. He took it for about five minutes. Then he said, "I was an idiot back there."

Laurel didn't look at him. "I know you mean to be nice, but I can't take your charity."

"Charity?" His fingers tightened on the steering wheel. "You're having my baby."

"Caleb, I wanted you involved, but not…" She hesitated.

He knew what she was trying to find a tactful way to say. In his mind they'd become a family. He was dad, she was mom, they were a unit. In *her* mind, he was a friend, a convenient male role model for a child. Somebody who spoiled the kid when he stopped by now and again. Involved, but casually.

Before she could finish the sentence, Caleb said, "I'm not asking for anything in return."

Her voice softened. "I know you're not. But I can't let you support me."

"Watching you struggle is going to kill me."

"Caleb, you've already insisted on paying child support. More than any court would assign to you. The majority of mothers in this country work out of the home, too."

But you don't have to. Caleb bit back the words. There was more he couldn't say, either, like *It might be different if you had a career you loved, not a job you're holding to pay the bills.* That sounded too much like a reproach.

Anyway, what difference did it make what kind of job she had? What counted here was her pride, her independence, her sense of dignity. They were what he threatened.

"This is what comes of running a business. I've gotten bossy."

She choked. Or laughed, he wasn't sure which. "You were always bossy."

"But hear me out," Caleb continued.

After a moment, Laurel gave a stiff nod.

"I make a lot of money. Even given that I put most of it back into expanding."

Another nod.

"I'd feel better—and more like a real dad—if I can make life easier for you and better for our child." He paused, glancing at her.

No rebellion.

"I can easily afford to pay your bills for a few months. Say, five or six." She opened her mouth. He hurried to finish. "You could start your maternity leave in the next few weeks. When getting to work and making it through the day becomes a struggle. Then enjoy the baby for four or five months before you start back. Give him a solid start with you."

Caleb felt a little bad about that last bit—guilting her wasn't a fair tactic. But he didn't take it back, either.

"Will you just think about it?" he concluded.

"I guess I can do that." She paused. "You always say 'him.' Will you be disappointed if we have a girl?"

They'd reached the ferry terminal. He shifted in his seat to pull his wallet out of his back pocket.

"Nope. I'm just being contrary."

"I say she, you say he?"

"Just reminding *you* not to get too attached to pink."

Like her old self, Laurel snorted. "I've never worn pink a day in my life."

"Not true." Caleb had looked through her family photo albums. "Remember your princess costume?"

"Oh, God." She laughed. "It was over the top, wasn't it?"

When the photo was snapped, she'd been maybe six or seven, plump, pink satin stretched across her stomach, layers and layers of sequined tulle ending just above pink satin high heels—with which her mom had made her wear socks, because it was cold out there trick-or-treating. A tiara had flattened her stick straight hair to her head. In one hand, she'd held a giant grocery sack, in the other a wand trailing pink and white ribbons.

Laurel had turned the page real quick on that picture. Caleb had thought it was cute.

"Actually," she said now, sounding thoughtful, "it wasn't until Mom died that I gave up wearing girly stuff. I became more of a tomboy, got more into school."

"Identifying with your father."

"I guess so."

Back in college, she'd talked about her mother and her regret at the fading memories. She actually looked a lot like her mom, while her sister took after their dad. Caleb had always figured that when she did stuff like paper her bathroom with sprigs of violets, it was the part of her that came from her mother popping out. He wondered if Laurel realized that.

They went up top for the ferry ride back, too. Everybody smiled at the sight of Laurel—pregnancy seemed to do that to people. A couple of times women asked when she was due, and he saw that they were itching to lay hands on her belly.

"Everyone wants to touch you," he observed, when they were alone at the railing.

"I know! Isn't it weird?"

"Does it bother you?"

"You mean, the intrusion on my personal space? Mmm." She pursed her lips. "Not as much as it should. There's something communal about having a baby. Have you ever noticed? It's a good thing, I think. I mean, on some level adults feel responsible for all children."

It was even more communal in some of the places Caleb visited, where everyone was an aunt or uncle or neighbor.

"I agree," he said. "But I was thinking more of you. You used to look uncomfortable when the sidewalk was crowded and people brushed you. Now I see these hands reaching out, and you don't flinch."

She looked at him, her eyes startled. "That's true. I hadn't thought. Maybe it's because it's not really *me* they want to touch."

"Hate to break it to you, but it is you that's the draw.

Right now, you're like a fertility goddess. Or maybe motherhood personified. They want to catch some of that glow."

"Did you see that woman's face back there?"

Caleb nodded. He knew which one she meant.

"She looked…wistful."

Sad, he'd been thinking.

Laurel shook herself. In a voice so soft, he thought she was talking only to herself, she said, "If she only knew."

Knew what? That this baby had been conceived by sperm donation? Or that Laurel saw herself as unfit for any other kind of close, loving relationship?

Today, with her ripe belly and palpable happiness, Laurel looked like someone who had everything.

If only, he guessed she was thinking, that other woman knew she didn't have everything. Didn't, and probably never would, thanks to the sick bastard who had hurt her irreparably.

CHAPTER NINE

LAUREL WOKE UP SCREAMING.

She hadn't done that in a long time. Years.

She sat upright in bed, gasping as if she'd run ten K, eyes staring, senses straining.

Over her gasps, she heard only city noises, all familiar. Freeway traffic, never stopping even in the small hours of the night. A siren a long ways away, fading. A dog barking a few blocks over.

The dream came clear in her mind, and a whimper escaped her.

She was having *his* baby.

Not Caleb's. *His.* The rapist's. The morning-after pill hadn't worked. Nobody could kill the hideous thing growing inside her. A child that would be born with his face, his angry eyes.

She shuddered and looked down at her belly with revulsion lingering from the nightmare.

What if...?

No! It's been years!

Oh, God. What was wrong with her? Why was she thinking something like this now?

Not once, in all the time she'd been pregnant, had she thought of the baby as an intruder, as alien to her body. Why now?

After a moment, she turned on the bedside lamp, then lay back down on her side with her knees curled up. Gently rubbing her belly, she whispered, "I'm sorry, baby. Did I scare you? It was just a bad dream."

Her stomach bounced, as if her unborn child had rolled in response to her voice.

"It's just…I've been thinking about things more. Maybe because of you."

The baby kicked.

"Or maybe it's because of Caleb. His making me go to the U District that day. Since then, I've been remembering more."

Another bounce, and suddenly she had to pee.

"Great, use my bladder for a trampoline, why don't you?" Sighing, she slid out of bed, managing to get her feet under her. The bathroom felt a lot smaller to her these days than it used to. She was beginning to have more sympathy for Caleb who often complained about it. She couldn't shut the door anymore until she was sitting on the toilet. Her stomach stuck out too much.

Falling asleep again wasn't going to happen. She thought longingly of a latte but heated water in the microwave for a cup of herbal tea, then settled on the sofa with a fantasy novel she'd started a few days before.

Somehow, she had trouble concentrating on it. She kept thinking about how tired she was going to be by midafternoon and wondering whether—just this once—she could call in sick.

What if she were to take Caleb up on his offer, and take maternity leave soon? She knew the firm would be okay with it if she gave a week's notice. And, as Caleb had pointed out, even if her position wasn't available again when she was ready to go back to work, an experienced legal assistant wouldn't have to hunt far to find another job.

Charity, a part of her argued, but weakly.

He did have money to spare. And this *was* his baby. Plus…they were friends.

Her dad would help, too, so she didn't have to take so much from Caleb. He'd offered plenty of times, but she'd been stubbornly determined to make it on her own. As if taking care of herself now could absolve her of the shame of *not* being able to take care of herself that one time.

Dumb, she knew, but the way she felt.

The sky outside turned from midnight to charcoal to pearl-gray, and she didn't turn a single page in the book that lay open on her lap.

Why the dream?

It seemed to her that lately everything she'd pushed way far down, everything she refused to think about or remember, was seeping back to the surface, as if it were a poison at a toxic dump site.

Because of the baby? Caleb? She didn't know.

Watching the sky continue to lighten, Laurel thought, *Maybe it was inevitable.* Head in the sand didn't work forever. Was nature giving her a nudge, suggesting that she deal with her fears before she became responsible for another life?

An hour before she would have had to get up, she jerked and realized she'd dropped off to sleep. Yawning, she went back to bed, reset the alarm so she could call in at nine, and fell immediately into a dreamless sleep.

WITHIN TEN DAYS, LAUREL had three baby showers.

She'd guessed that the women she worked with would

hold one. Wedding and baby showers were a regular lunch-time occurrence in the office. And from the moment she announced her pregnancy, everyone at the firm had been really nice, with no penetrating questions about who the baby's father was. Heck, they were probably relieved to find out why she was racing for the bathroom so often.

So many people brought gifts, one of the women attorneys drove her home after work that day with the trunk full of her haul.

Then Megan let her know she was having one. Nadia came, of course, and another old friend from college Laurel hadn't seen in years. Half a dozen other friends from recent years brought gifts, including Sheila Baker. There were even a couple of women there who had been friends of their mother's.

But it was the last shower that amazed her most.

Her rape support group met monthly, and when she walked into the last meeting before she was to give birth, her first thought was *Oh, everyone's already here.*

As one they grinned at her, yelled "Surprise!" and stood aside for her to see the cake, punch and gifts they'd brought.

She burst into tears.

Amid hugs, laughs and more tears, she opened their gifts, looking around the circle at the faces of these other women who understood what she had survived as no one else did.

At the end, she said, "I can't thank you enough. And I want to say something else, too. I don't know if I could have made it through these last five years without you."

Marie shook her head. "Yeah, you could have. You're strong, Laurel. But it would have been harder. And…I feel the same."

There were a lot of puffy eyes when they left that night, all helping to carry the baby clothes, receiving blankets and toys to Laurel's car.

She promised to let them know when the baby was born, and when she drove away she saw them still standing in a cluster in the parking lot, waving.

Two and a half weeks before her due date, Laurel began her maternity leave. Her ankles were puffy, just getting out of a chair was a major production, and it felt like she had to pee every ten minutes around the clock.

When she'd called her father one evening to ask if he would help, the first words out of his mouth were "Thank God! I thought you were going to go into labor on a Metro bus rather than ask for a thin dime."

"I didn't know you were that worried."

"I've been trying real hard to keep my mouth shut."

"Then you did better than Caleb."

"Good for him," her father said in a heartfelt tone. "You know you're always welcome to come home."

"Thank you," Laurel said meekly. "But actually, Caleb suggested I stay with him. He has a guest bedroom, you know." Why was she telling her father that? So he wouldn't think she and Caleb were going to share a bed and have wild sex? She looked down at her swollen body and almost laughed. Yup. That was going to happen.

"And then he'll be there when you go into labor. That's good."

"Were you with Mom when she had us?" She'd been thinking about her mother lately, too, wishing she were here to tell her what labor was really like, what to do if the baby was colicky, how to treat diaper rash, when a baby's cry meant she was sick.

"Sure I was," her father said. "It was my parents' generation when the dads were expected to wait in the hall. We took a Lamaze class when she was pregnant with you, and I counted breaths the whole way."

"How long did Mom's labor last?"

"Sixteen hours for you, only ten for Meggie. That's from the first contraction she felt at home."

"That doesn't sound too bad." She and Caleb had been attending Lamaze classes, too, and some of what the instructor told them had scared Laurel. Labor could go on for two days. And there were all kinds of other things that could go wrong: the baby presenting the wrong way, or the cord wrapping around the neck, for example.

"It really progressed fast once we got to the hospital. We were so excited." His voice sounded odd, wistful. "When the doctor handed you to me, I fell in love. And the expression on your mother's face…"

"I wish she was here."

"I think she's with you, Laurel. Whether you can see her or not."

"I thought of her that night," Laurel heard herself say. "When…you know."

Her father made an inarticulate sound.

"I told her I'd see her sooner than we both expected." Her throat felt thick. "And…and it seemed to me she said that I wouldn't die. That I should hold on."

When she woke up at last in the hospital, she couldn't understand why her mother wasn't there with her father beside the bed. Her sense that they'd talked, that she *had* seen her, was so strong, in her confusion she believed her mother was still alive.

She hated now to remember her grief when her father

said, "Honey, Mom's… She can't be here." And she knew. Her mother was dead.

Maybe *she'd* been dead, if only for a minute. How else could they have talked? The memory was as clear as ones of Mom kissing Laurel good-night, of her pain-ravaged face at the hospital right before she died, when Daddy took the girls to say goodbye.

"You never told me," he said now,

"It sounded crazy. That I believed she talked to me."

"Not crazy. If she could possibly be there to hold your hand, she would be."

A funny feeling of peace came over Laurel. "I really think she was. So maybe…"

"She'll be there when her granddaughter is born, too. I wish…" He swallowed audibly.

"Maybe you haven't needed her enough yet."

He was silent for a long time. Then said quietly, "Maybe."

After that conversation, Laurel thought more about what she'd believed to be a hallucination: her mother sitting beside her in that parking garage, butterfly touches on her ravaged face, compassion and love and strength in her eyes.

You'll live, sweetheart. I know you will. Just hang on.

The memory was part of the seepage, that awful night refusing to stay buried. But in this case, Laurel was grateful for her sudden conviction that her mother would be with her when she gave birth, too.

If only in her heart.

She heard Caleb's car out front, and went to let him in. Laurel had packed on her own, not taking all that much. Despite Meg's best efforts, her maternity wardrobe was pretty skimpy, and everyone told her she wouldn't fit back in her own clothes for weeks after the birth so not to bother taking any of them.

"Hey." He smiled at her when she opened the door. He was as vital and electric as always, and she felt like The Blob. "You all set?"

Butterflies fluttered in her stomach, squeezed above the baby. Was she ready to leave her cozy home? Ready to give birth? Ready to start a new life?

She made a face. "As ready as I'm going to get."

"You *sure* you have two more weeks to go?"

"You can count as well as I can."

"Yeah, I guess I was there, wasn't I? Sort of there," he amended, picking up her suitcase. Then, when he saw her reaching for the smaller one, snatched it up, too, as if it weighed nothing. "No lifting for you."

To his back, she said, "You're going to be really annoying, aren't you?"

"Yep," he said cheerfully, heading down the walk to the car.

Laurel looked around her small house and felt a pang, as if...oh, as if she wasn't coming back.

Of course she would be. That was silly. This was just a vacation, like the week she'd spent with him before. The chance to be pampered. And she definitely *didn't* want to find herself in labor in the middle of the night, and have to wait for him to catch the ferry and make it here from Vashon.

Her house would be waiting for her. The second bedroom was ready for the baby. Meg had painted it a bright, cheery yellow and helped Laurel put up a wallpaper border with frolicking lambs. Their dad had brought the crib they'd used as babies down from the attic and insisted on buying a new mattress for it. A few weeks ago, Caleb had set it up in the bedroom, hanging above it the bright mobile that was Meg's baby present.

The small suitcase held tiny sleepers, receiving blankets and the newborn size of disposable diapers as well as a couple of plastic baby bottles, a few cans of formula—just in case—and an unopened package of pacifiers. Laurel and Caleb hadn't talked about whether he'd bring her and the baby home right after they were released from the hospital, but she had a suspicion he'd refuse. Or else he'd insist on sleeping on her sofa, several feet too short for his lanky body.

Her suspicion was confirmed when she saw the bassinet beside the bed that was to be hers in Caleb's guest bedroom.

Her eyes narrowed. "You didn't mention buying that."

"I figured we should both have a place he can sleep."

She didn't really mind. Honestly, the idea of him dropping them off and driving away was a little scary.

In fact, the idea of leaving the hospital with a baby was scary all by itself. Baby in abstract was one thing; baby that screamed inconsolably and trusted her when she had no idea what she was doing, well, that was another altogether.

"We're going to do okay at this, right?" she asked, standing beside the bassinet.

"Yeah." Caleb put an arm around her. "We're going to be better than okay. Nobody will ever love their baby the way we'll love ours."

She gave a choked laugh. "Mr. Competitive."

"I won't insist he become a doctor." He paused a beat. "An engineer would be okay."

What about not-quite-a-lawyer? Laurel wondered. *Was that good enough?*

Oblivious to her thoughts, Caleb said, "If you want to settle in, I'll put dinner on."

She gave him a little smile and nodded. Once he left, instead of opening her suitcase she sat in the upholstered rocker he must also have bought recently and started it gently rocking.

Splaying her hands over her belly, she half sang, half murmured, "Rock-a-bye baby." When she got to the part about the cradle falling she thought there should be more upbeat lullabies.

CALEB'S FATHER CALLED the day after Laurel came to stay.

"Your mother's worried that you won't want us to see the baby," he began stiffly.

Caleb set aside the newspaper he'd been reading, glad Laurel was upstairs taking a nap. "You know I wouldn't do that."

"I'm supposed to apologize."

Despite the anger he'd nursed, Caleb couldn't help seeing the humor in his father's idea of contrition.

"But you're having a hell of a time getting the words out because you're not sorry at all?" he inquired.

Voice gruff, Clayton Manes admitted, "I regretted what I said the minute I said it. Laurel's a nice girl. I knew that. But I was afraid you'd get hurt."

And was still afraid, Caleb guessed. He was afraid, too.

"Apology accepted."

"You've been hard on your mother, ignoring us the way you have the last six months."

His eyebrows rose. "I talk to her every few weeks."

"But you haven't been to see her, have you?"

"I've been busy." Heaven help him, he felt like a teenager hanging his head sullenly and shuffling his feet as his father chewed him out.

"Uh-huh."

"Dad, I really *have* been busy. I've had to squeeze a lot in so I could take some time off now that Laurel's close to her due date."

"You need to delegate better, or you'll burn yourself out."

"Yeah, I'm beginning to realize that." He paused. "The Tacoma store isn't doing very well, Dad. I could use some advice."

"Why don't I go take a look at it?" his father suggested. "And then we can talk."

His mood lightened. "Thanks. And thanks for apologizing. Even if you were forced to do it."

"We're both stubborn."

"Yeah, we are."

"You'll let us know the minute our grandchild is born?"

"I will."

"And call your mother in the meantime."

"I will," he said again. "I love you, Dad."

His father cleared his throat and spoke words that had never seemed easy for him. "I love you, too."

Damned if Caleb's eyes weren't burning when he hung up the phone.

HE CAME AWAKE with a kick of adrenaline. The first thing he saw was Laurel standing just inside his bedroom, a dark silhouette against the light from the hall.

"Caleb," she said, and he knew somehow that she was repeating his name. "Are you awake?"

He shot upright. "Is it time?"

She nodded. "My contractions are still seven or eight minutes apart, but since we have to catch a ferry…"

Swearing, he all but fell out of bed. "Why didn't you wake me up earlier? You were fine when we said goodnight."

"I told you I was having contractions."

He shoved his hands through his hair. "Twinges! You said twinges! Damn. I have to get dressed."

"Me, too." But she didn't move, and a small gasp escaped her.

Caleb switched on the bedside lamp and saw her strained face. "You're having one. God." He hurried to her and took her cold hand. "Okay. Breathe. Remember? One, two, three… Come on, do it." Her eyes met his and she began to pant. "That's it. Three, four, exhale. There you go." He saw in her eyes the moment the contraction passed. "I'll help you get dressed as soon as I've got some clothes on."

"No, I'm okay. I'll hurry."

Fighting the urge to follow her, he looked down at himself. *Can't go to the hospital in nothing but pajama bottoms. Damn it, get dressed.*

He grabbed the first things that came to hand: jeans and a long-sleeved T-shirt. He yanked on socks and shoved his feet into athletic shoes. He screwed up tying a bow and ended up with a knot. His hands must be shaking. To hell with it. Almost to the door, he remembered to go back for his watch on the bedside table.

By the time he got to her room, Laurel was in the rocking chair panting. She'd managed to get into a jumper with a sweater over it, but had bare feet and held her hairbrush in her hand.

He crouched beside the chair and talked her through this contraction, too. When it passed, he said, "That wasn't eight minutes."

"No."

"I'll brush your hair."

She didn't protest. He eased out a few tangles and tamed the thick, silky mass in a somewhat askew braid, fastening it with a hair thingie that had been wound around the handle of the brush. Then he brought her shoes to her, collected the suitcase he knew she'd packed with what she thought she'd need and a few things for bringing the baby home. They waited out another contraction before walking downstairs to the car he'd left parked outside the front door.

The sky was still dark, and he glanced at his watch as he accelerated down the dark island highway, calculating ferry times. They should be okay, but...damn, her back was arching and she was panting again. By his calculations, five and a half minutes from the last contraction. She was progressing fast.

They got lucky and drove right on a ferry. Caleb helped Laurel lay her seat back. He didn't let go of her hand once.

"You're doing great," he kept saying. "One, two, three, four…"

He had to let go of her hand to drive off the ferry and accelerate up the hill. Thank God it was nighttime and not morning rush hour.

She let out a long, aching moan and he swore.

"We're almost there, sweetheart. You're doing great."

"It's going so fast," she said in panic.

"That's good. You don't want one of those forty-five-hour labors."

"No, but…" Her fingers tightened on his. "I'm glad you're here, Caleb."

"Where else would I be?"

"El Salvador."

"You notice I haven't gone anyplace for the past month. Babies come early."

"Ours has been watching the clock."

"Hey." A grin spread on his face. "Yeah. Today's your due date."

They'd talked about it at dinner, with him noticing how Laurel was picking at her food. He'd wondered, but not enough. Those "twinges" she'd mentioned oh, so casually had clearly been way more. She just hadn't wanted to get him excited.

Leaving the freeway at James Street, Caleb grumbled, "I don't like to think of you in labor half the night, not wanting to wake me up."

"I figured one of us should get some sleep. And I really was okay. When it got intense, I woke you up."

On First Hill, Swedish Hospital wasn't far from the freeway. Caleb pulled into the emergency entrance with Laurel panting in the midst of a contraction. A nurse and an orderly came out with a wheelchair and helped her into it, with Caleb going to park the car.

He all but ran from the lot. Since Laurel had already filled out all the preadmission forms, she was being wheeled down the hall when he caught up. She gave him a relieved smile and clung to his hand.

The birthing suite was nicer than Caleb had expected. Homier. A nurse pointed out where he could take a nap, and he looked at her incredulously. He was supposed to *nap?* And leave Laurel to struggle on alone?

Attaching the fetal monitors as a contraction seized Laurel, the nurse smiled. "Or not. Looks like this one is in a hurry."

He captured Laurel's hand and held her gaze as he counted breaths. "That's it, sweetheart." How many times had he said that? "There you go. It's passing."

That one had come less than four minutes after the previous contraction. This baby wanted to be born.

"We should have called your doctor from home," he realized.

"Dr. Schapiro is already here in the hospital," the nurse told them. "We've let her know that Laurel is here."

She came by a half hour later, smiling and telling them she'd just delivered a healthy baby boy. She put her hand under the drape that covered Laurel's legs. "Seven centimeters. We don't have long to wait. This is what I like. A two-for-one night."

Caleb lost awareness of anything but Laurel as her contractions mounted in intensity, racking her body one after the other. Her eyes never left his, as if her world, too, had narrowed to the two of them. He wiped sweat from her face, smoothed damp hair from her forehead, gently kneaded her back during the brief intervals.

He had given her back rubs during their birthing classes, but tentatively. He would feel her body stiffen when he laid his hands on her, but with the instructor watching he'd go through the motions anyway.

But tonight—no, this morning now—it was different. He found points of tension as if attuned to her. She arched like a cat against his hand, moaning in pleasure. Her skin was milk pale, her back so narrow he wondered at how she'd borne the weight in front. He learned the feel of the vertebrae from the curve of her neck down to her lower back. And, miracle of miracles, she accepted his touch gratefully, even with pleasure.

Caleb had a brief flash of hope. *Could she?* Then another contraction hit, one so intense a scream gurgled in her throat, and he forgot anything but her immediate need.

Permission from the doctor to push was a wild kind of release for her. Caleb had never seen anything in his life like the effort she made, her body lifting from the birthing bed as she strained to bring into the world the baby she'd cradled for nine months.

"I see the head," the doctor said urgently. "One more push."

She had mere seconds between contractions. This one bowed her up so that only her shoulders and heels still touched the bed. Through bared teeth, she let out a keening cry of effort and then triumph.

"That's it, that's it," the doctor chanted. "And here she is. Caleb, Laurel, you have a daughter."

Laurel, who had sagged back onto the bed, croaked, "Told you so."

Caleb gave a shaken laugh, then turned his head when a thin cry came from behind the drapes. Laurel's head lifted.

A moment later, he saw a baby, blood-smeared and with dark hair plastered to her head, her mouth open to let out a lusty cry. She seemed skinny to him, all flapping limbs, the colors shockingly vivid.

He watched as the nurse gently washed the baby and seemingly assessed her. Coming up with the...whatever. Apgar score? Something like that. Fear crowded his throat and kept his hand squeezing Laurel's. There wasn't anything wrong with their baby, was there?

Then the nurse came to them, her smile soft as she held their daughter, rendered even tinier now that she was bundled in a thin flannel receiving blanket.

"You have a beautiful little girl who already has a set of lungs," she said, offering her to Caleb who started in surprise.

He reached out and took the slight weight in his arms. In one moment, he looked down at his daughter's face and felt his heart squeeze and quit pumping blood. She had stopped crying and was staring at him with the vague, unseeing gaze of the newborn, but also with what he read as shock. She was beautiful and infinitely precious and he loved her so fiercely, he hadn't known it was possible.

"Look at you," he murmured. "Out in the world at last. I bet you want Mommy, don't you?"

He laid her in Laurel's waiting arms, and saw tears spring into her eyes.

"She's beautiful," Laurel said in wonder. "Oh, little one."

She didn't seem to feel any awkwardness about pulling down the neck of her gown to bare her breast. The nurse showed her how to help their baby latch on to the dusky nipple Laurel exposed.

Caleb's legs suddenly lost strength and he dropped into the chair beside the bed.

Tenderness swelled from somewhere in his chest and filled him until he wasn't sure he could contain it. Momentarily forgotten, he watched his tiny daughter nurse for the first time at her mother's breast, and he watched Laurel's face, soft with the same wonder he felt.

She looked up then, sought him out and smiled. The tenderness arced in his chest as if live wires had been implanted.

Was it possible to be any happier?

Yeah, it was. If Laurel was his.

His hold on her was so tenuous. Friendships came and went. He wanted more. Promises. Legal ties. Sex.

He remembered the feel of her fine-boned body under his hands while she was in labor, the way she had shivered and arched, and thought again, *Maybe.*

Right now, they were as close as they'd ever been. He was taking her and their daughter home with him once the doctor released them.

If he wanted more, it was up to him to campaign for it. To quit buying into her belief that she could never let a man touch her again, even though other rape victims did marry and love men.

But he had to sneak past her barriers, not demand she let them down. Laurel Woodall was a stubborn woman. Always had been. And now she was stubbornly holding on to her fear.

Convincing her she was wrong never had been easy. But he'd done it before and could do it again. Exhilaration, wanting, *love,* squeezed his chest even tighter.

Wrong, Caleb thought. It wasn't possible to be any happier. He had everything he needed right here in this hospital room.

He just needed to convince Laurel that making love had nothing to do with the vicious, degrading assault she'd barely survived, and that she, Caleb and their daughter were a family.

"So," Laurel murmured, "what are we going to name her?"

CHAPTER TEN

CALEB AND LAUREL took Lydia Ellen Woodall home from the hospital, Caleb driving ten miles an hour slower than he usually did and sneaking frequent glances over his shoulder at his baby daughter bundled in the car seat.

Of course, Laurel spent half the drive craning her neck to see between the seats, too, reluctant to take her eyes from Lydia.

She'd known all along, in her heart, that if she had a daughter, she wanted to name her after her mother.

Her dad had cried when she'd called him.

After telling him she'd had a baby girl, she had said tentatively, "Would you mind if I name her Lydia?"

There'd been a moment of silence. Then he said, in a thick, unfamiliar voice, "I can't think of anything that would mean more to me. And her."

"We thought Lydia Ellen. Ellen after Caleb's mom."

"That's a beautiful name."

Tears burned in her own eyes. "It is, isn't it? Oh, Dad. Do you want us to come by your house on our way home?"

"On your way? Last I knew, Shoreline wasn't on the way to the Fauntleroy ferry. No. If they aren't keeping you overnight at the hospital, I'll come over in the morning to see her, if that's okay with you and Caleb."

She sniffed. "Of course it is!"

Now, waiting in the ferry line, she watched Caleb watching their daughter sleep.

"She's so small," he murmured.

"Eight pounds three ounces isn't small as newborns go."

"No, but... Look at her! Damn it, I wish they'd kept you overnight. What if something goes wrong?"

Laurel was scared herself. Not so much that something would go wrong as that she wouldn't know what to do in normal situations. If Lydia couldn't latch on to her breast, or cried for no obvious reason, or...

No. Other new parents managed.

"Lydia is fine," she said stoutly. "She's nursing, she's not jaundiced, she's got a healthy cry. Why would anything go wrong?"

His fist bounced on the steering wheel. "It won't. I know it won't. I just don't think they *know* it's safe. It wasn't doctors who decided newborns didn't need to stay an extra day, it was the insurance companies."

Amused and touched, Laurel said, "Caleb. We're okay. Really."

"So you say," he growled, then shot a chagrined look toward the rear-facing car seat. Voice hushed, he asked, "Did I wake her up?"

"I don't think a cherry bomb going off under the car would wake her up."

Laurel was exhausted, but also full of this amazing love. It made her feel she could do anything for this tiny being born of her body, that she *would* do anything to keep her safe.

Imagine. She could so easily *not* have had Lydia.

It was funny, but she hadn't thought about Matt Baker as potential-father-of-her-baby in a long time. She'd had dinner a couple of times with Matt and Sheila while Caleb was away on trips, but even then she hadn't asked herself, *What if Matt and not Caleb was the father?*

She simply could no longer envision not having her baby with Caleb. She wouldn't have Lydia. She'd have… some other baby, with a different genetic makeup. Of course she would have loved that baby just as much. At least, she guessed she would have, although right now she instinctively rejected the idea of not having Lydia.

Because she was part Caleb's? Laurel stole a look at him. Despite her exhaustion, despite her soreness, she melted inside at how handsome he was, at thinking, *We're blended together in Lydia.*

If she'd been impregnated with Matt Baker's sperm, probably Meg would have been her labor coach. And right now, either Meg or her dad would be driving her home. Maybe she and Lydia—no, the other baby she'd have had instead—would be going to stay for a few days at her father's house. He wouldn't have let her go home alone.

But even that—even her father's care, which had been all she'd ever needed—wouldn't have been the same as Caleb's. She simply couldn't imagine setting off on this adventure without him.

She must have let out a sound, because he turned his head and his electrifying blue eyes caught her gaze.

"What are you thinking?" he asked, his voice a low rumble.

"That I'm glad you're Lydia's father. You and not…"

"I still can't believe you asked Matt Baker."

"I told you why I did."

"And it still ticks me off. Do you know how I would have felt if I'd gotten back from a trip and it had been too late? You were already pregnant?"

The rough emotion in his voice was new to her. "No," Laurel admitted, nearly inaudibly. "How would you have felt?"

He turned his face from hers and looked straight ahead through the windshield, his fingers flexing on the steering wheel. She doubted he saw the cars disgorging from the ferry and speeding, one after the other, past them up and up the hill.

"Betrayed."

Laurel gaped at him.

"Yeah, yeah, I know. You've never given me any reason to think…" He swallowed. "If you'd fallen in love, that would have been one thing. But Baker? Weren't we better friends than that, Laurel?"

Not wanting to admit too much, she said, "Yes. Maybe too good. You know? Asking something like this is emotionally loaded. Matt felt…safe."

He looked at her at last. "Yeah, I get that. It just hit me today. Lydia might not have been mine."

At the beginning of the line, cars were starting to board the ferry.

"It hit me, too. But Lydia wouldn't have been Lydia. She only exists because we did this together."

Caleb looked back between the seats, and his voice softened. "It's amazing, isn't it? That somehow we created her."

Laurel nodded, remembering the night he had handed her that plastic syringe, his cheeks flushed, and fled. Maybe it had been standing on her head that had done it.

Not the kind of memory most women had of the night their baby had been conceived.

"Thank you, Caleb." Her voice cracked. "For everything." She laid a hand over his on the steering wheel, feeling the tension and strength that belied the laid-back charm he projected most of the time.

As if instinctively, his hand turned to grip hers. "What are you thanking me for? I'm the one who feels so damn lucky right now…" He had to clear his throat.

A horn sounded behind them, and they both jerked.

Laurel snatched back her hand and Caleb muttered something under his breath, then put the car into gear to start after the pickup ahead of him.

A minute later, they bumped onto the ferry deck and parked where the orange-vested worker waved them.

The clanking sound of other vehicles driving on penetrated Lydia's sleep. She moved restlessly. At the deep sound of the ferry horn, she began to cry and thrash.

"I guess she wouldn't sleep through a cherry bomb after all." Laurel got out, opened the back door and unbuckled Lydia, lifting her from the car seat. "Are you hungry, sweetie?"

At the hospital, she hadn't been the least self-conscious about nursing in front of Caleb, but suddenly she was. He was so close here in the front seat that she could see the dark bristles on his chin. Which meant *he'd* get a bird's-eye view.

She hesitated, Lydia squalled, and after a moment Laurel inserted her hand under her shirt and unhooked one cup of her nursing bra, then cradled Lydia and lifted the hem only as much as she absolutely had to. Caleb, she saw out of the corner of her eye, was looking straight ahead, his cheeks dusky. She wasn't the only one who felt awkward.

For a moment Lydia struggled, letting out thin, frustrated cries, before she finally latched on and began to suck. It felt odd, almost sexual, and Laurel recalled reading that the tugging did cause the uterus to contract so maybe that made sense.

The car was awfully quiet, Laurel painfully conscious of the man beside her pretending not to notice what she was doing. To fill the silence, she ventured, "I hope she sleeps when we get home. I could really use a nap."

Caleb glanced at her, careful to avoid letting his gaze go lower than her face. "Even if she doesn't, I'll take care of her so you can get some sleep. The couple of hours at the hospital doesn't make up for last night."

"No." Laurel stroked the fine dark hair on her daughter's head. "I think she's going to have your coloring."

"Blue eyes can change."

"But hers are as vivid a blue as yours. You could tell right away that Alex's were going to be dark." They had been a murky blue, she'd noticed, which made sense considering Nadia's rich brown eyes and Darren's hazel ones.

"Her nose is yours."

She gazed fondly down. "How can you tell? It's a button right now."

"No, it's just miniature." His gaze, too, had lowered to their small, greedy daughter—and perilously near to the white swell of her breast.

Her cheeks felt warm. "Everything about her is miniature. I love her fingers."

One of Lydia's hands waved in the air, the tiny fingers curling and uncurling.

Laurel burped Lydia, then switched her to the other breast. A couple walked by the car, single file, both glancing in then averting their faces. Embarrassed, Laurel told herself to get over it. She'd have to breast-feed in plenty of public places in the months to come. Other women did.

She just wished she wasn't so buxom. Her breasts had been inconvenient before, but now they felt enormous. "Oh, you're built for this!" one of the nurses at the birthing center had told her in a repulsively perky voice, as though bestowing the ultimate compliment. Great. How was she supposed to nurse discreetly when she had so much to hide?

She was relieved when Lydia slipped from her nipple, mouth slack, boneless and relaxed in sleep.

"I'll take her," Caleb murmured, and Laurel was able to adjust her clothing while he restored Lydia to her car seat.

The drive to his house was short from the ferry dock. Laurel settled her baby into the bassinet, then showered and climbed into bed. She'd meant to call Nadia before she slept, but Caleb had earlier, and…she was so tired! Tomorrow, she thought. Her lids were heavy from the moment she lay back. Her body felt battered. Ah, sleep…

THE NEXT DAY, first Laurel's dad and sister and then Caleb's parents came to see Lydia. Caleb expected the visit with his parents to be awkward for Laurel in particular, considering how much they'd disapproved of him choosing to father her baby, but Lydia herself erased what otherwise might have been a stiff greeting.

"Oh, let me see her!" Ellen Manes cried even as she was getting out of the car. Inside, Laurel laid Lydia in her grandmother's arms. After a long moment of gazing down at the baby, Caleb's mother looked up with tears in her eyes. "Oh, she's lovely!"

"She is, isn't she?" Laurel agreed fondly. "I think she has Caleb's eyes."

His mother nodded. "Even the shape of them."

His father admired Lydia, as well, Caleb watching in amusement.

Ellen said, "Laurel, we want to apologize for not being supportive from the beginning. I suppose we've been old-fashioned, feeling Caleb should be married to the mother of his baby."

"I understand," she said. "I know this isn't what you hoped for. But I'm so grateful to Caleb for agreeing to do this. He's my closest friend, and I can't imagine anyone else as Lydia's dad."

"Oh, my dear." His mother hugged Laurel with her free arm.

His father gave a gruff nod.

And that was that.

After the first rush of visitors, Caleb and Laurel fell into a pattern that felt so natural, he began to believe it had been predestined. Maybe it had—mom and dad shaping their lives around the rhythm of an infant's schedule for sleeping and eating.

They talked about Caleb giving her a bottle occasionally, but Laurel didn't want to hurry. "Breast milk is important. And it's not as if I have anything else to do."

Caleb didn't go anywhere for the first week, and was away no more than eight hours at a time for the next couple. When *Sunset* magazine decided to feature the shopping district surrounding his new San Francisco store and wanted to interview him, he made a few comments on the phone and then told them to talk to his manager. He was too fascinated by his newborn daughter, and by her mother, to fly to California.

He now knew exactly what Darren had meant. He was madly in love with Lydia, and could sit by the hour holding her against his chest without feeling a trace of the usual boredom and restlessness that had made him ambitious and footloose. He couldn't imagine going weeks at a time without seeing her.

Rocking her now while Lydia napped, Caleb pressed a kiss down on his daughter's downy head and inhaled her scent.

Hell, he couldn't imagine going *days* at a time. He didn't want to be a long-distance father. He'd been crazy to agree to something like that. Then, the idea had been abstract. Now, it was concrete, embodied in the small body of his daughter and in her big, puzzled eyes, her pursed lips and hearty burps. He could hardly wait until she smiled at him. Said, "Daddy."

What if he missed some milestone? Had to learn his Lydia had taken her first step in an e-mail from Laurel?

He broke out in a cold sweat every time he thought about Laurel taking Lydia home, him relegated to a visitor.

His fear of exactly that kept him from advancing his campaign too aggressively. That, and the fact that Laurel was utterly engrossed in the baby and therefore oblivious to him except in his role as daddy.

He could tell partly because she'd gotten so much more comfortable nursing around him. It apparently hadn't occurred to her that the sight was incredibly erotic to him. At first he'd tried not looking, but how could he help himself?

Big breasts had never been especially important to him

in choosing a lover. In fact, he wasn't sure he was drawn to any particular physical type. He'd had girlfriends who were lean and athletic, lush and curvaceous, slight and delicate. With each woman, he'd been attracted by something different: a laugh, an unexpected way of looking at the world, a hip-swaying walk.

With Laurel, the package was incredibly complex. He'd always liked the way she thought, dreamed and schemed. He liked the shifting color of her eyes, her long toes and fingers, her hourglass figure. He'd teased her back in college that her face was so gentle and round, no one would ever guess what a shark she'd be in the courtroom.

"You mean," she'd sighed, "I seem to have no cheekbones."

"You have them," he had assured her. "They're just, ah…" The pillow hit him just as he finished the sentence. "Well-padded."

That was one of the many contradictions about her that had intrigued him from the beginning, and kept him from ever feeling that he knew her inside and out. He wasn't sure he ever would. Which was fine. Surprises, maybe even a few secrets, were good for a relationship.

He just wished she wasn't keeping such a big one. Caleb couldn't imagine keeping from her one of the defining experiences of his life.

You're a man. You wouldn't understand.

The memory of her voice, flat and even angry, still took him aback. Even pissed him off. It made him hold back.

If she felt the same way about him that he did about her, she couldn't say that. And if she didn't feel the same…

He swore under his breath. He couldn't deal with it. He just couldn't. Not now. She and Lydia were his life. If

Laurel was incapable of loving him, he'd made a colossal mistake by getting in so deep.

No! Caleb told himself sharply. Laurel might be damaged, but wounds healed. He sometimes wondered if hers had, and she just hadn't noticed. She wasn't *letting* herself believe in the possibility of love and marriage. He had to make her see it could work.

In the meantime, he'd suffer in silence when his infant daughter's mouth slipped from her mother's nipple to reveal the dark areola and puckered center on a breast that would overflow a man's hand.

Sometime while he brooded—and had lustful thoughts about her mom—Lydia had fallen asleep, her small body going slack and her head lolling against his shoulder. He eased the rocking chair to a stop and stood, carrying her to Laurel's room.

The door stood half open, the interior dim with the blinds drawn. He walked in as soundlessly as possible and laid Lydia gently down on her back in the bassinet, pulling her quilt up to her chin. She never even twitched.

After a moment, he lifted his head and looked at Laurel, sound asleep facing him. Her face was utterly relaxed, her mouth curved as if her dreams were happy ones. A strand of hair lay across her cheek and mouth, sticking to her lip, and his hand itched to smooth it behind her ear. Instead, he curled his fingers and turned away, feeling like a Peeping Tom.

She came downstairs a while later without Lydia. Caleb had been reading in the living room, having put a bean soup to bubble on the stove. He looked up in surprise.

"Did she wake up already?"

"No, I did. How long has she been down?"

He glanced at his watch. "An hour. Hey, maybe we can eat dinner for once without interruption."

"You're kidding, right?" Laurel plopped on the couch beside him. "She senses the moment serving spoon touches food."

He laughed as much at her fond tone as at the idea. "Figures we spawned a kid who resents anything that distracts her parents."

Laurel chuckled, a comfortable sound, and gazed dreamily at the dark window. "We'll have to go Christmas shopping someday, you know."

"And wrap everything, so we can unwrap it for her?"

"Of course."

He grinned at her, then took a chance by nudging her head away from the sofa back so that he could wrap his arm around her. Instead of stiffening, as she sometimes did, she reacted by snuggling against him.

"Do you ever feel as if there's no past and the future is hazy?" she asked unexpectedly.

He knew what she was saying. It was exactly what he had been thinking earlier, that *right now* was all that mattered. But something in him also rebelled. He'd be glad if the past as a barrier vanished, but by God, Caleb wanted a future.

With her and Lydia.

He said nothing for a moment. "It does seem as if there couldn't have been a time without her."

Laurel made a humming sound. "That's it exactly. A world without Lydia... Unthinkable." She shivered. "How do parents bear it when..."

He covered her mouth. "Don't say it. Nothing will happen to her."

She took his hand from her mouth and squeezed it. "I know. I should never have even let a thought like that cross my mind. I'll be good. I swear."

Was she thinking about her mother, gone so young? Or how her father had had to sit in the hospital beside Laurel's bed facing the fact that he might lose his oldest? Laurel of all people knew how vulnerable she and her loved ones were. Caleb had no way of comforting her beyond tightening his arm.

And turning his head to press a kiss against her temple.

She tilted her face up to look at him. "What was that about?"

"Mmm. Just felt like it."

She smiled at him so softly that he kissed her again, on the forehead. Then, when she didn't flinch, on the nose. And finally, a mere brush of lips, on the mouth.

He lifted his head to see her face still lifted to his, her eyes closed, as if she were suspended in the moment. Caleb reached up and stroked her cheek, and she shifted to press it against his hand. Then her lashes lifted and she smiled as naturally as if they always cuddled.

"So, what *is* for dinner?"

God. He was thinking about kissing her passionately, and she was speculating on the menu.

On the other hand, her voice was just a little husky, and she was edging away from him. So maybe she *didn't* care about food. Maybe it was simply the first topic that came to mind to break the mood.

He let her get away with it. "Bean soup and sourdough rolls," he said.

"I love your cooking."

"You mean, you love *not* cooking."

Her grin flashed, a hint of mischief that reminded him of a younger, more carefree Laurel. "Well, that, too."

He lifted his arms above his head and stretched. "I'd better get the biscuits in the oven."

Twenty minutes later, Caleb was taking them out of the oven when they both heard a distant cry.

Laurel, who was setting the butter on the table, said, "Told you so."

"Damn it, they're going to get cold."

"I'll nurse fast." Her hand snaked out to grab one. "And gobble quick." She detoured to slather it with butter, then ate as she headed for the bedroom.

Resigned, Caleb wrapped the biscuits in a cloth napkin and put the lid back on the soup.

They ended up eating with Lydia in her plastic carrier on the table between them, as she was during so many of their meals. She wasn't as quick to fall back asleep anymore, and was more likely to enjoy being held, head wavering on her immature neck as she tried to take in the world with eyes that didn't yet focus quite the way she wanted them to.

Caleb's parents came for a visit the next day for the third time in less than two weeks. His mother in particular had surprised Caleb. She'd never been the stereotypical parent who hinted strongly that she was looking forward to a daughter-in-law and grandchildren. But she was obviously delighted now that she had a granddaughter.

While she cooed over Lydia, who lay between mom and grandma on the sofa, flapping arms and legs, Caleb and his father sat in easy chairs facing their womenfolk.

Caleb's dad took a sip of his coffee.

"I've been thinking about taking early retirement."

Caleb stared at his father. "You?"

He raised an eyebrow. "Should I take offense?"

"No, no. I just…" He shook his head. "Wouldn't you be bored?"

"Bored? Hell, no! There's more to life than work. Your mom and I've been wanting to do some more traveling." He shrugged. "My golf game interests me more than adding a new account."

"You're only fifty-five."

"That's why it's called early retirement."

"Would you move?" Laurel asked.

"I think we might," Caleb's mother answered. "Not away from Seattle. Especially now that we have a grandchild." She tickled Lydia's tummy. "But, honestly, our house and yard are a lot to take care of. I don't want to give up gardening altogether." She smiled at her son. "Caleb came by his interest in it naturally. But I'd be content with a much smaller yard. I love playing with annuals in pots all summer, then being able to forget them in the winter."

Still stunned, Caleb said, "Well, then… Have fun."

"Of course, we might be willing to put off the traveling if we can help." His mother looked at Laurel. "I assume you're planning to go back to work."

Laurel nodded, and Caleb stiffened.

"I'd love to take care of Lydia for you." She gave a quick laugh. "Maybe not until she goes into kindergarten, but for now, anyway. If you'd be interested."

"Interested?" Laurel blinked, but tears trembled on her lashes. "I've been dreading having to find day care. I couldn't imagine who I'd be willing to leave Lydia with. Oh, if you mean it, I'd be thrilled."

She tried to mention payment. His mother pooh-poohed

it. "It would be my privilege, to be able to spend time with my darling granddaughter."

Caleb's father beamed benevolently. Caleb wanted to kick both of them and say, *Damn it, don't you see that you're making it* easy *for Laurel to go back to work?*

Yeah, they did see, he realized. They were trying to make up for their earlier resistance to the idea of their son having a child out of wedlock by helping. They had no idea how insecure he was, waiting for the day Laurel decided it was time to quit playing family and go home again.

Caleb wondered if they'd be able to refrain from saying "I told you so" if he confessed to his present state of mixed happiness and misery.

Yeah, of course they would. He knew them better than that.

Suddenly aware of his father's blue eyes resting thoughtfully on his face, Caleb tuned back in to hear his mom and Laurel making plans.

"If I can find halfway reasonable parking near work, I might start driving. I don't like the idea of Lydia's car seat unbuckled on the bus."

Caleb didn't, either.

"Plus, it would make my day a bit shorter."

Well, that was something. He'd hated the image of her standing on street corners waiting for the bus, icy drizzle coming down and Lydia bundled in her mother's arms. Downtown there were always street people hanging out at bus stops, and the nearest stop to his parents' house had to be two blocks away. Not far on a warm summer morning, but a hell of a long way at six o'clock in January with night having fallen.

On the other hand, Caleb knew Laurel didn't drive

much anymore. She kept a car, and did use it for her weekend grocery shopping and an occasional visit to her dad or sister, but not much else.

"Why would I?" she'd said. "The bus is cheaper, more ecological and less stressful."

He didn't find driving stressful, but hadn't argued. Then. *Then,* she hadn't been carting their baby around.

When Lydia began to get fussy, Laurel hugged his parents goodbye and retired to her bedroom to nurse, leaving Caleb to walk them out.

"Bet you're going to miss them," his father said.

You think? Caleb wanted to ask viciously.

Unclenching his jaw, he conceded, "You could say that."

His mother gave him a soft kiss on the cheek. "Oh, Caleb, I wish…"

She didn't finish saying what she wished before getting in the car. She didn't have to. He knew. He wished, too.

But wishing wasn't good enough. His businessman father had always believed in taking charge, and despite Caleb's more laid-back personality, so did he.

No, he wasn't going to let her go that easily.

He waved as his father started their car forward around the circular drive. Then he went back into the house filled with new resolve.

CHAPTER ELEVEN

LAUREL WISHED CALEB WOULD quit kissing her at all if he didn't really mean it.

Not that she wanted him to mean it… Yes, she did. What if, next time he planted a gentle kiss on her mouth, she parted her lips a little? Or even, daringly, licked his lips lightly?

Lying in bed, she moaned, muffling it at the last minute into her pillow. Lydia had been cranky tonight. She kept falling asleep in their arms, but every time Laurel or Caleb laid her down in the bassinet she woke screaming. Finally, thank God, she'd been so exhausted she had remained in a deep, limp sleep. But who knew how long before she'd wake demanding Mommy? Four hours? Two? One?

Sleep! Laurel ordered herself. She'd be sorry later if she didn't.

But despite her exhaustion she couldn't stop thinking about the kiss Caleb had dropped so casually on her mouth out in the hall, before he murmured, "Good night." As he'd taken to doing every night lately, or sometimes when he was leaving to go to his office at the Seattle store. Then, he might stop behind the sofa, bend over and kiss the edge of her mouth, or the back of her neck, his hands gently squeezing her shoulders.

Tonight they both stood holding their breath in the hall waiting to see if sleep would take. Laurel had eventually sagged and said, "I'm going to bed."

"You do that." Caleb clasped her upper arms, kneaded a couple of times, and bent his head oh, so slowly, his gaze focused on her mouth. The kiss might have been brotherly, except for the way his lips had lingered. They'd brushed one way, paused, then slid the other, while she had stood paralyzed, feeling this rush of heat.

Even now, that warmth continued to pool in her lower belly, and she was tempted to touch herself. As if that would help, when it was Caleb she would see behind closed eyelids.

She couldn't want him. She just couldn't.

Another moan caught in her throat. She pictured him sauntering down the hall to his room and changing into the flannel pajama bottoms that he wore slung low on his hips. The pajama bottoms that were *all* he wore to bed. And maybe those were in deference to her presence and to the fact that he often got up at night when Lydia cried.

She'd seen him shirtless back in college, but he'd been skinny then. Athletic, but bony enough that his shirtless state didn't induce womanly knee-buckling. But the night three weeks ago when she woke him because she was in labor, after he sprang out of bed and turned on the lamp, Laurel had stared. The only thing she could think was, *Wow. When did* that *happen?* A woman who was between increasingly close, intense contractions shouldn't have been able to notice how sexy a man's chest was, but she had.

Now she saw him almost nightly without his shirt. He was still lean, but with the addition of ten years, he'd acquired muscles that bunched at his shoulders and de-fined his chest. She tried every time not to let her gaze wander to his taut stomach, and especially not to the thin line of hair that led from his belly button down below the waistband of those pajama bottoms. He was all male, and, damn it, he'd buckle *any* woman's knees.

Laurel wanted to be an exception. She might feel these things, but she couldn't act on them. Not with him, not with anyone.

What if he were here right now, in bed with her? Eyes closed, she imagined splaying her hands on his chest, learning the feel and not just the look of those muscles. Kissing his neck, tasting his skin…

Her breath came fast between parted lips.

Tracing that line of hair, sliding her fingers beneath the elastic waistband…

Her belly cramped and she opened her eyes to stare at the band of dim light from the hall. Caleb knew she didn't like complete darkness, and had taken to leaving the bath-room light on.

Caleb, she thought, who would not lie passively in her bed, a warm living mannequin. No, his arms would come around her and his mouth would smother hers with kisses. His tongue would penetrate her mouth, and he'd rear above her, his shoulders blocking that dim light. His weight would bear down on her, making her feel small, weak, in-effectual.

Her breath still came fast, but for a different reason now. Incipient panic shivered beneath her skin, balled in her chest. No. She couldn't bear it. Shouldn't fool herself for a second that she could.

Or…could she?

She calmed her breathing. None of the other women in her rape support group were celibate. True, they might have been more experienced sexually than she was before the rape. Laurel suspected that would make a difference. But maybe it didn't matter. Maybe what she had to do was convince her subconscious that all men, and especially Caleb, were *not* like the monster who had raped her.

How did you communicate with your subconscious? Ask to have a chat?

Pushing the covers lower, Laurel flopped onto her back. Resentment stirred. Why did he have to stir all this up? Especially right now? She was muddled enough already. Not depressed—thank heavens, not that. But, postbirth, her mood didn't just swing, it did cartwheels. No, whole tumbling runs, Olympic class. One minute she'd feel dizzy with happiness, the next weepy. She could go from confident to frighteningly lonely in less than sixty seconds. It was hormones doing this to her, Laurel knew it was, but that didn't really help her cope.

And Caleb chose now to…well, whatever he was doing. Not flirting, exactly. But he was being tender, sensual. He was definitely hinting at possibilities.

Her eyes popped open in alarm. Was she *sure?* What if she did something incredibly forward when he dropped one of those kisses on her mouth, and he really didn't think of her as anything but a friend? She could ruin everything!

Her mood flip-flopped again, as capricious as a toddler's. *She* wasn't the one trying to ruin everything, Caleb was. Of course he was coming on to her. A man didn't look at a woman's mouth that way before bestowing a brotherly peck. Anyway, he'd said enough things suggesting that he'd been thinking about her in a different light for a long time for her to guess that he wouldn't be upset if she did some hinting of her own right back.

She wasn't supposed to be having this dilemma. Which part of "broken, can't be fixed" was she having trouble understanding?

What Laurel knew was, she hadn't felt these sexual stirrings in a long time—since Before—but the impulses were definitely alive and well. Not retired, gone, *fini,* the way she'd believed. And, boy, were they inconvenient for someone who was pretty sure she'd throw a major fit the minute some guy tried to climb on top of her.

Just like that, she was mad. Caleb *knew* this. So why was he giving her these not-so-subtle nudges?

She'd think he was just a flirt if she didn't know him better. See a woman, must come on to her. The thing is, Caleb wasn't like that. In the old days, they had flirted a little, but it was mutual. Otherwise, Caleb was friendly, direct, charming, but also often, to Laurel's amusement, oblivious to women trying to come on to *him.*

And since she was raped, he'd never once acted as if he were anything but a friend. The fact that he was a man and she was a woman never entered into it.

Okay, maybe, they'd both been a tad more conscious of those differences since his sperm impregnated her. How could they help it? But still, he'd been his usual supportive, occasionally overbearing self.

It wasn't until that first time he kissed her, after they visited Nadia in the hospital, that Laurel had caught these vibes of sexual interest from him. And then lately…well, lately, there was something in his eyes every time he looked at her.

And it sure wasn't because she was so stunning. Even if she started the exercise program she planned, her waistline would take six months to recover from Lydia's tenure. Her boobs dripped milk at inconvenient times. She had bags and dark circles beneath her eyes. Half the time, her hair was lank and scraped back in a ponytail, she'd just come from changing a diaper, and the most exciting thing she had to talk about was Lydia's sleeping schedule.

Miss America, she wasn't.

So what had gotten into him?

She gave one more frustrated flop and further tangled the covers.

If he didn't knock it off, she didn't know what she was going to do.

OVER THE NEWSPAPER, Caleb observed. "You look tense."

Laurel shot him a less than friendly look. "Walking for an hour straight with a screaming baby will do that to you."

"I offered—"

She cut him off. "I know you did. It's okay. No reason both of us should suffer. But my ears are ringing, okay? And I'm praying she stays down for a couple of hours."

"You should go take a nap."

Laurel mumbled what he took as agreement, but didn't move from her seat in the rocker. It thumped back and forth on the oak floor too quickly to suggest she was finding the act of rocking relaxing.

"Your dad still coming tomorrow? I may run down to the Tacoma store."

She shrugged. "Last I knew. We'll be okay anyway."

He nodded and pretended to go back to the sports news

while continuing to watch her surreptitiously. Laurel kept rocking, her fingers tight on the arms of the mission-style chair. She wasn't exactly frowning, but her face looked tight.

Enlightenment dawned and he lowered the paper again. "Headache?"

She started to nod and winced. "Yeah. I don't want to take anything while I'm nursing. Maybe a hot bath…"

"Why don't I massage your shoulders? You used to tell me I was missing my calling, I had such good hands."

"I'd forgotten." The rocking motion checked. "Do you mean it?"

"What do you think? Come on." He closed the newspaper and set it aside, then patted the couch between his knees.

After a moment Laurel stood and crossed the room, dropping to sit cross-legged on the floor in front of him. These days Caleb was keeping the house warmer than he liked for her and Lydia's sake, but Laurel seemed to be cold all the time anyway.

"You'd better lose the sweater," he said, tugging at it.

She lifted her arms and pulled it over her head. Beneath, she wore a white T-shirt and one of the sturdier-than-usual bras he often caught a glimpse of when she was nursing.

He laid his hands on her and gently squeezed the muscles that ran from her neck to the bony tops of her shoulder sockets.

A throaty sound escaped her and she let her head drop forward.

She'd sound like that when she was making love, he thought, and his body surged in response.

I'm healing here, not seducing.

He kneaded and applied pressure as he found hard knots of tension. He worked the ones out beneath her shoulder blades, then moved up to her neck. It felt tense, but also fragile beneath his hands, reminding him of how much smaller than him she was. Her personality was big enough, he never thought, *I dwarf her.* But she did have fine bones he noticed mostly in her hands and feet. Long fingers, long toes, but slender. Caleb vaguely remembered grumbles about how she had to buy expensive shoes at Nordstrom because she needed a narrow width.

As he took his time going up her neck, savoring the delicate line of vertebrae and squeezing and pressing the muscles, she kept making those throaty sounds. Probably unconsciously, Caleb decided. She wouldn't like knowing how erotic he found them.

When he reached the hairline, he kept going, his fingers slipping into her heavy fall of hair, rotating. Up to the crown, around the sides and just above her ears, to her temples and then forehead. Laurel tilted her head back and let him work on her face, from the bunched muscles at her jaw over to the cheekbones she swore were nonexistent, even to the bridge of her nose.

The nose he already knew their Lydia would have, too.

He could have kept stroking her forever, just for the pleasure of hearing her sighs and feeling the silky texture of her skin. She was the one who stretched luxuriantly, yawned and lifted heavy eyelids.

"I'm about to fall asleep."

"You can do it here on the couch." He patted the cushion beside him.

"Tempting. But I think I'll go to bed."

"It will be nice when she sleeps through the night."

"She and I'll probably be home by then." She didn't look to see how hard that hit him, instead yawning again until her jaws cracked. With a laugh, she levered herself to her feet. "Sorry. God. All I do these days is nurse, eat, sleep. Start cycle all over."

"It's bearable when you know what a short time it lasts."

She murmured agreement. "And when Lydia is so endlessly fascinating. Thank you, Caleb. You're better than a fistful of ibuprofen."

"Knew I was good for something."

Laurel smiled, her eyes clear and her forehead uncreased. "I'm sure you're good for something else. I'll let you know when I remember."

He whacked at her butt as she turned to sashay away. "I cook. I'm good for that."

"Yeah, you are." She gave him a wicked smile as she left the living room. Her voice trailed back. "And your sperm was dandy, too."

He flashed on the fantasy he'd had sitting on her bathroom toilet, surrounded by that violet-sprigged wallpaper, trying to come into a sandwich bag so he could offer it to her as an unlikely gift. Forget the bouquet of roses or box of decadent chocolates, he'd given her his genes.

Hadn't she known then and there that he'd give her anything?

No, why should she? After all, Matt Baker had been willing to give his sperm, too. *Bastard*, Caleb thought. *Who the hell was Baker to think his sperm had any business in Laurel's body?*

She'd *asked* him.

No excuse.

Half-amused by his own spurt of temper—but only half—Caleb picked up the newspaper again.

Should have kissed her, he thought with regret. Although putting his hands on her… That was good, too.

SLEEP CRASHED DOWN on her like a rogue wave, but Laurel's last thought was how wrong it had seemed to think of her and Lydia back in her cramped house without Caleb around.

Sure, that was the way she'd planned it, but… She couldn't formulate the rest of the thought. Her mind was too foggy.

His hands felt so good….

She was gone, just a plunge into the depths.

And awakened as suddenly by an unhappy squall.

It actually hurt to open her eyelids, so badly did they want to stay glued together.

Nurse, eat, sleep.

Please, please, please, go right back to sleep after I feed you, Laurel begged, as she crawled out of bed and lifted her tiny daughter from the bassinet.

Wet diaper. That meant a trip to the bathroom, where the light was shockingly bright. Lydia blinked and Laurel squinted as she unsnapped the lemon-yellow onesie, peeled off a soaked diaper and replaced it. Nobody needed to see this well.

She hoisted her daughter to her shoulder again and, with relief, snapped off the light and made her way to the upholstered rocker in her bedroom that Caleb had thoughtfully provided. The bedroom lights were still off, but the hall one was on now. Caleb must have heard Lydia crying and looked in. It was nice of him to leave it on.

Seated, Laurel opened the front of her gown and Lydia took to her breast as if her mommy had been trying to starve her. By the time she shifted to the other breast, her suckling had become less urgent, her body relaxed. She seemed to appreciate the yellow glow from the hall, too—just bright enough that she could see Mommy's face, not surgically bright like the bathroom.

Her mouth slipped from Laurel's breast. Then she jerked and began sucking again with new fervency, as if to say, *Wait! I wasn't done.*

Laurel began to sing, softly, for Lydia's ears only. How funny that she loved this quiet interval in the middle of the night, no matter how sleepy she was. Lullabies, folk tunes, her rocking slower and slower, her voice becoming a whisper, then fading when she realized Lydia was sound asleep again.

Laurel gently placed her back in the bassinet and spread the comforter over her, standing for a moment to look down at her face, so perfect.

Who will you be?

Every parent must ask the same question. The mystery, the possibilities, all waiting to unfold.

Smiling, she turned toward the bedroom door with the intention of turning off the hall light. But she stopped at the sight of Caleb standing in the doorway, wearing nothing but pajama bottoms.

He nodded toward the bassinet. His mouth formed the word "Asleep?"

Laurel nodded. "You didn't have to get up," she whispered.

He backed into the hall. She followed.

"I wanted to."

"But…why?"

"I like to see you with her."

"But…" she said again. "You do during the day."

His bare shoulders moved. "It's different at night. Your hair is loose and tousled, you have a pillow print on your cheek—" he touched it with one finger "—your face is so soft. And Lydia is less likely to be cranky."

Self-conscious, Laurel reached up herself to feel the crease in her cheek. Then she remembered unbuttoning her gown and looked down the dark crevasse of cleavage. She wore a bra, thank goodness, or her breasts would be hanging out, but the sight of damp spots on the front of the gown made her flush.

"I like this feeding," she admitted, keeping her voice low. "I was just thinking that I should be miserable after being wrenched from sleep, but I wasn't. It's so peaceful."

"You'll miss it, when she doesn't want you at 2:00 a.m."

"I suppose I will. Except an uninterrupted eight hours of sleep is beginning to sound like nirvana."

His eyes were dark, hooded, but his voice was tender. "You'll miss it anyway."

"Do you watch every night?"

"No. I was just…tempted tonight."

She was beginning to understand temptation, too. She wanted to put her hands on his chest so that his heart drummed under her palm. Find out if she could feel the things she once had. If she could block out her fear.

But Caleb was the worst person in the world with whom she should experiment. She had so much to lose where he was concerned.

Yes, but she also trusted him more than anyone else in the world, except maybe her dad.

But did she trust him enough? Laurel didn't know.

"What are you thinking?" Caleb murmured.

"I…nothing. How it's silly for us to be standing here in the hall whispering in the middle of the night."

"I'm thinking how beautiful you look in the middle of the night. When you were nursing, I thought, Madonna and child. Da Vinci would have loved your face."

Shaken, she said, "I'm so not beautiful. I've never been beautiful."

"I've always thought you were." He caressed her cheek, a touch so light it gave her goose bumps. "I figured we'd get together someday. Didn't you?"

Her heart slammed. After a moment, she nodded. "We flirted a few times. I thought maybe."

"I thought for sure. When the time was right." He bent his head, rubbed his nose against hers. "What do you think, Laurel? Is this that time?"

"But…I can't… You know I can't…" It came out as a piteous cry, and she clapped her hand over her mouth.

Caleb gently pried her fingers from her lips. "It's okay. She's still asleep."

Laurel sagged a little. She didn't object when he steered her a few steps down the hall.

"Why now?"

"We're living together. For God's sake, we had a baby together. It's not logical to think maybe we could have more?"

That was it? He was enjoying domestic bliss? Contrarily, she felt a burst of outrage. He wasn't saying *I'm passionately in love with you.* No, it was more *Having a family is nice. Let's not wreck a good thing.*

"You've been making big assumptions ever since I agreed you could be my baby's father."

He stiffened. "Big assumptions? Like being part of my kid's life?"

"Like assuming you could make decisions for me!" She felt like she had as a child, frustrated in an argument and grasping for any straw.

Caleb's voice took on an edge. "I offered to help. That's all."

"Help I didn't want!"

His face went still, expressionless. "That's how you feel?"

Laurel's vision blurred. "No," she whispered, her sinuses suddenly clogged. Oh, God, she was getting weepy. "You know it's not. I'm afraid."

"Of me?" He took a step closer, the words husky, tender.

"No. You know I'm not. Just of…of trying to pretend it never happened."

"Why should you have to? You can overcome fears without pretending they don't exist."

She knew he was right. She had, to some extent. She lived alone, a crucial step in regaining her independence. It had been weeks after moving into the house before she had a real night's sleep. Her father had seen to it that good locks were installed, but the kind of horror she'd experienced couldn't be kept out by braces on the windows or dead bolts. She'd stuck it out anyway, until the noises became familiar, and she went to bed one night hardly noticing the absence of dread.

But sex seemed impossible. Even with Caleb, no matter how she'd reacted to him lately, to his touches and his bare chest and his not-so-casual kisses.

"I don't know." She sounded pathetic.

"We can take it slow. See if one of these days you're ready."

"What if I never am?"

Some emotion passed over his face, hidden before she could identify it. "Then I suppose I'll get frustrated. But not mad at you. I promise, Laurel."

"I'm scared," she whispered.

"Of what?" He lifted one hand and stroked her cheek. "Does that scare you?"

She gave her head a small shake.

He bent his head until their foreheads bumped, then nuzzled her nose again with his. "This?"

"No…"

His hand slid to the back of her neck and squeezed while he pressed a featherlight kiss to her lips.

"This?" His voice was a soft burr, a mere vibration beneath her hands, which—astonishingly—had come to be flattened on his chest.

She shook her head again, shyly this time.

"Good." He kissed her again, this time opening his mouth so that she felt his warm breath.

Laurel hadn't moved beyond having lifted her hands to touch him. Perhaps to push him away, but she didn't want to. She stood suspended in the moment, her face tilted up, her breathing shallow and fast, a sense of wonder filling her.

Maybe I can…

She let her lips part, just a little. He nipped gently at her lower lip, tugging at it, sucking it. Heat washed through her. Her eyes closed and she made a sound. A moan? Something damp touched her mouth. His tongue. He was tracing her lips with his tongue. And it felt heavenly. She leaned in, and one of his hands went to her waist. It felt…different than all the other times he'd put an arm around her, laid a hand on her lower back as they went through a crowd.

Purposeful. That was it. Strong. He squeezed, slid it lower to her hip, even as he continued to toy with her mouth.

Feeling brave, she nipped his lower lip, touched it with the tip of her tongue. He was the one to make a sound this time, a growl that delighted her. Then his mouth captured hers in a kiss that felt harder, more urgent. Before she could know how she felt about it, he lifted his head.

"Slowly. We're going to take this slowly."

Laurel blinked in confusion. Who was he reminding? Her or himself? Anyway, wasn't that what they'd been doing?

He let her go and took a step back. His eyes were heavy-lidded again, with a glint that increased the throbbing she felt down low.

"You need your sleep," he said. "You just gave birth three weeks ago."

She almost said, *Haven't forgotten. I was there, you know.* Then she realized with a tiny shock what he was really saying. She wasn't supposed to have sex yet. The doctor had told her six weeks. Caleb must know that. He must think they could really make love.

Alarm fluttered in her chest and she wrapped her arms around herself. "I am tired."

His face seemed to soften. His smile was classic Caleb: sweet, a little crooked, somehow merry.

"We've gotta quit meeting like this."

Her in her nightgown, him in his pajamas, them lurking

in the hall like two guests having an illicit tryst in someone else's house.

A bubble of laughter escaped Laurel, more of a hiccup than a giggle. "Good night, Caleb."

"Good night, sweetheart," he murmured, and patted her on the butt as she turned to go back into her room.

She was still smiling when she got into bed despite the fifty-nine arguments, pro and con, that were already jumbled in her head.

I swore I'd never…

Caleb isn't like him.

He might be more like him than you know. He wants the same thing.

No! Not to hurt her, not to dominate.

Are you sure?

Yes!

But…could she let even Caleb that close?

There was only one way to find out, wasn't there?

CHAPTER TWELVE

LAUREL'S FATHER SAID, "Where's my granddaughter?" the minute he walked in the door.

Laughing, Laurel kissed him and said, "Great to see you, too. Lydia is in the living room."

He gave her a lightning appraisal and then a hug. "You look the best you have in years."

"Motherhood must agree with me," she said lightly, not about to mention lust, romance or any similar topic.

Lydia lay on her back on the multicolored wool rug in the living room, her pacifier bobbing in her mouth and the rattle Laurel had left in her hand ten feet away. As Caleb put it, his daughter had a good arm. Her understanding of what to do with strange objects in her grasp was pretty hazy as yet.

Laurel's father had a good cuddle with Lydia, telling her she was the prettiest girl in the entire world and amazingly smart, all opinions Laurel happened to share. Still, she was amused to watch him, a dignified man in his fifties, making silly noises and chucking a baby's chin.

Of course, she reminded himself, he *had* done this before. He'd even changed diapers in his time.

Lydia was going to get a big head from the stream of visitors exclaiming over her. Nadia had been over a couple of times, Darren in tow once, Caleb's parents *and* his grandparents who had flown up from San Diego, Megan, of course, and even Sela Sweeney, who much to Laurel's surprise had seemed envious.

When Lydia decided she was hungry, Laurel's dad handed her over to Laurel and pretended to inspect Caleb's bookshelves on the other side of the room while Laurel nursed. He was just old-fashioned enough to be embarrassed when she had to expose a breast, even though she knew her mother had nursed Megan and her.

"I'm glad you decided to take a few months off," he observed over his shoulder. "Looks like the two of you are thriving."

"I wouldn't have gone back to work until she was six weeks old anyway." Laurel gazed down at Lydia, still a slight weight on her arm, but developing some substance. As always when she thought about leaving her for up to ten hours a day, her heart cramped. How could she? Did she trust even Caleb's mom with her baby's welfare? And even if she knew Lydia was fine, how would she get through the day without seeing her? Holding her? Inhaling her baby scent?

She was dreading the day she had to go back to work.

"What's the plan now?"

"I'm not sure. Mr. Hern e-mailed the other day wondering when I'd be back. They've been good about it, but I've already been off for two months."

"Don't hurry," her father advised. "You and that baby need time together."

"Did Caleb bribe you to say that?" she asked, only half joking.

"You know I'll continue to help financially."

Caleb had been careful not to echo his offer lately, probably hoping Lydia would do his work for him.

But she'd already taken so much from her dad in the months after the rape and in buying the house, she hated to take more. And how could she live like a leech off Caleb and have any self-respect left? Besides…wasn't it going to get harder and harder to pack up and go back to her own house the longer she waited? No Caleb around to take Lydia when she wouldn't quit fussing, no one to make dinner at least every other night, no one to cuddle with?

No kisses.

"I know, Daddy." She bent her head so even if he looked he wouldn't see the mist she was furiously blinking away. "But I chose to get pregnant on my own, and I should be able to take care of us. I'm a big girl."

"You'll forever be my little girl. You know that, don't you?"

"Of course, I do." She eased Lydia away from her breast. "Let me put her down for a nap and then we'll have lunch. I made a shrimp salad. *And* lemon meringue pie."

As they ate, they tacitly agreed to let the subject drop. Instead, he told her about work, neighbors, friends.

"Did I tell you Frank Brisco is brewing beer now? He says microbreweries are popping up everywhere, and why shouldn't he make a go of one?"

"How's it taste?"

"Not bad."

Laurel already knew that Megan had ditched her latest boyfriend, the successor to the computer nerd.

Her father shook her head. "Says he spends more on clothes than she does."

In tandem, they both said, "Which is saying a lot," then laughed.

He left at two, hoping to beat the traffic. Lydia had just

awakened, so he got to kiss her goodbye. "I haven't seen any new pictures lately," he said, as he was getting into his car.

"Oh, Caleb's been taking them. I'll remind him to e-mail some to you."

"He's a good man, Caleb. He's taken responsibility."

There was that old-fashioned attitude again.

"Dad, he didn't knock me up. He donated sperm because I asked."

He raised his brows. "What's the difference?"

In exasperation, Laurel said, "Sex, Dad. That's the difference. *He* didn't get anything out of it."

"He got a daughter, didn't he?"

Her father was hopeless. If she'd used an anonymous sperm donor, would he have railed about the irresponsibility of a man just letting his sperm be frozen and implanted anywhere? Probably.

"Your granddaddy is a stick-in-the-mud," she told Lydia, going back in the house.

Laurel had put dinner on later and laid Lydia down for yet another nap when she heard Caleb's car outside, then the front door opening and closing.

Smiling, she went downstairs to meet him.

Once in a blue moon, he felt compelled to dress up for a business meeting. Today had been one of those days. She'd barely caught a glimpse of him this morning, so now she looked him up and down.

"Nice."

He grimaced and stripped his tie from around his neck.

Why was a well-cut suit so sexy on a man? Laurel had no idea, but this one sure was. Dark, charcoal-gray, the coat fit his wide shoulders and hung in the way only incredibly expensive fabric could. It was open to reveal the slacks, pleated below a narrow black leather belt. His throat and face were tanned above a white shirt. He'd probably loosened the tie and unbuttoned the collar the minute he got in his car, Laurel thought with fond amusement.

"Lydia down?" he asked.

"Ate like a pig, conked out. I put dinner on. We might get to sit down alone tonight."

It had become a private joke. They never sat down at the table without her squalling.

"Counting on it," he said, straight-faced. "Hey. Come here."

When she took a step forward, he grabbed her by the waist and bent to kiss her. Laurel stood on tiptoe to meet him halfway. Already, it felt natural. They kissed hello, goodbye and six dozen times in between. She *liked* kissing, she'd remembered. Liked it even more with Caleb than she had with her previous boyfriends.

Knowing they couldn't go beyond kisses for three more weeks—two now—had freed Laurel to explore these new/old feelings without anxiety building like a thunderstorm in her chest the minute he touched her. And he'd kept his promise about taking it slow. Once in a while, she'd sense raw need, the scrape of teeth, the tightening of his grip, but he always pulled back before she panicked.

What would happen when these weeks were up…? Well, she wasn't letting herself think about it. Right now, she could make out with a guy. She hadn't believed she could do even that. She suspected she still couldn't with anyone but Caleb.

Actually, she couldn't imagine *wanting* to make out with anyone but him. She thought back to her couple of boyfriends in college and wondered why she'd bothered.

Even then, she knew she'd rather spend time with Caleb given a choice. She just hadn't ever let herself admit to what that meant. And, of course, she'd denied feeling anything but friendship to everyone including Nadia, in whom she confided just about everything else.

Well, you couldn't confide what you didn't know, could you?

But she knew now. She was in love with him. Always had been, always would be. Whether that would be enough… No. Laurel stopped herself from even going there. Two more weeks to savor what she could only call his courtship. *Then* she would worry.

Lifting his mouth from hers now, he smiled down at her. "Brought you something."

"You shouldn't do that everytime you go anywhere."

Flowers, chocolates, a hair scrunchie made of fabric woven in Guatemala, a picture frame. Little things, but sweet. Especially the chocolates—she'd really enjoyed those.

"I miss you." He reached in the pocket of his jacket and, like a magician, pulled out a scarf. Gossamer fine, scarlet and sparkling with gold, it kept coming and coming.

"Ohh," she breathed with delight. "It's beautiful!"

"Even mommies need to remember they're sensuous women."

Her gaze caught his. "You remind me of that every time I see you."

A light flared in his eyes, but he banked it, only smiling lazily. "A service I perform with pleasure."

She punched him, then took the scarf. It was unbelievably lightweight, like holding a spiderweb spun with scarlet and gold. Laurel draped it around her shoulders and spun.

"Or maybe around my hips." She tried that, knotting it on one side.

"You know, instead of step aerobics you could try belly dancing," Caleb suggested.

"You wish."

He succeeded in sounding woebegone. "Don't my wishes count for anything?"

Laurel kissed him on the cheek. "Of course they do. Just…" She hesitated.

"Not yet. And that's okay." He covered her mouth with a quick, hard kiss, then let her go. "I need to change."

"I'll put the noodles on." Reluctantly, she untied the scarf, held it briefly to her cheek then folded it and set it on the hall table as he started up the stairs.

Somehow, she wasn't the slightest bit surprised when he came back down ten minutes later with Lydia against his shoulder.

"Guess who woke up?"

"That was hardly a nap," Laurel said indignantly, turning from the stove. "She was *pretending* to sleep. Setting me up for disappointment. Isn't that right, sweetie?" She kissed Lydia's plump cheek. "See, she's not even hungry. She'd be crying."

"Nope. She wants to dine with Mommy and Daddy." He hoisted her so that father and daughter were nose to nose. "Daddy understands all, Lydia. Never forget it."

Lydia's arms flapped. He grinned at her.

"Will Daddy understand when his little girl sneaks out her bedroom window to meet her boyfriend?" Laurel asked.

He looked momentarily appalled, which she thought was cute.

"My Lydia will never do that. Will you, kiddo?"

Laurel laughed and dumped the noodles into the colander, gave it a shake, then poured them into a bowl. "Dinner is ready."

Still carrying Lydia, he crowded Laurel as he peered into the second serving bowl. "Stroganoff. Smells great."

While they ate, Lydia once more in her plastic carrier on the table, Caleb told Laurel about his meeting.

"Guy owns a bunch of import stores in the Midwest. Chicago, St. Louis, Kansas City. More upscale than, say, Pier 1. Sells mainly stuff from Asia. He's interested in adding products from Latin America, but it takes time to develop the sources for high-quality art and textiles. He'd like to buy from me."

"Make you a middleman." She mulled it over. "You'd either have to pay the artists less, or shave your profit."

"Shave my profit, of course. But think of the payoff. Some of the co-ops I work with could expand." He spoke faster, leaning forward in his enthusiasm. "Maybe double production. It would be good for the artists, for the villages where they live."

She listened as he talked about delegating more buying and organization. He'd hired a PLU graduate two years before and had let him start negotiating and working with existing cooperatives this past year. Now he was thinking about adding another buyer or two. "Especially since I'll want to travel less," he added, squeezing Lydia's toes.

She kicked, her gaze staying on his face. She was getting really good at tracking interesting sights, and faces were her favorites.

"You know, I'd swear her hair is getting curly," he said, easily distracted.

"I noticed. She didn't get it from me."

"Mine does have some waves." He tugged at it. "A nuisance."

"But pretty on a girl."

They both smiled at their daughter, besotted parents.

"It's growing, too," Caleb said.

"Hair does that."

"Doesn't babies' hair sometimes fall out? I read that somewhere."

"Yes, but they're usually a little older. Like four months, I think. And I don't know why hers would. She definitely has your hair."

"But your nose. And mouth, too, I think."

"Your eyes. And your dad's." Her thoughts segued to the inevitable separation she'd brooded about all day. "I'm so glad your mother offered to take care of her. I really was dreading handing her over to a stranger."

"Could you have done that?"

Stomach twisting, Laurel pushed her plate away. "Of course I would have." It came out snappish. "Most parents do. Until you have a baby, you don't get to know a lot of day-care providers."

He leaned back in his chair, his tone carefully neutral. "I didn't mean that as criticism."

"Didn't you?" She knew she sounded grouchy and didn't care. Or maybe she did, but she couldn't stop herself. That was the thing with her emotions these days: they ebbed and surged, pulled by a stronger force than her.

"I admire your determination to take care of you and Lydia."

She sniffed. Oh, damn. The teary phase couldn't be far behind. "But you wish I'd let you take care of us anyway."

"I want us to be a family. To pool our resources. I can't nurse her. I can pay the bills."

Was he talking marriage? Big jump. More than she could think about.

"It's unequal. You take care of her, too. I had her because I wanted her. She's my responsibility."

Anger darkened his eyes. "However it happened, she's my daughter, too. My responsibility."

"You sound like my father. Old-fashioned."

"I should be like Matt Baker? Hand over sperm and say, 'Best of luck'?"

"Matt has nothing to do with this."

"But he almost did, didn't he?"

"I told you why I asked him."

"But you and I, we had a different deal. I said I wanted to be involved, and I do. Don't try to tell me Lydia is yours now. She's *ours*."

Laurel's voice rose. "I never said…"

Lydia, who had been looking from Mommy to Daddy in astonishment, now burst into tears.

"Now look what you did." Caleb scooped her up and held her against his shoulder.

Laurel burst into tears, too.

"Oh, damn." He got out of his chair and came to her, bending over to hold her, too. "I'm sorry, I'm sorry. I was being a jackass. Don't listen to me."

"I'm sorry, too!" she wailed, burrowing her face into his chest next to her daughter's small body.

Lydia kept crying. Laurel couldn't seem to stop, either. Was this *normal?* Would she ever get over being so emotional?

Caleb crouched awkwardly beside the chair and continued to pat her and bounce Lydia, saying over and over, "God, I'm sorry. I know you're not ready… I'm sorry. So sorry."

Now he felt bad, too, and she hadn't meant to upset him. She was just scared, Laurel knew dimly. Scared of losing him because she couldn't give him what he needed. Scared of being on her own, of life never getting any better. Scared she wouldn't be an adequate mother.

She wept harder.

It was the escalation of Lydia's screams that eventually penetrated. *She* was the one upsetting her baby, who couldn't begin to understand why Mommy was crying, too. It was time she acted like a mommy, not the terrified, damaged woman she knew herself to be inside. Cry when Lydia was asleep if she had to, but not in front of her.

And not in front of Caleb. She'd just reinforce his belief in her emotional fragility.

Somehow, somewhere, she found the strength to silence her sobs, gulp, then give a watery laugh. "Oh, dear." She sat up, away from Caleb, and rubbed her face. "I'm a mess. It's these damn hormones! I'm sorry, Caleb. Let me go wash my face."

She fled, and was horrified at the sight of herself in the mirror. Her face was puffy, red, wet, snotty. With a moan she turned on the tap and splashed cold water on herself, over and over, until the red patches faded and the puffiness subsided enough that her eyes weren't squinty raisins.

Lydia had quit crying by the time Laurel returned, but she and Caleb looked at Laurel with identical expressions of wariness.

"I'm sorry!" she said again, the minute she saw them. She

held out her arms to Lydia. "Come here, sweetheart. Mommy won't cry, I promise." She took her, nuzzling her head.

"I was a jerk," Caleb said.

She shook her head. "No. It was me. My emotions are all over the map. I don't even know what I was crying about. Everything that's ever made me sad in my life. Who knows? It's the postbirth form of morning sickness. Trust me to get a bad case."

He let it slide, leaving her to nurse while he cleaned off the table. Then they had pieces of the pie she'd baked for her father's visit.

Conversation was stilted, both of them trying really hard not to say a word about anything important.

She ventured, "Your parents open presents on Christmas morning, right? What if we go to Dad's on Christmas Eve, then your parents' Christmas Day?"

"Works for me. Are we going to get a tree?"

For what might be her one and only Christmas in his house. Fighting a wave of melancholy, Laurel nodded. "Of course we are! It's Lydia's first Christmas."

"Then let's go get one tomorrow." Caleb ate his last bite. "Laurel, I've been pressuring you. I'm sorry. I just don't want to lose this." He gestured vaguely with his fork. "Having you two here."

"I know." She sniffed, mad that her eyes instantly filled with tears again. "I don't, either. But I'm all mixed up still. I think I need to prove to myself that I can take care of us. Of Lydia and me."

"And I need to suck it up and let you."

She saw on his face that he was grieving already, and realized she shouldn't have agreed to let him father her child. She shouldn't have asked Matt, either. She'd been selfish, not thinking about the consequences to either one of them. And staying here like this, pretending they could be a normal family when she wasn't sure whether they could be…that had been selfish, too. Giving him a taste of being a regular dad, of being able to kiss his little girl goodbye when he went to work, change her diaper and play "This Little Piggy" with her toes, put her to bed. And then she was going to scoop Lydia up and go home, leaving him to his empty house.

That wasn't love, she thought, appalled. It was… She didn't know. Self-centeredness to the nth degree. Her striving through motherhood to make *her* life satisfying, never mind the casualties.

Even the kisses. Wasn't she being selfish indulging in them, too? Being a tease, when she didn't know if she could ever give herself fully? She didn't even know if she could *try*. But she was having fun, so never mind how much she frustrated Caleb.

Right at that moment, she despised herself. Had she ever really thought about another person since she awakened in the hospital? Or was everything about her suffering, her damage, her needs?

Caleb was talking. She didn't even hear what he was saying. She sat stunned, seeing herself clearly for the first time in years.

She'd rejected her friends because *she* couldn't bear to see the contrast between them and her. If they got hurt… well, that hadn't occurred to her. She'd taken her father's and sister's support and worry for granted. Caleb's, too. She'd had a baby because *she* was lonely.

Mothers were supposed to be unselfish! Giving, teaching, loving and, in the end, opening their hands and letting their children go as they hid their tears. Given her recent record, would she be able to do that?

"Laurel?" Caleb's voice was hard, urgent. He leaned toward her. "Are you all right?"

She wanted to cry again, but self-disgust washed over her. *Poor me. I'm so sad.* What about him? What about Lydia?

"I just…" Her voice faltered and she stared down at her half-eaten pie. "I'm just having an unwelcome revelation. Somehow I never let myself realize you were going to get hurt. I shouldn't have let you talk me into coming home with you like this. No matter *how* good friends we are."

"Is this your way of letting me down?" His voice sounded almost…detached. "Sorry, Caleb? Not interested in anything long-term?"

"*No.* But I said I'd never be with a man, and I've let you think I can."

"You haven't even tried."

"But you're counting on it. On me…" She couldn't even say it. Submitting? Lying beneath him as he pounded into her? Her throat closed and she shrank away from him without thinking.

Caleb swore, his face twisting. "You're still afraid of me. Nothing I do is going to change that, is it?"

"I'm not afraid of you. It's me. How *I'll* react."

There she went again. Me, me, me.

"You're right." He shoved back his chair. "I have been deluding myself. My fault, not yours. I wouldn't listen when you tried to tell me you'd changed." He shook his head, as if disgusted. "I'll clean the kitchen if you want to go to bed."

You're dismissed. No, more like *Do me a favor and get out of my sight.*

She could only nod dumbly, push back her chair, too, and scoop up Lydia. Hugging her so tight she squirmed, Laurel walked out of the room.

I've ruined everything, she thought in shock. *Killed even the* chance *that he might have loved me and I might have been able to love him back.*

All because she'd suddenly seen herself in a harsh, clear light.

She was damaged, all right. Just not in quite the way she'd thought.

CALEB DIDN'T GET UP that night when he heard Lydia cry. He lay rigid in bed and let Laurel take care of her.

That's what she wanted, right?

What he wanted was for his anger to be straightforward, pure. Undiluted with pity or a sense that he'd been the one to screw up, that he was responsible for the misery he'd seen on her face.

But she *had* warned him enough times. God! She'd tried to drive him away. She'd only let him take Matt Baker's place as stud when he damn near begged. And then, because she agreed, he'd been like some kid in love for the first time, imagining some glorious, unrealistic future.

Laurel encouraged me.

Yeah, maybe she had. But he'd also known that what he and she were doing wasn't a normal prelude to passionate sex. She'd been as nervous as a girl who'd never kissed a boy. From the beginning, Caleb had felt her innocence, as if in walking through fire she had become new again. Fumbling, shy, surprised at every sensation. She'd been nervous, but determined to experiment.

He'd played along, keeping every kiss gentle, hiding the raw desire that would have scared her. He had counted on her innocence becoming knowledge in the way a young woman's does, without reminding himself of the dark knowledge she possessed and would never be able to forget.

He continued to lie there berating himself long after the silence from her room told him she and Lydia had gone back to sleep. Ruthless, Caleb made himself picture her leaving the law library, carrying her bag with books and laptop. It had been spring, the night only a little cool. The lilacs might have been in bloom, the air scented with them as she followed the familiar path to the parking garage. It would have been mostly empty, but other students stayed late at the library, too, or had left their cars and gone home with someone. She might not have thought twice about it when she heard footsteps. As they neared, she'd have turned, her car keys in hand.

Okay, she turned, expecting to see a familiar face. And then…what? He rushed her. Slammed her against the car. Stifled her screams with his hand, or his mouth. Wrestled her to the concrete, ripped her clothes from her. And as she struggled, hit her, over and over. Shattering her jaw and cheekbone. Mounting her, raping her, as her struggles became feeble. Perhaps she'd been unconscious by the time he was done. Caleb prayed she was.

Dragging her behind the car, where she wouldn't be seen. Not noticing that her feet stuck out.

What if they hadn't? Dumb question. Caleb knew what. Laurel would have been dead by the time someone came to claim the car a day or two days or three days later.

An anguished groan tore its way from his chest. Caleb

realized that on both sides of his body he'd gripped sheet and mattress pad in fingers that had balled into fists.

Had he really thought it would be so easy for her? He could forget. But how could she? She'd never hear footsteps behind her again without terror spinning her to face who knew what. She would never forget her helplessness, the way she had been degraded, hurt, left to die.

All she had wanted, he thought dully, was to be friends. And, in bearing a child, to have the only kind of family that she thought possible for herself.

But him? He'd had to horn in. Start thinking *We have a baby together, why not the whole enchilada?* He'd planned a campaign, for God's sake, with the goal of seducing her. Laurel. A woman who had been used as brutally as it was possible to use her and for her to have survived.

Him, he'd gotten his feelings hurt because she was starting to panic. Yep, Mr. Sensitivity. Sure he could have it all, to hell with her lingering hang-ups.

Bleakly, he thought, *Got what I deserved.*

But *she* hadn't. He bet she, too, had gone to bed and lain rigid, unable to sleep. Maybe cried again.

All he could do was try to patch it up tomorrow, maybe give them a chance to take back the trust and friendship he'd damn near ruined.

If even that was possible.

CHAPTER THIRTEEN

LAUREL COULDN'T BELIEVE how easily Caleb smoothed things over between them.

"We should talk," he said, and they did, with him relaxed, charming and a bit goofy, the Caleb she'd always known. His fault, he'd just gotten caught up in the whole fantasy.

"And, yeah," he admitted, "maybe I'm more old-fashioned than I knew. Obviously I am, since I was trying to turn you into a hausfrau."

He didn't want her to go yet. "Stay for Christmas, at least," he urged.

She agreed, telling herself she was relieved although she roiled with conflicting emotions.

There *was* relief, that she no longer had to test herself. And, of course, that she wasn't losing Caleb as her best friend.

But she was also outraged and hurt that he could revert so effortlessly to the status quo. It was as if he were saying it would have been great if they'd worked it out, but, hey, he was okay with just being buddies, too. If he'd been desperate for her body, he couldn't have dropped the seduction without any apparent regret, could he? If he were truly in love with her, not just friends-forever love, how could he be so casual again? How could he give her quick hugs in passing, tease, not once even *hinting* that she had hurt him?

He didn't get up at night anymore, a fact for which she was determined to be grateful. No more shirtless man lounging in her doorway, capturing her hands and pulling her out into the hall, placing those hands on his chest so his could wander...

A couple of times, having put Lydia back in her bassinet after their 2:00 a.m. feeding, Laurel had stepped into the hall. She didn't know why. Just to see if he'd come out of his room. He never did. Maybe he was relieved to be able to turn over and go back to sleep.

They did buy the tree, an eight-footer that wouldn't have fit in her tiny house, and decorated it together. He had lights, and red and gold glass balls, plus miscellaneous ornaments from his childhood that his parents had passed on to him when he bought his own house. A plastic elf waved a banner that read My First Christmas. Laurel carefully hung a clay candy cane with spotty glitter that Caleb said he'd made in first grade.

"Or so Mom says. God knows, I don't remember." He inspected it. "I think it used to have more glitter. You can leave it in the box if you want."

"Don't be silly," she said. "Of course it should be on the tree."

He grinned. "Gee. Why am I not surprised?"

With it dangling from her hand, she turned. "What's that supposed to mean?"

"You're sentimental."

She bristled. "Is there something wrong with that?"

"Not a thing."

"Then why'd you say, 'Gee, I'm not surprised'? Like you were laughing at me?"

"Because you were Ms. Feminist when I first knew you. You had a great facade. It was a long time before I discovered how girly you could be."

"I'm not girly!"

"Are too."

"Am not." Before he could utter a rejoinder, she said, "When am I girly?"

"Your bathroom? Your bedroom?"

She sniffed. "They're rooms with no architectural distinction. Pretty was the only way to go. I didn't have floor-to-ceiling fir-framed windows looking out on woods to work with. Or wood floors, or…"

"You just don't want to admit you *like* girly stuff," he taunted.

She would have thrown the ornament at him, if it had been replaceable. Instead, with stiff dignity she hung it on the tree.

"Women can be powerful *and* like pretty things. We don't have to be manlike to prove our worth, you know."

"Never said you did." He gave her a sunny smile. "Just making an observation."

"That I'm sentimental."

"Yep."

"You're just as sentimental, or you would have chucked all these." She gestured at the box that held the ornaments his mother had given him.

"Never said I wasn't." He sounded completely agreeable.

Way back, when they had this kind of stupid, going-in-circles argument, she'd have punched his shoulder, he would have wrestled her to the ground and there would have come a moment when they both went still and looked at each other. After which they'd scramble apart and pretend they hadn't felt that jolt of sexual attraction.

The memory made her sad. Why *hadn't* they acted on it? Because they thought they had forever? A person should never assume that. Never.

Lydia was entranced by the Christmas tree. Whenever one of them plugged in the lights, she would stare and stare, the shimmer of colors reflected in her wide eyes.

On the twenty-second of December—date for the baby book—Lydia smiled for the first time.

It was the 2:00 a.m. feeding. The house was quiet. Laurel had turned on the bedside lamp, which provided just enough light for them to see each other. Lydia suckled eagerly at first, then contentedly. When she let the first nipple go, Laurel shifted her.

"Daddy is right," she murmured. "I will miss getting up with you, pumpkin."

Her daughter gave her a wide, delighted smile.

"You smiled!" Her own face stretched into an equally delighted one.

Lydia wriggled like a puppy, grinned again, then happily latched on for her second course. Laurel cradled her, bubbles of elation fizzing through her. She'd smiled. And earlier than the baby books said she would. She was developmentally advanced, brilliant, well-adjusted and she loved her mommy.

Wait until Caleb sees, Laurel thought. He was going to be as excited as she was. If only he'd been awake so she could have called him in.

It was a letdown to put Lydia back in her bassinet and

not be able to tell him. Which was silly. Lydia would smile again tomorrow. It was just that Laurel wanted to tell him *now*.

She tiptoed out in the hall. The dim light from the bathroom lay across the floor. His bedroom door stood ajar, as he left it most nights, but his room was dark. Laurel went to the bathroom, then paused again in the hall on her way out. He hadn't stirred. Disappointed, she went to bed.

In the morning, Lydia cried until she had on a dry diaper and fuzzy sleeper, after which she nursed as if she'd been deprived for twenty-four hours, at least. Laurel had just hooked her bra and was burping her when Caleb glanced in.

"Want me to take her while you shower?"

Forgetting that her hair was wild and her nightgown open halfway down to her navel, Laurel said, "She smiled last night. Twice. I almost woke you up."

"Our Lydia smiled?" Already showered and dressed in jeans and a sweatshirt, Caleb came into her room. "You should have woken me."

"It was the most beautiful smile in the world. Wasn't it, pumpkin?" She patted, and their baby gave another inelegant belch. "Are you going to show Daddy?" She lifted her so she could see her face.

Caleb bent over and they both grinned at her. She looked from face to face with suspicious blue eyes. They must look like idiots.

"Maybe it was gas," he said out of the corner of his mouth.

He was so close, she could smell his aftershave.

"It wasn't!" she exclaimed indignantly. "It was a real smile. I know the difference."

"Was Mommy just dreaming?" he asked, tickling his little girl's tummy.

She chose to exhibit her new prowess with an arm-flapping grin aimed at her daddy.

He swooped her away from Laurel and lifted her in the air, laughing exuberantly. "She did! She's beautiful. Aren't you, sweetie?"

They stood close together, Lydia smiling at both parents with such unaffected happiness, all they could do was coo and laugh and make faces until she did it again.

Eventually, Laurel let him take Lydia so she could shower and get dressed. Once she was downstairs, they had to call their parents to tell them of their granddaughter's achievement.

Christmas came and went, with a ridiculous amount of gifts under the trees for Lydia, who grabbed the wrapping paper happily but exhibited no interest in the toys and stuffed animals and cute outfits her parents opened for her.

Caleb gave Laurel a spectacular woven wall hanging from Peru, an entire village of people and animals and crops embroidered from top to bottom, while she bought him an espresso machine after listening to him grumble about coffee.

Her gift from her father was a check for enough money to pay her bills for six months.

"But…Daddy, it's too much," she said after tearing open the envelope and gaping at the number of zeroes in his dark scrawl. "You don't have to do this."

"I want to." He stood, came to her to kiss her cheek and give her a clumsy hug, then resumed his seat. "I don't want you to go back to work until you're ready. Enjoy Lydia's first year."

She launched herself at him for another hug. "Thank you. I love you."

"I love you, too."

She'd have sworn he was crying, too, although through her mist of tears she couldn't be positive.

Megan was watching with amusement. "If you want the good stuff from Dad, you've got to have a baby, huh?"

"Yeah, but that means changing diapers, too." Laurel swiped at her cheeks.

"I can do that. Once in a while." She grinned at Lydia. "When Auntie Meg is babysitting and spoiling her niece."

Lydia, lying on her stomach on the carpet, lifted her head. It hardly wavered, and the adults all exclaimed. She'd be rolling over before they knew it. Crawling. Walking. Into everything, Laurel's dad said, ominously.

Caleb's parents were equally thrilled on Christmas morning by their granddaughter's new accomplishments. They'd spent an outrageous amount on clothes and toys, many of which wouldn't fit her or she couldn't play with for ages. They'd also bought Laurel a set of high-end cookware that must have cost four hundred dollars or more.

"I'm not going to have to buy Lydia anything until she's in kindergarten," Laurel said, hugging them goodbye midafternoon. "And I can hardly wait to throw out my awful collection of pans. Thank you for everything, for her *and* me."

During the drive home, she and Caleb talked at first, about presents and his surprise at how much his dad was looking forward to retirement and how spoiled Lydia was going to be as an only grandchild on both sides of the family.

But gradually, it became quiet in the car. At first, Laurel thought they were both tired, or had run out of things to say. And they often sat together without talking in the evening, both reading. But this, she realized, felt different.

Christmas had given them something to focus on. Lydia's first Christmas. It had to be special. For it, they could be a family. But they hadn't talked about what would happen *after* Christmas. And now, that after had come.

Lydia would be six weeks old on December 30. Laurel knew the law firm expected her back at work soon. If she wasn't going to go, she ought to give them the option of replacing her. And that idea induced a flutter of panic. Of course she could get another job, but... The familiar, the known, was so important to her. She had seen herself as going back to work at the same place. Enough else had changed that she hated to think of launching into the unknown by job hunting.

No matter what, she had been living at Caleb's house for two and a half months now. She'd only been back to her house a couple of times to pick up clothes and make sure everything was okay. The last time, she'd stepped inside and smelled mustiness, as if the house had been empty for too long. It had felt chilly, cramped and dark. Not like home. She'd been glad to pack some clothes and lock the door again.

But it *was* home, and she and Lydia belonged there, not on Vashon with Caleb. Already it was going to be hard to leave. Hard for all of them.

He turned the car into his driveway and a moment later they emerged from the trees to see the swooping beds of rhododendrons and his shingled house with tall glinting windows. And just like that, Laurel knew.

It was time for her to go. And Caleb knew that, too.

They did have things left to say, she realized sadly. It was just that neither Caleb nor she actually wanted to say them.

He pulled into the garage and turned off the engine. "Well," he said into the silence, "we have quite a haul to carry in."

Hurting, Laurel said, "Let's leave it until tomorrow."

Why carry it in and then have to carry it all out again?

His eyes met hers and he nodded. Once again she thought, *He knows.*

So maybe they actually didn't have anything left to say after all.

WATCHING CALEB DRIVE AWAY ranked right up there with the most agonizing moments of her life, and that was saying quite a bit. Which was absurd. This was *not* life or death. She would see him again, and often.

Slowly going into the house with Lydia, Laurel had a sense of unreality.

This was exactly what she'd planned. So why did she feel as if she was letting go of a dream she'd nourished her entire life?

The phone was ringing when she got inside.

"Welcome home," Megan said. "You want company tonight?"

Laurel's eyes flooded with tears. "I would love company."

"Are you crying?"

She sniffled. "Maybe."

"You *are* in love. I knew you were." Meg wasn't crowing. Instead she sounded sad. "How come? Never mind. I'll bring takeout. And ice cream. Lots of ice cream."

Laurel's sister showed up an hour and a half later with cartons of Chinese food and a quart of decadent vanilla ice cream swirled with fudge and caramel. Her hair was in a ponytail and her face bare of makeup. She wore jeans and a couple of layered T-shirts and flip-flops despite the rainy day. She looked like Laurel's kid sister instead of the smart-assed adult she'd become.

They ate until they were bursting and talked like they hadn't in years.

Megan, it turned out, had been in love with the style-challenged computer nerd. Stunningly, *he* had been the one to fall for someone else.

"I hate the fact that I have to see him regularly at work." Megan suddenly groaned. "I think I'm going to puke."

"Good practice for when you get pregnant," Laurel said heartlessly.

"Do you intend to have another baby?"

Not unless it's Caleb's.

The knowledge was quick and certain.

But that wasn't what Megan had asked. "Lydia is worth every minute." She was just as sure of that. "If it seems right…maybe."

Megan nodded. "Tea. That might settle my stomach. Do you still have some?"

"I'm sure I do." Did tea become stale? This had been on the shelf since pre-pregnancy. "I'll even make it for you," she offered.

Lydia had been asleep for a couple of hours. Laurel had been working toward getting her on a schedule and should have woken her a while ago, but it was so nice to have the time with Meg she hadn't.

Now she heated water and poured them both cups of

tea, herbal for her and caffeinated green tea for her sister. She was still avoiding caffeine since she was nursing.

When she carried it to the living room and set the two mugs on the coffee table, Megan asked. "What about you? Are you okay?"

Laurel opened her mouth to lie, and suddenly couldn't. Sinking onto the sofa, she shook her head. From someplace raw inside her, she asked the unanswerable. "Why did it ever have to happen?"

"The rape?"

Laurel gave a jerky nod.

"I don't know. Because bad things happen." She searched Laurel's face. "Is it keeping you and Caleb from…?"

Laurel nodded again. Her face contorted and she bent her head to bury it in her hands. Hot tears smeared on her fingers.

"Oh, sweetie." Megan scooted over and grabbed her in a fierce hug. "It's not fair. None of it's fair."

Laurel cried against her sister's shoulder. She had to go to the bathroom for tissues when she was done. The face she saw in the mirror was becoming familiar: blotchy and swollen.

Blowing her nose, she returned to the living room. "I really think Caleb and I could have been happy if I weren't so screwed up. But how do you have a relationship if sex can't be part of the deal?"

"Are you sure it can't? Because…" Megan bit off whatever she'd begun to say.

"What?"

She hedged for a moment, then said, "Because it can be wonderful. With the right person."

"I never…"

Megan's eyes widened. "You weren't a virgin!"

She sounded so horrified, Laurel laughed. "No. I was going to say, none of my experiences were that stupendous. I guess they weren't with the right person."

Caleb. They weren't with Caleb.

"Have you *tried?*" Megan paused delicately.

"Um…not exactly." Laurel told her about Caleb's kisses and the evening when she'd realized how selfish she was being. "The thing is," she concluded, "he seemed okay with it. Like, Oh, well, we tried. Big shrug."

"He does have his pride." Megan took a swallow of tea. "Maybe not just that. Maybe he loves you enough that he wants to stay friends no matter what. And he thought if he made a big deal out of being rejected, that wouldn't happen."

Laurel hadn't thought of that. Was it possible she'd hurt him? That all his casual, it-was-no-big-deal attitude was *fake?*

Yeah, she realized, it was possible. That would be like Caleb. He wouldn't have wanted to hurt her by letting her think she'd done anything wrong.

Then, maybe it wasn't too late. *If* she was next thing to positive that she could go through with it, so she wasn't just sucking him into another great experiment for her benefit, never mind the fallout.

"I'm going to have some more ice cream," she decided, getting up again.

"You have no idea how tempted I am to say, me, too," her sister confessed. "The tea helped."

"No. Absolutely not."

Megan grumbled. She'd bought the ice cream. Couldn't she decide if she wanted some or not?

When Laurel went back to the living room, she set

down her bowl on the coffee table, then bent over and kissed the top of Megan's head.

"I'm really glad you came tonight. I needed this."

Her sister smiled at her. "Yeah, me, too. We look like hell, don't we? But we should do it more often."

"Way more often," Laurel agreed, feeling teary again.

Right now, she wasn't letting herself think about the fact that Megan wouldn't be here tomorrow night, or the next night or the one after that.

Any more than Caleb would be.

CALEB PROWLED HIS EMPTY HOUSE, unable to settle at his computer or with a book, uninterested in the television offerings. All he wanted to do was call Laurel. See Laurel. Hold Lydia.

He'd mucked everything up. Gone too fast. Pushed too hard. If he'd just been more patient…

It might not have made any difference.

He swore out loud, his voice startlingly loud in the quiet house.

Damn it, she'd responded to him. Yeah, going from kisses to hot sex was a leap, and one that probably looked scary to her given her history.

Was that why she'd backed off so fast? She'd panicked? Or had something else happened?

He wondered if she was glad to be home. She'd pretended to be yesterday, when he dropped her off.

"Look at the garden," she'd tsked. "I didn't cut anything back. I didn't mulch…. I've got a ton to do."

"Spring is a few months away."

"I want to get the beds cleaned up before the bulbs start coming up."

She'd gone inside and talked about airing the house out, washing bedding before she used it. Housewifely, already making lists of everything to be done. He felt extraneous even before he left.

He'd driven home, paced for two hours and thought about calling.

Too soon. Too needy.

But tonight, phoning seemed reasonable. Lydia was his baby, after all. It was natural for him to wonder how she'd handled the move. Although Lydia had her own bedroom and a crib waiting, Laurel had taken the bassinet so that their daughter could continue to sleep next to her bed for a while. Even so, the shadows and smells and sounds would be different. Would she wonder why her daddy wasn't there?

If so, he realized with a sinking feeling, she'd forget him soon enough. He'd be relegated to that category of people who appeared occasionally instead of being an everyday part of her life. He hated that.

Caleb grabbed a beer from the refrigerator, popped the top and took a long swallow. He wasn't much of a drinking man, but for this call, he needed to be fortified.

"Caleb," Laurel said, after she'd picked up the phone and he had identified himself. "We're fine. Were you worried about us?"

You could say that.

"Just wondered how Lydia handled the change."

"As if we'd been on the road since she was born." Amusement suffused her voice. "You know the drill. Eat, poop, sleep. As long as she gets clean diapers and Mommy's breast, she's okay."

There was the confirmation: Dad was not needed.

And he was just feeling sorry for himself. "Great," he said, as heartily as he could manage. "Glad to hear that."

Silence. Neither of them knew what to say.

"Megan came over last night," Laurel offered.

"Yeah? How's she?"

As if he didn't know. Hadn't seen Laurel's sister at least weekly since Lydia's birth.

"Fine. We stuffed ourselves on ice cream and talked. Girl bonding."

Versus hanging with the guy who'd provided the sperm and was otherwise irrelevant.

Getting pathetic here.

"Have to be in Seattle Wednesday," he said. "I was hoping to stop and see Lydia if you plan to be home."

"Oh, sure. We can be. When are you coming?"

They set a time, said goodbye with what sounded like relief on her part.

His house was just as empty. Wednesday was still three days away. Caleb opened another beer and thought, *How am I going to live like this?*

WEDNESDAY'S VISIT WAS awkward. Lydia got woken early that morning and was now ready for a nap, but Laurel had kept her up for Caleb's sake. She kept apologizing for Lydia's crankiness, which made Caleb grit his teeth. It was if she was rubbing in his visitor status.

He claimed appointments, thrust his by-then-screaming daughter at Laurel and left.

In the car, he said aloud, "This sucks," and shoved the key in the ignition with a shaking hand.

That night at home he thought seriously about cutting his losses. Distancing himself. What kind of real father could he be with occasional visits? Maybe it would work better later on, when he could take Lydia for the weekend now and again, when she'd remember him during absences.

But for now, holding Lydia for a half hour and then having to give her back… Seeing Laurel happy in her home with the baby she'd wanted… Why not just dig out his heart and hand it to her the next time he said goodbye and see ya, grinning as if he was okay with this whole, screwed-up arrangement?

An arrangement, he couldn't let himself forget, to which he hadn't just agreed, he'd actually volunteered. No, he'd done more than that. He had *demanded* that Laurel let him father her baby. With full knowledge that these visits were all he was ever going to get out of it.

He just hadn't known how much he would love his daughter from the moment she was laid in his arms.

And he hadn't understood that what he felt for Laurel wasn't friendship that might have blossomed into love if they'd ever had a chance. Nope. It had already been too late. He was in love with her. The can't-imagine-ever-loving-another-woman kind.

So now he had two choices.

Back off. Way, way off. Continue providing child support. Maybe try later to build a relationship with Lydia separate from her mom.

Or, option two, keep torturing himself. Be Laurel's best buddy. Hold Lydia fleetingly once or twice a week. See them both just often enough to keep his wounds raw. Keep pretending, somehow, that he was fine.

He didn't want to abandon Laurel. He'd refused to even when she did her damnedest to get rid of him. He thought she still needed him now even if she was determined to embrace single parenthood.

But Caleb didn't know if he could keep doing this.

He got drunk that night for the first time in years. Woke feeling like crap.

Staring at his haggard face in the mirror, he realized he couldn't walk away. Lydia needed to grow up knowing he cared. And Laurel...damn it, he'd promised friends forever, and he'd deliver, even if it hurt.

So he stopped by Saturday for another short, uncomfortable visit. Thursday the next week for a longer one, staying for dinner. Saturday again. Wednesday again.

Laurel was vague about when she might start back at work. Soon. But the partners at the firm were being nice about her taking extra time.

With his twice-weekly visits, Caleb had a routine going. Laurel relaxed, seemed to welcome him as her old buddy Caleb again. He hugged her a few times, kissed her cheek when leaving. He kept thinking, *It's got to get easier.*

The visits did. Leaving didn't. In between, he counted the days. The hours.

He should start doing some traveling again, after taking a lengthy sabbatical, but the idea of not seeing Laurel and Lydia for a couple of weeks or longer kept him from making firm plans.

Two months old, Lydia was able to hold her head steady without a hand supporting it. She cooed; she squealed. She was starting to rock as if she meant to roll over. Every time Caleb saw her, she'd changed. It was a daily thing, and he didn't want to miss a single accomplishment. He didn't want to go from being a person she recognized as regular in her life to a stranger.

There were problems in Bolivia. Deliveries weren't arriving, items were missing from the ones that did. His contact in Tarija in the south wasn't returning calls or e-mails. The region was dangerous enough, the politics so touchy, he was reluctant to send anyone else in his place.

He had to go sooner or later. Sooner would be better. This was his life. Ten days, two weeks, he'd be home. He'd send Chad to Mexico and El Salvador, look for another eager PLU grad this spring to learn the ropes.

The next week, Caleb was in the back at the Seattle store, checking a shipment of Honduran pottery, when his cell phone rang.

"Caleb?" Laurel's voice was barely recognizable.

He swung away from the open box and his associates. Dread dug claws into his gut. "What's wrong? Is it Lydia…?"

"*No!* No. She's fine. I didn't mean to scare you. I'm sorry. You're probably busy. I shouldn't have called during the day…"

He interrupted. "Now's fine." Covering the mouthpiece, he said, "I'm stepping outside," to the store manager and assistant manager. They nodded, and he opened the heavy metal door.

"Caleb?"

"Yeah, I'm here." A fine mist wet the ground and the cars. He stepped close to the wall, under the eaves, gravel crunching under his feet.

"Detective Garner called. He's the officer who investigated after I was raped," Laurel said unnecessarily.

Caleb tensed.

"He thinks they've arrested him. My rapist. He attacked someone else. In the same parking garage." She was breathing as hard as if she'd been running. "They want me to identify him. Oh, God, Caleb." Her voice broke, regathered, thick with anguish. "What if I don't recognize him? What if I can't be sure? And then they let him go?"

"They won't let him go, not if he got caught in the act."

"But he'd get away with what he did to *me*."

"You're not going to let him. You're too strong to do that."

"I don't know if I am." She sounded frantic now. "I don't know if I can look at him. I can say no. You're right. He'll go to jail anyway. I don't have to do this."

"You have to do it. For your sake."

All he heard was her hard breathing.

"Are you home?"

"Yes."

"Stay there. I'm on my way."

Good thing he hadn't yet made reservations. He wasn't going anywhere.

CHAPTER FOURTEEN

THE GLASS WAS SUPPOSED to be one-way, but Laurel knew the moment she stepped into the room that it wasn't. Couldn't anyone else see how thin it was? As a line of orange-suited men filed in on the other side, Laurel felt the first flutters of panic.

They can see me. Oh, God, they can see me.

All six men ignored the people flanking Laurel and stared straight at her. Several smirked. *He* was there, fourth in the row. His mouth formed the word *bitch*. He'd called her that while he raped her, his voice guttural. *You bitch. That's all you are. A bitch.* Such hate.

She reeled back. Suddenly the glass exploded, disintegrating into glittering shards. There was nothing between her and him. Eyes on her, he stepped forward, the glass crunching under his feet. This time she heard him.

"Bitch."

The police officers did nothing. She swiveled. They were gone. They'd stepped out without her realizing. How? How? She backed away, her heart slamming…

And awakened sitting straight up in bed, one hand clasped over her mouth, her body heaving with dry sobs.

For a moment Laurel stared uncomprehendingly around her dark bedroom. Thin slats of light leaked through her window. Another band of light from the one she'd left on in the bathroom. The bassinet within arm's reach. Lydia made a tiny snuffling sound. The numbers on Laurel's clock glowed: 4:13 a.m.

Real memories settled back into her mind. Laying Lydia down to sleep just before midnight. This week she had started skipping her 2:00 a.m. feeding if she had one at eleven or eleven-thirty.

Before that… Caleb. He'd been here. Was still here?

Needing reassurance, Laurel pushed the covers aside and put her feet on the floor. She tiptoed around the bassinet and out of the bedroom, pulling the door partially shut behind her. Around the corner, the living room was darker. She peeked over the back of the couch and felt a huge swell of relief at the sight of him sprawled on his back, one foot on the floor, another propped on the far arm of the couch. For some reason that foot, long and bony, was the most visible part of him, caught in the faint light from the bathroom.

She wasn't alone. Thank God she wasn't alone. It had been a bad dream. A nightmare.

He shifted on the couch. Voice soft, he asked, "Are you all right?"

"I had a bad dream. I didn't mean to wake you. I just wanted to be sure…"

"That I was here?" He jackknifed to a sitting position, pulling the blankets with him. "Come here." He patted the cushion beside him.

Laurel circled the couch and sat, grateful when his arm came around her and tugged her against him. He wore a T-shirt, no bare chest, but she still felt his warmth and the solid, reassuring beat of his heart, so much slower than hers.

"Was it the rape?"

She shook her head against him. "I was identifying him. Only the glass wasn't one-way. He could see me. And then…" She shuddered. "Then it shattered, and he walked through the opening."

"You won't be alone."

"In the dream, I was. Everyone else had left."

He swore under his breath and his arms tightened.

"It was so real."

"You saw him in the dream. So you do know what he looks like."

She frowned, remembering. "I'm not sure in the dream he looked like he really does. I just *knew* it was him. But…I think I'll recognize his face. And his hands."

After a minute, Caleb asked, "Why his hands?"

"He's missing part of a finger." She closed her eyes to concentrate. His hand over her face. His left hand. It had to have been his left hand. "From the last knuckle. He must have had an accident."

"You told the police that?"

She nodded, then shook her head. "I don't know. I must have. But I can't remember."

"Call the detective in the morning. Tell him."

"Then maybe I won't have to go look at this lineup." Her relief was immediate and intense.

Mouth against her hair, Caleb asked, "Did you study his face while it was happening and think, I have to remember what he looks like so I can describe him?"

"Only for a minute, at the end. I think I must have been losing consciousness. I was floating down, seeing him through a tunnel. I was sure I was dying. But then I thought, just in case I don't, I need to remember him. I tried to take a snapshot. You know?"

He nodded. She'd always had a photographic memory for words on a page. When she was taking a test, she could close her eyes and see the paragraph she needed from the textbook. Faces were different, but this time, she'd made an effort.

"It was because of Mom." She surprised herself, telling him that.

"What?" He sounded startled, as well he might. Her mother had been dead over ten years on the night Laurel had been raped.

"I saw her. She said I wouldn't die, to hold on. So I looked at him. He was a blur, because one of my eyes must have already been swollen shut and the other one wasn't so good, either, but I tried."

"My gutsy woman," Caleb murmured, voice like a torn piece of velvet.

"It happened so fast, Caleb." In the cocoon of his arms and her memories, she didn't know why she'd never told him about the attack. "But when I remember, it's as if it lasted for hours. So much else has happened in my life, but it's *huge.* No matter what I'm thinking about, I can feel it, casting this shadow. It dominates me, and I hate that."

"Putting him away might help."

"I'd have to testify. I'd have to tell a whole courtroom full of people what happened."

He was quiet for a minute. Then he said, "Why would that be so bad? You didn't do anything wrong. He did horrible things to you. You survived despite him. Now you have the chance to look him in the eye and say, 'You picked the wrong woman. Guess what? You lose.'"

Voice a thin thread, she said, "I don't want him to see…" She couldn't finish.

"See what?" Caleb asked gently.

"What he's done to me," Laurel whispered. "Because then he'll know that really he won."

"Won?"

Caleb took one arm from around her and reached for the lamp. Laurel blinked in the sudden brightness. He gripped her shoulders and held her so that she couldn't look away from his fierce gaze.

"That scumbag didn't win. And don't you think for a minute that he did! You recovered from your injuries, you live a full life. You're a mother, a daughter, a friend. You recovered. You'll keep recovering. He's going to live his life in a windowless cell. And then, if there's any justice, he'll rot in hell."

Laurel gaped at the fury on his face. She hadn't known he carried so much anger. He'd hidden it from her.

"I used to think that's why I'd lived," she confessed. "So I could describe him and he'd be put in jail before he raped another woman. But when months went by, and then a year and another year..." Her mouth twisted. "I thought I'd failed."

Caleb's eyes flared, as blue as the heat at the center of flames. "But you were wrong. Because now you have your chance."

She pressed her lips together, nodded. "Will you come with me?"

"If they'll let me."

"I have an advocate, too. She's supposed to call and tell me what to expect, and then she'll go in with me."

"If they won't let me, I'll be waiting right outside."

"Okay." She smiled, even as her eyes filled with tears. "Thank you for coming today, Caleb. I've been so...flaky lately. So changeable. And you're always patient. I don't deserve you."

"Yeah, you do." He leaned forward and kissed her forehead, his mouth resting against her for a moment. His breath shuddered out. Finally, he sat back. "You deserve a hell of a lot more than you think you do, Laurel."

Looking into his eyes, his grip lending her strength, she almost believed him.

"Thank you," she said. "I love you, you know. Friends forever."

For a moment something had flashed in his eyes, as if she'd jolted him. Then he smiled. "I know, Woodall. Now go to bed." He jerked his head in the direction of her bedroom. "Lydia is going to be up in less than two hours."

She nodded and stood. "You, too. Thank you for…"

"Thank me one more time—" his voice had a sudden edge "—and I may lose my temper."

She backed away, bumped into the coffee table and had to readjust her path. "Okay. No more. Just… No. I'm going. I promise. Good night."

"Good night." He waited until she reached the hall, then turned off the lamp, plunging the living room into darkness.

Back in bed, Laurel listened to the silence from the living room.

I love you. She'd never said those words to him before. She'd barely jumped to recover. *Friends forever.* Uh-huh, but that's not what she'd meant.

The look in his eyes… Laurel shivered, remembering. If he felt that way, why were his kisses always so gentle? Why had he let her go so easily?

Was Megan right? Was Caleb waiting for her? If he was,

would she ever dare find out what he was like when he wasn't being gentle, when he quit worrying about scaring her?

My gutsy woman.

If only…

IT HAD TO BE TODAY that Caleb's luck at finding parking spots ran out.

He put on the turn signal and Laurel realized he was going to enter a parking garage that was ahead on the right.

"If we go around one more time, maybe we could still find street parking." Her voice was high and thin.

"What?" He looked at her, saw her face. "You don't like… Oh, damn." Shaking his head, he turned off the signal. "I'm sorry. God. I'm an idiot. I should have realized."

Her hands were clasped on her lap, her nails biting into her flesh. She was stretched like wire, quivering with the strain.

"It's silly," she said.

"No. Not silly." Turning the corner in what she knew would be another fruitless trip around half a dozen blocks, he said, "That's why you don't drive to work, isn't it?"

"Parking is expensive, too."

He didn't say anything. Laurel stared straight ahead.

"If there was a lot at street level, I would."

"How is it that in five years, we've never once gone into a parking garage?"

"Because, when you're driving, a spot always opens up right in front of wherever we're going. And also because…" She hesitated, then thought, *Oh, why not admit it.* "I plan ahead. We don't go anywhere that would mean having to park in a garage."

He shook his head again. "I can't believe I was that dense."

They circled, and circled again. Laurel looked at her watch, her tension increasing until she thought she'd snap. What if she was late? Did they hold police lineups if the witness was late?

The next time around, she said, "Go in the garage."

"What?"

"Caleb, we're going to be late. Anyway… You're with me. I can't live the rest of my life this way."

"I can drop you off while I park."

"No. I mean it." If she could face her rapist, she could walk through a parking garage.

Still staring straight ahead, she felt his quick assessment. Then he put on his signal again, and a moment later turned into the low, concrete-framed opening.

If it was possible to get any tenser, she did. Completely rigid, she sat silently as he took a ticket from the machine and then drove down a ramp to the first subterranean level of the garage. Her breathing grew shallow. It looked…not the same, but close enough. Dim, with a low ceiling. Dark corners, shadows between cars.

Only, in this garage today the slots were full, row upon row of cars. Two well-dressed women were just leaving one, tote bags over their arms. Brake lights flickered ahead as another car made the same turns Caleb was.

"Ah," he said with satisfaction, and she, too, saw a couple leaving an elevator and going straight to an SUV parked nearby. Caleb paused, the SUV backed out, and he took the slot.

Laurel got out, trying not to look at the concrete abutments or the painted yellow line underfoot.

But I have to remember.

Today, she was going to point at her rapist and say, *Him. It was him.* She had to remember everything.

Caleb laid a hand on her back. A moment later they were in the elevator, then emerging onto the street.

In the public safety building, the middle-aged detective who'd handled her case and the advocate from the rape center both waited in the lobby. Esther Smith was no more than Laurel's age, and had herself been attacked when she was a teenager. She and Detective Garner talked to Laurel, repeating things they'd already said, and she let the words wash over her. They ended up standing around waiting, with her feeling as if she were having an out-of-body experience. There she was, Laurel Woodall, apparently composed, nodding as people spoke to her, and yet already she didn't know what they were saying.

She did hear the summons, and the detective telling Caleb he had to wait outside. The squeeze of his hand, warm and strong, worked as nothing else had to bring her back into her body.

"Go get 'em," he murmured.

She gave a shallow, jerky nod and let Detective Garner escort her through a doorway.

The room he led her into was small, almost a hall, but the glass was reassuringly thick, nothing like that in her dream.

Even so, she gasped and tried to back up when the row of orange-suited men filed in on the other side of that glass and turned to face her. She hadn't expected them to be so close to her.

She saw *him* right away, the second in line, and stared fearfully. His hair was longer, and he was shorter than she remembered. His hands were curled at his side, so she couldn't see whether he was missing part of a finger, but she knew.

"Look carefully at their faces," Detective Garner said, voice low and calm. He'd talked to her in advance, too, but he must have sensed her panic. "Don't hurry to give a number. Study all of the men in the lineup."

She drew a deep breath and nodded. Even so, wrenching her gaze from that face took a painful effort. She was momentarily jolted when she looked at the man at the end, who held the number-six placard. He looked so much like *him*. Did they all? She scanned the faces. They'd picked a physical type. They did all resemble each other. Maybe number two wasn't him. How could she be sure?

Her heart raced and her breathing came even faster.

"Carefully," the detective murmured. "Feature by feature. Face by face. Take your time."

Another shaky breath and she nodded, turning her attention back to number six. There *was* a resemblance, but his lips were full, fleshy. No, it wasn't him.

Reassured to have eliminated one man in the lineup, she studied number five. He was beefy, thick, his face too broad.

Number four's nose was thin, his chin receding enough to give him a ferretlike appearance.

Number three was the closest. She skipped past him and eliminated number one next. Although he'd shaved, the shadow on his jaw was still dark, and hair peeked above his collar. No. *He* wasn't that hairy.

Back to three, then two. They did look a great deal alike, both staring defiantly at the glass, their mouths curled as if in contempt. But she knew.

Finally, to be sure, she said, "Will you ask them to hold out their hands?"

Detective Garner stepped forward to a speaker. "Spread out your fingers."

The police had done their jobs well. Number five, the beefy one, was missing an entire finger on his left hand. But *he* lacked only the last inch or less on the index finger.

"Number two," she said, surprised at how strong her voice was. "That's him."

"You're certain?"

"Yes."

"Then we're done."

The tension left her in such a rush, Laurel's legs went weak. She nodded and started to turn toward the door, then stopped and took one last look. She wanted to remember him like this, in an orange prison jumpsuit, in a police lineup. Powerless. Smaller than she remembered, more ordinary.

Despite the sneer, there was fear in his eyes. He was sweating heavily, and his hands had curled into fists again.

She thought with surprise, *He's afraid of me.* And then, *He* should *be afraid of me.* She was going to send him to jail for a long, long time. If some of the other women were able to identify him, too, or if the DNA from the one attack was a match, it might be for a lifetime.

Released by the knowledge, she turned and walked out. Caleb had been pacing. He froze midstep, spun and covered the distance between them in a couple of strides. He studied her face but said nothing, only placing a supportive arm around her.

She turned to Detective Garner. "It was him, wasn't it?"

The detective grinned at her. "Damn straight. You did fantastic, Laurel. I always knew you'd be a great witness.

We rarely get descriptions as detailed as yours, and especially from a victim in the shape you were in. I still remember the way you closed your eyes and just painted him with words. I'm only sorry it took this long to nail the bastard."

"The other woman…the one he just raped. How is she?"

"She's out of the hospital. She got lucky. Luckier than you were. A med student was napping in his car. He'd put his seat back and was so low, our guy didn't spot him. The victim doesn't think she screamed, but something woke him. He peered at his side mirror, saw this guy assaulting her and jumped out. The slimeball was too busy to see him coming. The student's a big guy. He was able to wrench him off the woman and sit on him while she found her phone."

"Are you able to pin other rapes on him?" Caleb asked.

"He was smart enough to use a condom, but it ripped in one case. We've sent off DNA, and if it matches we'll get him for that one, too."

"Thank you for everything you've done." Laurel held out a hand. "You always seemed to care. That meant a lot to me."

He shook her hand. "We'll be in touch, Laurel. We're putting him away."

She thanked the advocate, too, and then Caleb and her left the building. It was a rare, sparkling-clear winter day, and the chill outside made her skin tingle. Her senses felt heightened, every sensation enhanced. It was as if they'd been muffled before. Smells from a deli, a hearty guffaw from one of a pair of expensively dressed businessmen who passed her and Caleb on the sidewalk. A Metro bus stopping half a block up, brakes squealing. Her own muscles and skin, the pavement under her feet.

"How are you?" Caleb asked.

"I…" Laurel searched herself. "I'm okay. No, I'm good." She stopped in the middle of the sidewalk. "I did it. I feel amazing!"

He laughed, and she realized she was, too.

"I knew you would. What have I always told you?"

"I'm a gutsy broad." Her knees were still shaky, but ebullience bubbled in her. "Caleb, he was afraid of me. He was sweating fear."

Something dangerous flashed in Caleb's eyes. "And he should be."

"Testifying in court doesn't seem so scary now. I *want* to testify. I hope they don't plea bargain him."

"Let the D.A. know how you feel."

"I will." She drew in a deep, clean breath. "Let's get Lydia at your mom's and go home. No." She smiled at him. "I'm starved. Let's go out to lunch first."

"And celebrate." He nodded. "I like your plan, Woodall."

They walked into the parking garage, getting on the elevator with a group of women carrying full shopping bags. The women left the elevator on the next level, Caleb and Laurel continuing down. When the doors opened again, they went to his car.

Laurel waited while he unlocked. The air in here had that hushed, thick quality, even as the sound of a car a level or two away was magnified. This time, she looked at the many black marks on the concrete where drivers had misjudged, down at the painted yellow line so much like the one in which her face had been ground, and thought with a dawning sense of wonder, *I'm free.*

A part of her inside surfaced to protest. The frightened woman she'd been these past five years argued, *It's not going to be that easy.*

It had still happened, that cautious side of her pointed out. There were other monsters walking around.

Yes, but *this* one wasn't anymore. And knowing that made her feel different. As if… She struggled to understand what was breaking loose inside her. Then, almost in puzzlement, she identified a part of her she hadn't known still existed.

She felt strong. Certain of herself. Able to overcome fear. She'd spent the past five years debilitated by fear and an overpowering sense of helplessness. She felt as if she'd been drugged but had suddenly refused to take another dose. Suddenly she was aware of the confidence that had her able to look around and think, *I will never be afraid of a parking garage again.*

Maybe it *wouldn't* be this easy. Maybe she was just giddy. But she didn't believe it. Refused to believe it.

The Laurel she'd once been hadn't died that night after all. She'd just been hiding.

But I'm not hiding anymore.

"Laurel?"

Startled, she realized Caleb had gotten into the car and reached across to open her door while she stood oblivious. He looked worried.

"Sorry," she said, getting in. "I just had a little moment there. But I'm back."

His brows rose as he studied her face. "So I see."

She grinned at him, as brash as the old Laurel. "What are we waiting for? I'm ready to pop the champagne."

AFTER LUNCH AT WILD GINGER, Laurel and Caleb went to his parents' house to pick up Lydia. She hadn't gotten up from her nap, for which Laurel was grateful. Her breasts ached, and she would have had hours of discomfort if Lydia had just guzzled a bottle.

Caleb's father was at the office, but Laurel had to sit down and tell his mom what had happened.

She gave Laurel an affectionate hug. "How frightening. I'm so glad Caleb wasn't in Brazil or someplace, so he was here to take you."

"Dad offered, too." Laurel had used Caleb's cell phone to call her father at work and tell him what had happened. Tonight she'd call Nadia, too.

"I'm proud of you," he'd said.

It was the first time Laurel had felt a prickle of tears. She liked feeling as if she deserved his pride.

Now his mother cocked her head. "I think I hear Lydia."

Laurel went up to the bedroom and nursed in private, smoothing the soft curls on her daughter's head and savoring her weight and the tug at her breasts.

"I love you, pumpkin," she murmured, as she burped her afterward.

Lydia beamed at her.

"I bet Grandma took good care of you, didn't she?"

Lydia waved her arms.

Laurel hugged her hard and whispered, "I wish your other grandma had had the chance to spoil you, too."

Shaking off the moment of grief, she repacked the diaper bag and she and Caleb left after profusely thanking his mother.

"Home?" he asked.

"Are you going to go to work?"

"Nope. I'm yours to command."

"I'm low on diapers. If you wouldn't mind…"

He swore he didn't. They grocery shopped, and he carried her bags in while she managed Lydia in her totable car seat.

He put away groceries, then played with Lydia, bouncing her, swooping her above him into the air, making her grin when he made funny sounds.

Feet tucked under her as she sat at the other end of the sofa, Laurel watched. He was going to be the world's best father. Just as, she suspected, he'd be the world's best husband once he gave his heart. Caleb had been loyal to their friendship beyond what she'd deserved. For all his looks and charisma, he'd be as loyal to the woman he loved.

She wanted suddenly, terrifyingly, for that woman to be her.

Lydia began to wind down, and he changed her diaper and then handed her over to Laurel.

"Poop, eat, sleep."

She laughed to cover the emotions swirling inside her.

"I assume you don't need me to stay over tonight." He reached down and zipped his overnight bag, stowed next to the coffee table.

He was going home. She should let him go. Think about this. Not jump into something she wasn't ready for.

"You don't have to go," she heard herself say.

He looked up in surprise. "You nervous?"

"No." Laurel bit her lip. "I just…um, I like having you here."

"If I'm going to do many sleepovers, you'd better buy a new couch. This one is at least a foot too short. Why don't *you* sleep over at *my* house?"

Lydia was asleep at her breast. She eased her away, not realizing how she'd exposed her nipple until she saw Caleb's gaze lower to it, and then his head turn sharply.

She fastened her bra with a hand that shook. "Just a minute," she said, standing.

For the first time ever, she carried Lydia into the second bedroom and laid her on her back in the crib. She stirred, and Laurel held her breath hoping she wouldn't wake up and be alarmed. But she sighed and sank deeper into sleep. Laurel pulled a fleecy blanket up to her chin, then slipped out of the room.

Caleb was standing in the living room, his gaze meeting hers the minute she appeared.

His voice was slightly hoarse. "Trying out the crib?"

She nodded. "It seemed like time I have my bedroom back."

"You might both sleep better."

Sleep wasn't what she'd had in mind.

Say it. Laurel crossed her arms tightly in front of her. Talking fast, she said, "I thought that maybe if you stayed, you wouldn't have to sleep on the couch."

He went completely still, only his eyes fiercely alive. It was the longest time before he asked, "Are you propositioning me, Woodall?"

"I…I think I am."

Caleb said something, low and rough, that might have been "Thank God." Then he came to her, stopping a foot in front of her, still not touching her. Sounding shaken, he asked, "Are you sure?"

She tried to smile and failed. "No, but I want to try. If you'll try with me."

He let out a ragged sound that widened her eyes. "Oh, yeah. I'll try."

Finally, his arms closed around her and with a sob she rose on tiptoe to meet him.

CHAPTER FIFTEEN

IF YOU STAYED, YOU wouldn't have to sleep on the couch.

Caleb had come damn close to giving up, accepting that he'd never hear those words from Laurel. Now that he had…God help him, he was terrified.

He'd never in his life wanted anything as much, and never been so afraid he would foul something up. Sex for the first time with anyone was weird. Sometimes awkward, or even downright embarrassing. Sometimes good, too, of course, or nobody would make it to a second time.

But this…sex with his best friend after ten years of a platonic relationship. Sex with the woman he suspected he'd loved for those entire ten years.

Sex with a woman who'd been brutally raped and had never intended to let a man touch her intimately again.

What if he lost control? Wasn't gentle enough? What if she freaked?

He had one shot. One. And if it went bad, he wasn't the only loser. Or even the main loser. Laurel was. He could see in her eyes that she'd grabbed for every ounce of courage. If she panicked and couldn't go through with it, Caleb couldn't imagine that she'd ever be willing to take a chance again.

Talk about performance anxiety. Their futures depended on his skill as a lover.

When he took her in his arms, she uttered a little sob and lifted her mouth to his. For just an instant, he let himself crush her mouth with his. Her response was eager, helpless, as if she'd given herself into his hands, and that awareness penetrated his powerful arousal.

Caleb lifted his head and looked down at her. At this moment, the sight of her stopped his heart. Why this face, this woman and no other? He didn't know, just savored the sight of her flushed cheeks, her parted lips, her lids lifting to reveal eyes filled with tumultuous emotion.

"What?" she whispered.

"You're so beautiful."

Always before she'd argued. This time she lifted a hand to his cheek and murmured, "I've always thought you were the sexiest man I've ever seen."

Caleb gave a choked laugh. "Do you know what that would have meant to me when I was nineteen and skinny?"

"Well, maybe not *always*."

They shared another laugh, quiet and tender, before he kissed her again, softly this time. They tasted and suckled and nipped. The tip of his tongue touched hers, teased, stroked, as if they had all the time in the world. He'd give them that time, even if the need he'd bottled up for years had him aching to be inside her.

He backed her into the hall, with them bumping the corner, then the doorframe to her bedroom, shushing each other. When she giggled once, he swallowed the sound with a kiss.

Just inside her bedroom, Laurel went tense when she realized where they were. He stroked her arms and kissed her neck until she sighed and tipped her head back, her hips bumping his as she arched to give him access to her throat.

Caleb licked the hollow at the base, then nuzzled between her breasts.

Against she stiffened. "I'll leak."

Caleb laid both hands on her breasts and gently rubbed. "Do you have any idea how hard it's been to watch you breast-feed?"

"Oh!" Her startled gaze sought his. "No. Really?"

"I've been dreaming about your breasts. Your nipples." He squeezed, rubbed, cupped. "You're a mother. Leaking doesn't make you any less sexy."

This "Oh" was more of a gasp.

He paused to wrestle his shirt over his head. "Touch me." He took her hands and laid them on his chest.

Her exploration was curious and both delighted and innocent, as if she'd never felt a man's nipples harden or his muscles spasm beneath her hands.

She didn't protest when he eased her shirt off, too, only momentarily crossing her arms in front of herself. "My bra is so ugly."

He laughed, the sound husky. "We can take care of that."

Shyly, she let him unhook her bra. Her teeth sank into her lower lip and her gaze stayed downcast as he looked for a long, aching moment at her glorious, full breasts with large areolae and stiff, puckered nipples. He wanted to suckle but wouldn't, not this time anyway. Instead, he contented himself with touching and stroking and teasing until she let out small, throaty whimpers.

When he gripped her buttocks with sudden urgency and fitted her against him until her breasts flattened on his chest and his arousal pressed her belly, he said, "If we get all our clothes off and then Lydia starts to cry, I'm going to have to kill myself."

Laurel's laugh was as much a moan. "I think…" Her breath caught as he kneaded her buttocks. "I think we might have to ignore her."

Would she be scared if he laid her on the bed? He didn't want to ask, *Are you ready?* and get her thinking. Thinking was bad. Once she started examining her feelings, she'd find anxiety, then keep searching for it.

"Milady." He picked her up, plopped her on the bed in a sitting position, then knelt on the floor in front of her before she could react to his manhandling. He slipped off her shoes, stripped off the socks, then massaged her feet as he studied them.

She had long toes, just as she had long fingers, and an unusually high arch in her instep. She giggled as he hit a sensitive spot, murmured when he tugged on her toes.

"Your feet are too soft. You don't go barefoot often enough."

"I never go barefoot anymore. I don't know why. I get out of bed and put on flip-flops."

"You need to feel the grass under your toes." He lifted a foot high enough to kiss it, then to nip her littlest toe.

She squeaked. "You should talk. I noticed last night how white your feet are."

"Last time I went for grass under my toes, I stepped on a slug."

Laurel giggled again.

Good, Caleb thought. Laughter and panic weren't natural partners.

He stood and kicked off his own shoes, then pulled off his socks. "We'll compare feet."

He sat next to her on the bed and they held out their feet. His bony size twelves and her far daintier size… He didn't know. Six maybe? Seven? Her feet just *looked* feminine.

"You have sexy feet," he decided.

She turned laughing eyes on him. "*Can* feet be sexy?"

"Yours can." He bore her backward as if it was the most natural thing in the world and began to kiss her again. There it was again, that innocent pleasure. The surprise, as if she hadn't expected to feel this way.

He reached down and unbuttoned her slacks. She sucked in a breath, but didn't go rigid. Startled, a little nervous, but not scared, then. Encouraged, Caleb unzipped.

He kissed her again, then murmured against her mouth, "Your turn."

"Oh." If anything, her cheeks turned pinker. "Okay."

She rose on one elbow so she could see what she was doing.

As erect as he was, his pants were painfully tight. She struggled momentarily with the snap. He gritted his teeth as she inched the zipper down with excruciating slowness, her fingers trailing in its wake. *God.* He wasn't going to make it in her, not at this speed.

Hang on. He struggled to empty his mind, to concentrate on breathing. If women could forget pain in childbirth, he could regain patience.

"Your underwear…" She hiccuped. "They have, um…"

Oh, damn. He'd worn ones given him as a gag. He'd grown rather fond of them. They had pink hippos on a navy-blue background.

"Yeah, yeah," he growled. "Are you laughing at me?"

"Do you know how funny it looks to see an erect penis and…and pink hippopotamuses?" She fell onto her back, her hand clapped over her mouth, her eyes watering at her effort to avoid howling with laughter.

"Yeah, well, yours have…" He looked. "Violets. I told you! You're girly!"

A giggle exploded around her hand. "You're…you're… I don't know what you are!"

"One of a kind," he said with dignity.

"Oh!" Laurel held her sides as if they ached. Then she said guiltily, "Oh, dear. We should be quiet. We don't want to wake Lydia."

"God forbid," he agreed fervently.

He kissed her again, tasting her laughter as if it were wine lingering on her tongue. Then he slipped his hand inside those violet-sprigged panties, feeling muscles quiver in her belly as his fingers curled in her hair.

Suddenly impatient again, Caleb sat up and pulled her pants down with her cooperation. There she was, hips deliciously round, belly still a little soft from childbirth, dark curls rioting. With his fingers he parted her, found her hot and wet. As he stroked, she made the most erotic sounds: sighs and moans. Her hips lifted from the bed and he kept pleasuring her, watching her face. Even if it killed him to wait, he was going to give her a sample of what was to come, relax her body so that it accepted him more easily.

With his fingers he made insistent circles. He felt the first quivers as soon as she did, kissed her deeply as she came against his fingers.

As she lay lax and flushed, he stripped off his slacks and pulled out the condom he'd optimistically put in his wallet back when she and Lydia were living with him.

He parted her legs and started to fit himself between them, his weight on his elbows to each side of her.

And that was when her body went rigid and her eyes opened wide, her stare so blind he knew she was fighting to hold on to the image of him above her and not that monster. "I…I'm sorry," she gasped.

He got off her. "No. It's okay," he lied.

"It's not!" Her voice was high, unhappy. "I want…"

"You can touch me."

"No! Just do it."

Just do it. Climb on top of her and screw her while she lay there stiff and scared out of her mind. Sure. There was the path to happiness.

"Hey, sweetheart." He pulled her against him, felt the dampness of tears.

With her head on his shoulder, her hair tickling his skin, he had an inspiration.

"Hey. Your turn to make love to me."

"What?" She lifted her head.

He stayed flat on his back, spread his arms out. "You're in charge, lady. Have your way with me."

There was a hitch in her breathing. She sneaked a look down the length of his body. "Really?"

"Really." *And please, have mercy, do it fast.*

"Oh." She sat up, touched his chest. Tentative at first, her exploration grew bolder, his suffering more acute.

Then she climbed atop him, bent over to rub her breasts against his chest. "Does that feel good?"

"Oh, yeah," he said, in a strangled voice.

The sight of her above him, white belly, voluptuous breasts, eyes as green as he'd ever seen them, brought him close to exploding.

"Take me into you," he managed. *"Now."*

Fingers awkward with inexperience, she lifted him to

her opening, then settled back. It was all he could do not to grab her hips and thrust upward.

Let her stay in control.

His fingers dug into the mattress.

She sank slowly, slowly onto him, the tiny muscles inside her flexing. The feeling was exquisite, water to a dying man. A groan felt torn from his chest as she paused with his entire length inside her.

"Again," he croaked.

Her teeth caught her full, lower lip as she lifted, lifted, then sank. Did it again. Made excited sounds.

He held on to a ragged shred of patience. He had to make this good for her. For her sake.

For his.

Finally he couldn't bear it. His hips shoved upward to meet her. He grabbed her buttocks and ground her down against him. She let out a shuddering cry as he lifted her, pushed her down, rolled his hips.

This time when her muscles contracted and her back arched with surprise, he let himself go. He pushed as deep within her as he could reach and let his release blast through him like Fourth of July fireworks, glittery and huge, filling his world.

Laurel subsided onto his chest, seeming as spent as he felt.

After a long, long time, he lifted a hand to stroke it down her spine.

"You okay?" he finally asked.

"Okay?" She croaked as if she'd lost and had to rediscover her voice. "I'm...I'm better than okay. I'm fantastic. I feel incredible! Caleb, that was..."

"Amazing?" He grinned at her when she lifted her head to look at him. "Did it blow your socks off?"

"You've already taken them off," she pointed out, his ever-literal Laurel. "But if you hadn't, they'd have gone flying."

"So, we should've done that ten years ago."

"Maybe." She thought about it. "But maybe it was better this way. Heightened anticipation, and all that."

"Oh, it was heightened."

Her laugh lit up her face and made it even more beautiful. "It was heightened."

"It could be again."

"Really?" She sounded equal parts skeptical and hopeful. The hopeful part, he liked.

"You're a genius, you know."

"I am?"

"Letting me, um…"

"Climb on top?"

She nodded, for a moment looking shy again. "I don't think I'll ever be scared again."

"Yeah, you will. But it's okay. We'll work through it."

Right now, Caleb felt so optimistic he had complete faith he could lift a semi if he had to. Leap Lake Union. Climb the Space Needle without a rope.

Only one thing held him down. Besides having her contentedly sprawled on him.

He was scared to death that he'd freed her sexually, but that she hadn't translated any of this into undying love.

He was afraid if he said, "Will you marry me?", her eyes would shy from his and she'd say, "This was wonderful, but…"

Five years ago, she'd written off the possibility of sex,

love, marriage. What he didn't know was whether she'd written off the possibility of the others only because she couldn't imagine ever having sex.

Worse yet would be if she said yes just because she trusted him, felt safe with him, not because she couldn't live without him.

Only one way to find out.

Before he could open his mouth, she said, "It's too bad we didn't make Lydia this way."

Sidle through the door. "Now that we've figured out the new, improved technique, we could make her a brother or sister this way."

Laurel wriggled. "We could."

"It's probably a little soon."

"Actually…" She lifted her head to take a peek at him. "There's something I was thinking about today."

He was careful to hide his wariness. Somehow, he suspected she wasn't thinking about having another baby yet. "Something?"

"I want to go back to law school." In her eagerness, she sat up, then looked down at herself and grabbed a pillow to hold in front of her. "I think I'm ready."

Damn, she didn't do anything by half.

"You're sure?"

"Pretty sure." Her eyes searched his and her voice became uncertain. "You don't think I am?"

He rolled onto his side and propped his head on his hand. "I've thought you were ready for a long time."

"Really?" She sucked in a breath. "The thing is, now that I have Lydia, the only way I can do it is if you and Dad are still willing to help me financially."

Abruptly angry, Caleb sat up. "Here's a thought. Since we're having sex anyway. Why don't you marry me?"

Whoa. Great way to propose, dude.

"Marry you?" she echoed.

At her shock, he grabbed for his pants and underwear draped over the footboard. Naked wasn't so good when you felt vulnerable in other ways.

"Is the idea that outlandish? We do have a kid together."

"It's not outlandish." She sounded mad now. His fault. "You just don't sound like you *want* to marry me."

Zipper up, he froze. She'd jumped off the bed, too, and was scrambling for clothes. As he watched, she hopped on one foot so she could pull up her panties.

"I want to marry you."

"You don't sound like it!" she yelled, then clapped her hand to her mouth.

Neither moved; both waited for Lydia's cry.

Silence. Ten seconds, twenty, thirty.

Caleb breathed again.

A sound escaped Laurel that might have been a sob. She went back to getting dressed.

"I want," he said again, quietly.

She had on panties, bra and a T-shirt she'd yanked from a drawer. When she looked at him, her eyes were awash with tears. "I don't believe you."

He hadn't even gotten his slacks buttoned, and now he had to strip himself bare in a different way. "I think I've been in love with you for ten years."

She sniffed and took an angry swipe at her eyes. "You *think?*"

"The early years, I'm a little muddled about."

"You've never said!"

He still didn't make a move toward her. "How could I, when you'd publicly vowed never to let a man touch you?"

"You aren't a man." Another swipe. "I mean, you are, but you're *Caleb*."

He stiffened. "What's that supposed to mean?"

"You're my friend!"

"And now your lover."

"I never felt about you the way I did other men. I mean, not exactly. That's why…"

"You let me kiss you." He squeezed the back of his neck. "But then you panicked anyway."

"I didn't! You misunderstood, and I didn't know how to tell you. And you just shrugged and said, 'Oh, well, that's fine.'"

All that suffering, and he'd *misunderstood?*

"I don't get it. What was it you said? That you didn't know how you'd let me talk you into coming home with me? Oh, and let's not forget you apologizing because you'd let me get my hopes up that you might actually go to bed with me someday."

Her shoulders hunched. "I didn't exactly mean it that way."

Unclenching his jaw, he asked, "How *did* you mean it?"

"I just…" She bit her lip, then straightened with a visible effort. "I realized how selfish I was being. All I've ever done is take from you. I was happy there, but I knew Lydia and I had to go home eventually. I never thought about how that was going to hurt you."

"Then why wouldn't you stay?" Caleb's voice was hoarse.

"How could I stay if I *couldn't* make love with you?" She sounded despairing.

"But now you have."

"I know, but then I was so mixed up. And you didn't seem to care when you thought I wanted you to quit kissing me."

"I was afraid to lose what we had. It just about killed me to pretend it was okay. But I love you, Laurel. If being your friend was the only way you'd let me…" His voice broke. God. He was begging. *Love me. Please, love me.*

Tears still sparkling on her lashes, she searched his face. "You…you really want me? As messed up as I am?"

"I love you," he repeated. "Always have. Looks like I always will."

Her face crumpled and she flung herself at him. His arms closed around her with bruising force. Her wet face against his chest, she seemed to be trying to burrow inside his skin. They rocked, his face against her hair.

Finally she gave what seemed to be a last, hiccuping sob and pulled back, just a little. Caleb loosened his arms.

"Yes." Her face was a mess, and damned if he didn't still think she was beautiful. "If you mean it…yes. I'll marry you."

"*Mean* it? God." His eyes closed for a moment as relief flooded him. She'd be his. She and Lydia.

But beneath the relief, a niggling voice whispered, *She said yes because you're Caleb. You're her friend. The two of you managed to have sex, and she's on a high. Is that enough?*

He forced the words out. "You're not going to want to be free someday?"

"Free?" Laurel took a step back to see him better. "What are you talking about?"

"I know I feel safe to you…"

Her mouthed formed an *O*. Then she actually laughed,

although it had an hysterical note. "Caleb, I'm desperately, head over heels in love with you. I'm pretty sure *I've* been for ten years, too. I will never want to be free if that means being without you."

He actually staggered and had to grab the footboard of her bed. "You love me."

"I said so once before."

"You said friends forever."

"I didn't know—" she gestured at the bed "—whether I could do this."

He pulled her into his arms again and kissed her, deep and hard, holding nothing back. Laurel flung her arms around his neck, rose on tiptoe and gave herself as he'd never believed she could.

"I'm still a mess," she whispered when they came up for air.

"Don't care," he managed to say. It was lucky he hadn't bothered to button his pants; she was pulling the zipper down again even as he pulled her shirt over her head.

They both kept saying the words "I love you."

This time, she lay on her back, held out her arms and took him inside her without hesitation. He flipped once and she rode him astride. Then they rolled again when he had to plunge hard and fast.

She gave a keening cry. He groaned. When they pressed their cheeks together, he didn't know if they were wet from her tears, or his.

"Thank you," she said, in a voice he didn't recognize. "Thank you for never giving up on me."

He inhaled her scent. "I did say forever."

"People don't always mean it."

"I did."

THREE AND A HALF YEARS LATER, he held their daughter on his lap and watched as his wife, pregnancy hidden beneath billowing academic robes, accepted her Juris Doctor degree. Beside Caleb sat her father and sister. He hadn't known it was possible to be so proud, and could tell they felt the same.

Afterward, they found her on the lawn outside Hec Edmundson Pavilion. Her hair was in a French braid, her face glowing beneath the cap with its dangling tassel. Laughing, she accepted Meg's hug and her father's kiss.

"I just wish your mother could have been here," he said.

She smiled at him. "Oh, she's here. I know she is."

Then she handed Caleb her diploma and took Lydia in exchange.

"Could you see Mommy?" she asked.

Lydia's forehead creased. "Daddy said it was you."

"I was a long way away, huh?"

"Looks legit," Caleb pronounced, after inspecting the diploma.

She just laughed again. "I'm taking the slow track to a law career, aren't I?"

He patted her distended belly. "You'll have plenty of time to study for the bar."

"With two preschoolers? Uh-huh."

He kissed his wife soundly. "You know what? You made it through law school. You, sweetheart, can do anything."

"Hear! Hear!" said her father.

Megan never cried. But when she said, "My sister, my heroine," her eyes sparkled.

"This might be the best day of my life," Laurel decided

aloud. "Unless it was the day Lydia was born." She bounced her three-year-old. Her eyes met Caleb's. "Or the day we got engaged."

The sun was shining, and they would soon be celebrating with his parents and Nadia and her family, as well, all of whom—except maybe Nadia's kids—would have loved to be here if Laurel could have gotten more tickets. Their family circle was strong and complete.

Today, Laurel had accomplished something so difficult, most people would never understand.

"I'm voting for today," Caleb said. Although every day of the trip they'd taken to Belize and Guatemala once Lydia was old enough to stay with Grandma and Grandpa had ranked close. "But tomorrow might be just as good."

"And the next day," she murmured, for his ears alone. "And the next…"

Friends and lovers forever.

Turn the page for a sneak preview of
IF I'D NEVER KNOWN YOUR LOVE
by
Georgia Bockoven

From the brand-new series
Harlequin Everlasting Love
Every great love has a story to tell.™

One year, five months and four days missing

There's no way for you to know this, Evan, but I haven't written to you for a few months. Actually, it's been almost a year. I had a hard time picking up a pen once more after we paid the second ransom and then received a letter saying it wasn't enough. I was so sure you were coming home that I took the kids along to Bogotá so they could fly home with you and me, something I swore I'd never do. I've fallen in love with Colombia and the people who've opened their hearts to me. But fear is a constant companion when I'm there. I won't ever expose our children to that kind of danger again.

I'm at a loss over what to do anymore, Evan. I've begged and pleaded and thrown temper tantrums with every official I can corner both here and at home. They've been incredibly tolerant and understanding, but in the end as ineffectual as the rest of us.

I try to imagine what your life is like now, what you do every day, what you're wearing, what you eat. I want to believe that the people who have you are misguided yet kind, that they treat you well. It's how I survive day to day. To think of you being mistreated hurts too much. If I picture you locked away somewhere and suffering, a weight descends on me that makes it almost impossible to get out of bed in the morning.

Your captors surely know you by now. They have to recognize what a good man you are. I imagine you working with their children, telling them that you have children, too, showing them the pictures you carry in your wallet. Can't the men who have you understand how much your children miss you? How can it not matter to them?

How can they keep you away from us all this time? Over and over, we've done what they asked. Are they oblivious to the depth of their cruelty? What kind of people are they that they don't care?

I used to keep a calendar beside our bed next to the peach rose you picked for me before you left. Every night I marked another day, counting how many you'd been gone. I don't do that any longer. I don't want to be reminded of all the days we'll never get back.

When I can't sleep at night, I tell you about my day. I imagine you hearing me and smiling over the details that make up my life now. I never tell you how defeated I feel at moments or how hard I work to hide it from everyone for fear they will see it as a reason to stop believing you are coming home to us.

And I couldn't tell you about the lump I found in my breast and how difficult it was going through all the tests without you here to lean on. The lump was benign—the process reaching that diagnosis utterly terrifying. I couldn't stop thinking about what would happen to Shelly and Jason if something happened to me.

We need you to come home.

I'm worn down with missing you.

I'm going to read this tomorrow and will probably tear it up or burn it in the fireplace. I don't want you to get the idea I ever doubted what I was doing to free you or thought the work a burden. I would gladly spend the rest of my life at it, even if, in the end, we only had one day together.

You are my life, Evan.

I will love you forever.

* * * * *

Don't miss this deeply moving
Harlequin Everlasting Love story
about a woman's struggle to bring back her kidnapped
husband from Colombia and her turmoil over
whether to let go, finally, and welcome another man
into her life.
IF I'D NEVER KNOWN YOUR LOVE
by Georgia Bockoven
is available March 27, 2007.

And also look for
THE NIGHT WE MET
by Tara Taylor Quinn,
a story about finding love
when you least expect it.

presents a brand-new trilogy by

PATRICIA THAYER

Three sisters come home to wed.

In April don't miss
Raising the Rancher's Family,

followed by
The Sheriff's Pregnant Wife,
on sale May 2007,

and

A Mother for the Tycoon's Child,
on sale June 2007.

Silhouette®
Romantic
SUSPENSE

Excitement, danger
and passion guaranteed!

USA TODAY bestselling author
Marie Ferrarella
is back with the second installment
in her popular miniseries,
*The Doctors Pulaski: Medicine
just got more interesting...*
DIAGNOSIS: DANGER is on sale
April 2007 from Silhouette®
Romantic Suspense (formerly
Silhouette Intimate Moments).

*Look for it wherever
you buy books!*

REQUEST YOUR FREE BOOKS!

2 FREE NOVELS PLUS 2 FREE GIFTS!

HARLEQUIN®

Super Romance®

Exciting, emotional, unexpected!

YES! Please send me 2 FREE Harlequin Superromance® novels and my 2 FREE gifts. After receiving them, if I don't wish to receive any more books, I can return the shipping statement marked "cancel." If I don't cancel, I will receive 6 brand-new novels every month and be billed just $4.69 per book in the U.S., or $5.24 per book in Canada, plus 25¢ shipping and handling per book and applicable taxes, if any*. That's a savings of close to 15% off the cover price! I understand that accepting the 2 free books and gifts places me under no obligation to buy anything. I can always return a shipment and cancel at any time. Even if I never buy another book from Harlequin, the two free books and gifts are mine to keep forever.

135 HDN EEX7   336 HDN EEYK

Name _____ (PLEASE PRINT)

Address _____ Apt. _____

City _____ State/Prov. _____ Zip/Postal Code _____

Signature (if under 18, a parent or guardian must sign)

Mail to the **Harlequin Reader Service®**:

IN U.S.A.: P.O. Box 1867, Buffalo, NY 14240-1867
IN CANADA: P.O. Box 609, Fort Erie, Ontario L2A 5X3

Not valid to current Harlequin Superromance subscribers.

Want to try two free books from another line?
Call 1-800-873-8635 or visit www.morefreebooks.com.

* Terms and prices subject to change without notice. NY residents add applicable sales tax. Canadian residents will be charged applicable provincial taxes and GST. This offer is limited to one order per household. All orders subject to approval. Credit or debit balances in a customer's account(s) may be offset by any other outstanding balance owed by or to the customer. Please allow 4 to 6 weeks for delivery.

Your Privacy: Harlequin is committed to protecting your privacy. Our Privacy Policy is available online at www.eHarlequin.com or upon request from the Reader Service. From time to time we make our lists of customers available to reputable firms who may have a product or service of interest to you. If you would prefer we not share your name and address, please check here. ☐

HSR07

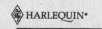

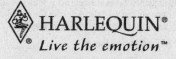

HARLEQUIN®
Super Romance®

COMING NEXT MONTH

#1410 ALL-AMERICAN FATHER • Anna DeStefano
Singles...with Kids
What's a single father to do when his twelve-year-old daughter is caught shoplifting a box of *expired* condoms? Derrick Cavennaugh sure doesn't know. He turns to Bailey Greenwood for help, but she's got troubles of her own....

#1411 EVERYTHING BUT THE BABY • Kathleen O'Brien
Having your fiancé do a runner is not the way any bride wants to spend her wedding day. Learning it's not the first time he's done it can give a woman a taste for revenge. And when a handsome man gives her the opportunity to do just that, who wouldn't take him up on it? Especially when it means spending more time with him.

#1412 REAL COWBOYS • Roz Denny Fox
Home on the Ranch
Kate Steele accepts a teaching job at a tiny school in rural Idaho. The widow of a rodeo star, she's determined to get her young son away from Texas and the influence of cowboys. Then she meets Ben Trueblood. He's the single father of one of her pupils— and a man she's determined to resist, no matter how attractive he is. Because he might call himself a buckaroo, but a cowboy by any other name...

#1413 RETURN TO TEXAS • Jean Brashear
Going Back
Once a half-wild boy fending for himself, Eli Wolverton is alive because Gabriela Navarro saved his life. They fell in love, yet Eli sent her away. Now she has returned to bury his father. He, like Eli's mother, died mysteriously in a fire—and Eli is accused of setting both. When Gaby and Eli meet again in the small Texas town they grew up in, one question is uppermost in her mind: is the boy she adored now the man she should fear...or the only man she will ever love?

#1414 MARRIED BY MISTAKE • Abby Gaines
Imagine being jilted on live TV in front of millions of people.... Well, that's not going to happen to this particular bride at Adam's TV station—not if he can help it by stepping into the runaway groom's shoes to save Casey Greene from public humiliation. Besides, it's not as if it's a real wedding. Right?

#1415 THE BABY WAIT • Cynthia Reese
Suddenly a Parent
Sarah Tennyson has it all planned out. In two months she'll travel to China to adopt her beautiful baby girl. But that's before everything goes awry. Apparently what they say is true...life *is* what happens when you're busy making plans.

HSRCNM0307